Dani Argyle Takes on the Universe

VIVIAN M. JEWELL

ShelteringTree.Earth, LLC Publishing
PO Box 973, Eagle Lake, FL 33839

Did you enjoy this book?

We love to hear from our readers.

Please visit the author at
ShelteringTreeMedia.com

About the Cover:
Artist: Betty Martinez
Title of Piece: Girl with Golden Leaves

DEDICATION

To Elissa and Nathan, my willing muses.

And, of course, to David, my beloved, my ally.

CONTENTS

FOREWORD

English, as every speech-reader knows, is only partially visible on the lips. Cued Speech is a visual mode of communication in which mouth movements of speech combine with [handshapes or] "cues" to make the sounds (phonemes) of traditional spoken languages look different. Cueing allows users who are deaf [or] hard of hearing... to access the basic, fundamental properties of spoken languages through the use of vision. Using Cued Speech in addition to American Sign Language (ASL) ... can be beneficial.[1]

With cued speech, words such as "cake" and "cook" or "base" and "vice" (and all words that could not be distinguished with lip-reading alone) can be understood.

VMJ

---

[1] Karla Giese "Cued Speech: An Opportunity Worth Recognizing" *Odyssey: New Directions in Deaf Education*, v19 p54 ~ 58 2018

ACKNOWLEDGEMENTS

Many brilliant students do not thrive in our educational system, and if you are one of them ~ if you relate to Dani ~ then know that you are admired. To you, my readers and fellow travelers, I offer my deepest thanks. If you ever want to discuss issues that are relevant to this novel, you may communicate with me through my author's website at VivianJewell.com, at my substack at vivianjewell.substack.com, or at shelteringtreemedia.com/

Stories cannot exist in a vacuum: they only come alive when told. Thank you to the people who kept Dani alive through her first iterations:

To Judy Ventimiglia, my friend and ally, I cannot heave my heart into my mouth. Your wisdom and support have been a continual lifeline.

To my early and generous readers: Kathleen Ortiz, Mary Rouvelas, Eileen McLaughlin, Tim Ready, Mary Macpherson, Sophie Macpherson, Doug Macpherson, Richard Washer, and Ina Lynne Jewell, thank you for your enthusiasm and kindness.

Virginia Herrick, Sophia Bonjiovi, Andrew Scronce, and Evelyn Rainey with Sheltering Tree Media: thank you for the guidance and insight.

PART I:
STILL.
LIFE.

VIVIAN M. JEWELL

Dani Argyle Takes on Grief.
And Breakfast. And Memories of the Past
Monday, March 3, 2025
2:00 a.m.

My father slips into my room at night.

It's creepy, I know. But not for the reasons you'd think.

My father is dead. Has been for years. But not everyone believes he is dead since, officially, he's listed as Missing.

But I know better. If he's missing, how could he slide past a locked door and sit on the edge of my bed? Men who are actually missing do not materialize before their daughters at night. Fathers who went forth to save the world ~ or at least the citizens of Kunimi, Japan, the ones who were trapped under collapsed condominiums ~ do not displace the covers to perch on the pillow next to a stuffed effigy of Sailor Moon. The missing do not do that.

Only the dead do.

My father has not always left the halls of heaven or Valhalla or whatever afterlife he was awarded in order to visit my room at

4245 Stone Tower Drive. For two years, he was silent.

Now, I can't get him to shut up.

I wish he would go visit his wife. She's never believed he's dead. I can't wish for him to visit his son. My brother doesn't remember him, and my brother would need to touch him ~ not just hear him ~ and he'll never be able to do that.

Hear, that is.

So all my father's angst ~ and all his fatherly wisdom ~ is saved for me: the only relative he has who owns ghost eyes.

Tonight, he has a new request.

Not the typical I'm-proud-of-you-but-please-take-school-more-seriously request. Not even the things-will-get-worse-before-they-get-better-but-you-need-to-handle-it request.

Tonight, there is silence before he speaks.

Since when do ghosts grope for words?

He opens his mouth, but no words come out.

And then they do:

"You need to take care of your mother."

I stare at him. *Hard.*

"Crap, Dad. I'm not even sixteen. I think *Mother* needs to take care of Mother. It's enough of a muck-fest just holding my own crap together."

His eyes soften, crease at the edges, and he smiles at me with that Dad-smile that's saved only for me and for no other person on this planet. My heart aches, tightens, and squeezes in on itself, and I want to fling myself into his arms ~ except I know that would end badly for him. And maybe for me, too.

Dad's eyes narrow with concentration. "I'm not asking you to bathe your mother or feed your mother or even clean up after her. But try seeing things from her perspective. She's wounded and needs help. Focus on her. Be there for her. Move at Mom speed. Listen."

"At Mom speed? Dad, Mom-speed is slow. *Glacial*. It's been three years, and she's still stuck ~ mired in ~ "

"Denial."

"Denial doesn't even *touch* this. What she is, really, is willful. Belligerent. Aggressive. She won't listen to anyone who mentions you and death in the same sentence." I try to look at him directly ~ to stare at a beauty that makes me squint. And ache. What can I do for a mother who isn't connected to reality? "Dad," I hear my tone sharpen to a whine, but I seem helpless to stop it, "the only thing she wants is you. Or her delusion of you."

"You can help her with that."

I stiffen. "You're asking for the impossible." I slump, shake my head, and then straighten again. "Can't *you* do something to help her? Lead someone to your body? Give someone a hint?"

"It's not that easy, Dani-Boo." He shimmers, quietly. "But if you help your mother, you might just help me, too."

I shake my head. "So no pressure, then."

"No pressure." His eyes shine. "Just a suggestion. A nudge. Try to be open. Aware. People can be works in progress. Not all personalities are final."

And then he's gone, leaving me in the dark, alone. Only Sailor Moon for company.

Mornings at the Argyle house can be stressful: I never know which Mom I'm going to get ~ the one who loves me with her careless beauty, or the one who's thinning before me, ghostly and vacant.

I come out of my room and face the Argyle house: I scan the living room and assume Mom is around the corner, in the dining room. There are no upstairs rooms for Argyle children: the upstairs bedroom and bath are for adults only.

I peek around the corner and see Mom slouching at her coffee, staring at its dark loam, its whiffs and steam. In this Mom-iverse, where some days are worse than others, this day seems like a bad one. Today, Mom seems more like a husk than a human, as if someone has reached within her and scooped out her insides with a spoon, scraping the sides clean, like a pumpkin at Halloween. She has some remnants of her dark-skinned beauty, but sadness has a way of pulling everything down, so her face looks long and weary with weight. And Gabby ~ as if Newton's Third Law applies to people and not just to thermodynamics ~ comes jumping into the kitchen like some giddy hopscotch star, dazzling the air with his exuberant light.

He stops in front of Mom, cups her face in his perfect, pink, six-year-old hands, and says, "Mom, you're so beautiful to me."

Except he doesn't ~ because he's been mostly deaf for most of his life, so his words come out as:

"Ah. Ur oh ee-oo-ih-uhl oo ee."

But we speak Gabby.

Mom smiles weakly, closes her eyes and kisses his forehead. Then her stare returns to her coffee.

How can I take care of this woman? How can I help her when her grief has become a chasm, and my mother is distant, lost in the depths?

I consider mentioning that Gabby needs a new speech therapist, but is this another thing that I need to take care of? How would I find a new language pathologist? And how could I pay her?

Gabby tries to make eye contact with Mom ~ he signs, "Hungry," and "banana," and then jumps ~ but Mom's eyes have steadied and hollowed, become stuck in a space only seen by her.

Breakfast, therefore, is up to me for its making. "C'mon, Bo-Bo," I say, cueing with one hand and gesturing to his chair with the other.

Breakfast is not a friend of the fat girl, so on most days, I'll skip it. It's still a fact, however, that no one loves working with food more than I do, but I don't have to eat it to enjoy it. I place before Gabby the remnants of food from his very belated birthday party (I promise you, I had more fun than the kids: I made a Mario-themed landscape with paper-mâché Gumbas and a Bowser Pinata and snacks in the shape of fire-flowers and gold coins). I also fill up his bowl with heaping scoops of fruit. It's hard to keep this kid fed. I have, in fact, made my brother the object of wagers with friends. Five dollars says the five year-old can eat five bowls of fruit in less than five minutes. But then word got around: the deaf kid can EAT.

Either that, or I ran out of friends.

He eats one bowl and then I fill up another but let him eat it as we walk to Lainie's house. Drop him off by 7:23 so I can be at the bus stop by 7:38 and at school before the first bell.

At school, the day stops. I don't really mind being in charge at breakfast because there, at least ~ things HAPPEN. Food gets eaten. Texts get texted. But at school, no one seems to be in charge ~ least of all, me. It's like entering a numb wasteland where everything is still or mindless or rote. They tell us we're preparing for life, but no one is letting us live it right now.

Wait! The teachers tell us. *You need to study the past before you look at the present. You need to write about other people's writings ~ no one cares about what YOU write. You should know about cell division because you need to learn it in order to forget it one day. And math will always be useful in the future.*

Except I've never met a person who's been saved from suffering by Algebra II.

And some of us need saving more than others.

At least in second block, I get to sit by Sophia.

I slide next to her, and she leans in conspiratorially. "Dani," she whispers, "what did Ms. Russel talk about today in history?"

I shake my head lightly. "I don't know."

"Dani. What the hell! There's a test coming up, and I need

to know what she's going to review."

I drop my voice to make it more persuasive. "Seriously, Sophia, I don't remember."

"Seriously? The class happened five minutes ago! Seriously, girl, sometimes, I do not understand you." She leans back in her seat with a huff.

How do I tell her that, sometimes, I come back to myself after an hour has passed and I do not know where I am? Or who I am? I have gazed around school rooms, startled at my own presence, as if I've dropped in and out of time and don't know where I am. Or *when* I am. Some days, World History II and Imperial Russia seem to be the least of my concerns.

I shrug.

And then Mr. Wright skims in; Mr. Wright and his extravagant white hair ~ settling atop an ageless face, a face too young to be shocked with white. He's tall and thin and impossibly pale, and he slices through the room and materializes center stage, swaying a little as I imagine he would do in a reasonable breeze.

Of all my classes, I should like English best. Human beings are natural linguists. And storytellers.

Leave it to high school to make Dante dull.

I sigh and slump. This day is going nowhere.

Mr. Wright starts in with Canto 33 something something, and something about the ultimate punishment being frozen in something or stuck in something, and something about grief consuming us and something about cannibalism and how people can get trapped in their anger, and something about something else until his voice becomes a background noise ~ like an air conditioner's fuzzy hum ~ and the other sounds that are closer to me are commandeering my attention, the thin scrape of pens on paper, a nearby chair's insistent squeak, the surly grumble from an empty stomach, and then I sense a flourish at the door and Niko Kaneko walks in the classroom.

Walks in the class and slides next to *me*.

There's some collective sighing from the Chorus of Pretty Girls in the corner, and even my own stomach feels scrungy with floops, as if deep down, something inside me is beating and alive, and I decide to really try to pay attention to the lecture so that Niko won't think I'm weird because I'm so aware of his heat.

Damn. I can't do it. Someone is stuck in the ice of Hell and I think he's getting his brain chewed for eternity, and my mom is still lost in her own frozen wasteland, but all I can think about is that Niko Kaneko is wearing a white shirt and sitting next to me and the Chorus of Pretty Girls loves him because he's tall and tan and positively luminous, and when he smiles, you wonder what joy is present in the universe that could make anyone smile a smile like his ~ you wonder what you could have possibly done to deserve a smile like that, you wonder, for a second, if you cured cancer or won a Nobel prize because how else could you deserve that luminosity, that light, and his skin seems to shine from within ~ I can see him on the inside ~ I *am* seeing it, without looking at him, without eye contact, and that's when Mr. Wright calls my name:

"Daniella?"

Crap. Damn. CrapDamnCrap. My hand was NOT raised.

Why do teachers feel the need to volunteer our voices when we do not want to speak? I've been silent for seven months. Why does Wright think I want to speak today?

"Yes?" My voice is thin and ridiculous, and the question mark at the end of my word is palpable.

"Why are there no accidental baths in literature?" He raises his eyebrows and waits.

There's silence. Endless, agonizing, and lengthening before me ~ ghastly in its stillness. And everyone in the class is looking at me. Eyes can pierce. Throughout my skin, I feel the holes.

"Come again?" My ability to be spontaneously acerbic stuns me.

Mr. Wright sighs. "Again: Gilgamesh has a bath, Odysseus has several. Sundiata is radiant after he bathes. Now Dante is crossing the River Lethe. In literature, all baths are symbolic. Why is water imagery important? Why are there no accidental baths in literature?"

Niko pipes up: "What about accidental showers?"

The adoring Chorus giggles from the corner.

But I've got something. A glimmer of an idea, and I grasp at it. "Because bathing reveals change. It's like a Catholic sacrament."

No one mentions religion in Wright's class without provoking an argument ~ even *The Inferno* is his personal opportunity to rail against religion. "Now hold on a second," he commands.

But I will not hold on, "an external expression of an internal reality. The bath doesn't change these guys: the bath just reveals the change that's already happened: it's a purification, a cleansing ~ "

Mr. Wright does not like to be interrupted. "You cannot apply Catholic sacraments to Greek and Babylonian literature."

"But you can apply *purification rituals* anywhere."

"Yeah," Niko agrees. "The bathing shows change."

The Chorus squeaks in agreement.

"So, the lesson is," I'm trudging on, "if you're a literary character, you need to bathe often, because bathing signifies change, and nothing is worse in literature than stillness and stagnation."

Silence. People are staring at me, but it's not as pierce-y as before.

Mr. Wright chuckles approvingly. "The girl speaks!"

I nod my head. "Yeah. They let us vote, too."

There's a collective gasp across the class. No one is talking, so the squirms can be heard: around the room, there are rustles and creaks.

Sophia's eyes are wide, and she leans in, whispering, "Dani, do you have a death wish?"

Mr. Wright ~ who has given detentions for remarks less obviously on the smart-ass scale ~ commences the tongue-clicking. "Daniella," he intones, "we need to talk after class."

Throughout the room, there's some squiggling and some

oooh-ing and then the whirlwind is over and my gut feels heavy and tight and I think Wright's saying something about Lethe forgetting something and something something about stars and dawn and next class, we'll meet Cato because, apparently, there's more to life than Hell.

There's also Purgatory.

And then time disappears and space disappears and then I hear a bell.

People pack up and leave, and Sophia squeezes my shoulder as she escapes, but I sit. I know Mr. Wright expects me to go to him, but I'm curious to see if *he* will come to *me*.

He does. *After* shutting the door.

He stands over me. "Daniella," he begins, "do you have anything to say?"

I pause and squint. I nod my head, a little theatrically. And then I say, "No."

His exhalation is something between a sigh and a whistle.

"Wait," I begin, "I *do* have something to say." I straighten a little. "In the world of teachers and students, why do *you* get to make fun of *me*, but I don't get to say anything back? How is that fair?" I stare at him, hard. I promise you: being a large girl in this country is a horror, but, on occasion, I can make other people feel some weight.

"I did not make fun of you."

"So *you* get to laugh under your breath, and *you* get to act startled that I have a voice, but *I* shouldn't then use that voice to explain that I have a voice?"

"Dani ~ "

(*so he does know my name*)

He tips up lightly on the balls of his feet. "You need to use your voice in a respectful way."

"Why?" I see the shock on his face.

He's startled still as if someone hit a *pause* button. But then I watch him gather himself. He straightens a little ~ bones lift from within ~ making him more angular than he was before. "Respect is a tool that will help *you*," he asserts. "It will make people want to work with you. And to like you."

I feel my eyes narrowing. "What if my goal in life is not to win a popularity contest?"

He looks surprised. Respectful, even. "Understood. But showing respect can help you towards *any* goal you have. It can help propel you towards success or admiration or friendship." He pauses. He tries to look at me with that meaningful teacher-look. "Dani, what *is* your goal in life?"

So much is whirring through my brain at once ~ save my mom? Save my dad? Save my brother? But I hear my breath escaping, and, somehow, it's forming the words before I can control them: "To survive this hell-hole without blowing out my brains."

Wright's eyes startle open and he takes a step back. I see him trying to form words, but nothing is coming.

"Listen," I'm consoling him ~ I'm focused now, I have to be ~ "I'm not a nut case" (*not true*), "and I don't own a gun," (*a little true, but Dad does, but I need to reel this thing back in before I'm crushed in the parade of agitated adults*), "but school is something that must be endured ~ not enjoyed ~ and my goal is to simply survive this institution for long enough that I can get out into the world where my real life will begin."

As I hear the words, I realize how true they are. I feel a lightening in my core. Perhaps my mom is not my responsibility. Perhaps the only person I need to save is myself.

"Daniella," Wright is sighing and using his lecture-voice again, "school is a gift. It's free. People across the world are trying to get into our country to experience what you are trying to throw away. You need to look for the good. School is not all bad."

And school is an institution I can discuss with assurance ~ its flaws are visible for everyone to see (unlike my family, which is hidden and sad). "It's not all bad if you're a *teacher*." Why I have to remind adults of these basic truths is beyond me. "You get to make all the rules and do all the judging. But we students are in a fishbowl, and we bump into it every day, and we're judged not just by teachers but by other students and there is nowhere in this building we can go and be free."

Something seems to be shifting; students are crowding in the hallway outside the room, and a warning bell is warning us that time is short and getting shorter, but Wright seems to be stretching into a figure who is even taller and thinner.

Wright tips again on the balls of his feet; he always seems stiff, as if he's made out of cardboard and not of flesh. "I need to give you some kind of consequence for today's ~ *digression* ~ but let's do it this way. You choose your consequence. Something other students would see as a punishment, but you do not." He pauses. Is he smirking? "Any ideas?"

My mind begins orienting itself to this novel situation. Mr. Wright might not be the person I thought he was, but time is short, and I don't have a lot of it left for reflection. "I'm intrigued," I admit. There's more sophomoric clamoring in the hallway, and the bell is ringing ~ for real, this time ~ yet Wright seems patient. I float a suggestion: "How about I read the books of *The Odyssey* that we skipped in class?" Maybe I won't have to focus on my own problems if I can lose myself in Telemachus'.

He chuckles quietly, a light, approving ticking in the back of his throat. "The *Telemachia*? And Books 6-8 and 15?" He whistles. "Yes, that will work. But it won't be over quickly. Reading this text will be longer than any detention."

"But, unlike detention," I explain, "it will be worth the time." I start shoving papers into my backpack ~ they act like they won't fit, but I force my will upon them ~ and then I stand up, swing around, and I open the door, pushing my way through the squalor of students in the hallway.

After school, I walk to Aunt Lainie's house to pass some time before Gabby gets home. Being Lainie, my aunt has an open-door policy ~ or perhaps, more truthfully, an open-oasis policy ~ but when I open the door and call out, "It's just me ~ no one's robbing you" and start slipping my backpack from my shoulders, she's nowhere to be seen, and a half-naked man is lounging in her living room, watching ESPN.

Not just *any* naked man. Manny.

Ugh. Not again. I reposition my backpack and feel its weight sagging me towards the floor.

Lainie flows into the room in a sheer, translucent nightrobe ~ the woman always seems to glide and never to plod ~ and she lowers herself next to Manny and snuggles into his torso and sighs. He drops his arm around her. Owningly. And stares at me.

I look at him but speak to her. "What's *he* doing here?"

There's a silence as he looks at me as if I'm carnage, as if I'm *vermin*. He shakes his head, slowly, and his words gutter out: "She *is* my wife."

"No, she's not." I'm glaring at him now. "My aunt is not a prize to be owned. She's a woman to be loved."

There's some silence as he processes the fact that a woman ~ or at least me ~ is standing up to him.

"Listen, you ~ " he's posturing himself to get up, but Lainie has positioned her hand on his shoulder.

"Dani," Lainie soothes ~ her voice is light and shimmers like silk ~ "Sweetheart. Settle down. Manny's dropped by for a little visit. No matter what you might think about the state of our marriage,"

(*ex marriage*)

"we can still be friends."

"Mostly naked friends." I'm staring at her now. She's looking at me and shaking her head lightly, warningly.

"You don't get to ~ " and he's rising off the sofa ~

Lainie's pulling the elastic band on his boxers, guiding him back to his seat. "Sweetie, Dani, listen, I know I'm not wife material. That's just me, and I learned it too late. But I'm not going to blame Manny for my faults. We can still have a relationship. He's a good man."

I look at her and say, "You're a good woman, Lainie, too good for ~ " and then at him, "You put my aunt through hell."

He's rising now, and no womanly restraint will stop him. He's not tall, but he's boulder-chested ~ broad as a boat ~ and menacing. He approaches me, glowering. My pulse tightens, and I do the quick mental arithmetic: he will not hit me, and, if he does, Lainie *will* walk and never see his sorry ass again.

"Listen up, you stupid bitch. You leave now." He pretends to point out the door but his finger is up in my face. I close my eyes and wait for ~ not a punch, he won't hit me ~ but a shove or a solid finger pushing my sternum, but all I hear is his guttering voice, growling: "You do not get to barge into this house like you own the place."

So, he's punching with his words ~ "stupid" and "bitch ~ " but they do not hurt as much as he thinks they do. I take a deep breath. "Actually ~ " I begin.

"Dani!" My eyes startle open at Lainie's voice, and she's

rising from her seat, shimmering but concerned. "I really think it would be best if you met your brother at the bus stop. Look," she gives a sweeping gesture out the window, "it's finally March, and it's gorgeous outside. The weather is warm again. Go enjoy the sunshine."

So she's choosing Manny over me. It's the same old story: she loves me a little, but she loves men more. "Fine," I fume as I turn around and start pulling on the door. "I'll go the bus stop, but it's *not* gorgeous and I *won't* enjoy it. And by the way," I need some words that will punch, so I say loudly as I slam the door, "anyone who knows me knows that March sucks."

I stand on the front stoop and seethe, and I don't even know who to hate more ~ him, because he's Manny and he acts like he owns the world and all the women in it ~ or her ~ because she's gorgeous and vibrant and loving and smart in every way *except* for the men she's always falling for. But I can*not* let her go back to this one. She might have forgotten how Manny treated her, but *I* have *not*.

If I have to be the only accurate memory for every broken woman on this planet, I will do it.

And then I hear, "Ay, Anne Ee," and Gabby is on the street waving his excited Gabby-wave, as if seeing me on the stoop of Lainie's house is the best thing that ever happened to him, as if this is what he's been waiting for his entire life, and the anger seeps away and I watch him hop up the driveway with a backpack that swamps his first-grade frame and that bobs up and down on his back like a buoy. And I go to him and kneel down and hold him and hold him and he kisses my cheek and sinks into me and holds me and hugs me like he'll never let me go.

Back home, the Cape Cod is awash in other people's clothes. There are dresses and skirts and pants and shirts and I swear ~ even a pink tuxedo ~ and Mom is at her sewing machine doing the magic things Mom does to make other people's clothes look new or fit better or become fashionable again. When Gabby and I walk in through the front door, she looks up and smiles ~ she SMILES ~ but she doesn't stop the machine. Today, she has a purpose; she's a woman on a mission ~ to push back the chaos of her life and this world with one repaired zipper at a time.

"I'm sorry. I got a little behind at the shop," she's explaining as if we've never heard this before, "so I brought some work home."

Although part of me wants to, I choose not to argue with her or tell her that, if she brings work home from the dry cleaners, she should get *paid* for it. No fair being paid part-time wages for full-time work. Today, I will support her. I let my bitterness seep out and mellow.

"No need to apologize, Mom." I have to raise my voice over the sound of the machine – so I'm not sure if I sound supportive or annoyed ~ and I drop my backpack on the floor. It thumps and tips ~ spills out a few of its innards ~ and Gabby runs to Mom and kisses her on the lips, and she responds with a boisterous, playful,

"MWAAHHH" and Gabby smiles and beams and then hops toward the kitchen.

"Wait up, Gabby-Boy," I say ~ I'm calling to his back and there's no way he can hear me ~ but I continue calling out like an idiot, "I'll cut you some fruit."

Later, when the fruit has been cut and cut again and the snack has lasted long enough that I made some pancakes and called it dinner, Mom has finally finished in the living room. She takes her seat at the table, and I fix her a plate.

"Thank you, Dani," Mom nods. "You're such a good cook."

"It's just pancakes," I explain.

"No. Don't diminish ~ " she remembers and starts cueing as she talks, "don't diminish your skills. There are good pancakes and ordinary pancakes. These pancakes are good."

"It's just flour and buttermilk and…"

"Just say 'thank you.'"

"Thank you, Mom."

And Gabby chimes in with a thank-you in sign language ~ a thank-you that's both a thank-you and a sign for "good" and that ends with the slap of a back hand against the palm of another, and I feel fully, exuberantly, excitedly thanked.

Later, after I've washed the pan and done the dishes ~ by which I really mean folded paper plates and dropped them in the trash ~ after Gabby has gone to the basement to play MarioKart and Mom's returned to her sewing, I wonder if I should mention to Mom that an almost naked Manny was at her sister's house, but when I wander into the living room and watch her repairing a hem, I decide against it. Mom never forgave Lainie for so actively leaving her husband when Mom's own husband ~ in the Gospel According to Mom ~ is lost on the other side of the world and struggling to return home.

There are some wounds I refuse to pry open.

So I sit on the one chair not covered by clothing and remember the room as it used to be when Dad was alive ~ not clean, never clean, but filled with a different type of fabric, and with paints and with canvases and with easels that could spin. Mom's artwork used to be part painting, part sculpture, part magic, with fabric elements that swirled and danced and reached out to embrace the viewer. She had orders from around the world, and some pieces were still ~ to be hung inside a house on a wall ~ but some pieces were all fabric that flowed and billowed in the wind, and these were a garden's master works ~ like an infant's mobile grew up and got courageous ~ and when the finished design was blossoming outside, the final sculptor was not my mother at all, but, ultimately, the wind, who puffed and gusted and breathed and blew and who made different masterpieces with each passing mood.

My mom has finished with the hems now, and she's moving on to the ripped seams.

Oh, how the gorgeous have fallen.

My mom used to make masterpieces that sailed in the wind. Now, she does repair work for people who don't know how to sew their own buttons.

Dani Argyle Takes on Tweeting
Tuesday, March 4, 2025
7:51 a.m.

The next morning, Sophia and I are in class together before the bell rings ~ but this time it's Japanese II, and, since Sophia has some spare time, she has her notebook out and she's practicing her *kanji* ~ writing the pictographs for numbers over and over again, starting with the 四 and going on up. Waters Sensei is at his desk, staring at his laptop, and all the students adore him, even though he makes it his goal to ignore us entirely. Japanese II is actually a class that I actually like. This is where I feel whole. This is where I feel *new*. This is where there is a possibility of a world opening before me, and although some people don't know that it's possible, this is where I fall in love ~ not with a person ~ but with a *culture*. And often this class is all movement and motion ~ until it's not, but even the stillness is good ~ and in the middle of the period we race up to the whiteboard to have Kanji-drawing contests, or trace characters with our fingers on classmates' backs while asking them to guess the word, or play teachers while telling our classmates what to do, or stand in two lines like the Virginia Reel but this dance is language and movement and not just music. And then, in the midst of the energy, in the midst of the motion, we stop, and we find something to revere, because reverence, too, is a part of Japan. So on our desk, throughout the period, there is one beautiful thing: a vase or a plate or a teapot or a cup ~ a single piece of art to gaze at in wonder.

My phone buzzes. Lainie is texting.

LS Found these on the floor...

She's taken photos of old reports ~ schoolwork that got left behind:

Sophia Brown

Mr. Wright *Concise and well phrased—A*

English 10

24 February, 2025

Inferno Book Report

Midway through his life, Dante realizes that he is lost in sin, and he doesn't know how to get out of it. He wants to live a good life but feels powerless to do so. Dante, therefore, uses his reason (which is symbolized by the Roman poet Virgil) to guide him so that he can understand what sin is. In order to understand the nature and consequence of sin, Dante travels through three main regions of Hell (where sins of bodily weakness, violence, and fraud are punished). Dante talks to many sinners and eventually comes to understand that they deserve their punishments. When Dante understands sin, then he can leave Hell.

Dani Argyle

Mr. Wright *Some gravitas would be helpful* - C

English 10

24 February, 2025

Hell: A Traveler's Guide

Dante Alighieri has been having a bad day. His city is at war, he's lost in the woods, and three beasts have been prowling about and hunting him. What's a medieval Florentine poet to do? Why, get his own personal Roman-spirit-guide, of course! Enter Virgil: Dante's personal hero and representative of all things reasonable and Roman. Virgil has been sent by Dante's dead girlfriend to lead Dante away from the sins of lust, violence, and fraud (Yup, Dante suffers from all three), and into the light of divine illumination. All Dante has to do is go through Hell. Literally. So Virgil leads Dante ~ and all of Dante's readers ~ on a personal guided tour of the infernal regions... which just happen to be populated by all of Dante's personal enemies. What a coincidence! Dante gets his literary revenge, and Dante's enemies get eternally remembered for really pissing Dante off.

LS Are they important?

DA No!

I'm shaking my head when Waters Sensei rises from his desk, walks to the whiteboard and writes in an obnoxiously red marker: "Chapter 17 Lesson Due Today."

He returns to his desk to stare at his laptop, and I realize that the educational world is conspiring against me.

The Japanese culture might be a beautiful thing. But school? School is *not*.

Crap. Crap. This will not end well.

Here are the mathematical probabilities of Daniella Argyle handing in homework:

Chances of using phone during class to set-up a reminder? 23% depending upon the teacher

Chances of remembering, after a class is over, to set a reminder? Small. 15%

Chances of writing down the assignment in a school-sanctioned planner? Not bad. 75%

Chances of bringing planner home? Reasonable. 65%

Chances of checking the planner once at home? Poor. 33%

Chances of finding the entry where the homework is? Touch and go ~ about 45%

Chances of doing homework if the planner is checked? *Satisfactory.* 60%

Chances of remembering to bring the work to school the day it's due? *Abysmal. About* 20%

Chances of remembering to retrieve the assignment from the backpack and place it in the teacher's hands? 25%-75%-*depending upon the class.*

Overall chance of Dani Argyle handing in homework? *I'm not good in math, so I'll give a general estimate:*

Ridiculously small.

I sigh and rip open my backpack, digging through layers of past notes, neglected assignments, old tissues.

Deep down, I know the assignment is *not* in here. Not because I didn't do it. I *did*.

But if I know me ~ and I believe I do ~ the assignment is still in the printer on Mom's desk.

And just as I'm excavating an old layer of candy wrappers, Niko walks into class ~ Niko Kaneko, Japanese IV student extraordinaire and runner-up in last year's freaking national JAPAN BOWL ~ *he* walks in, quips about the Weaboo babies in Japanese II even though he's our age ~ and he wanders over to where Sophia and I are sitting and looks at *me*.

I startle up straight and zip up the backpack so its insides do not spill across Niko's feet.

"You guys are in Wright's class," he announces, as if he's had a revelation worthy to be shared.

"Yes?" I reply. Brilliantly. *Why is it so hard to breathe right now?*

Sophia grunts lightly and continues her *kanji* exercises.

Niko smiles. He's luminous. "You're the bath girl."

I nod. I'd like to have a different epithet, but....

"If we're gonna hafta sit through Wright's class together," he shares, "we might as well have some *fun*." His eyes gleam mischievously.

"What were you thinking?" I shift my foot and slide it next to Sophia's, trying to break her out of her *kanji* reverie. I might need her help if I'm going to form a sentence with over four words while Niko and his eyes are gleaming at me.

"I'm thinking...." He pauses for dramatic effect, "a texting chain." (Sophia starts at this ~ looks up from her notebook.) "The three of us. We text while Wright talks. Kind of like we're live-streaming commentary on his lectures." He grins and looks back and forth from Sophia to me, awaiting our approval.

"We can't have our phones out in class." Sophia is indignant, and she continues, a little sharply, "And if he takes our phones and reads our texts, we're DEAD." She nods at me: "We'll have to do more than read books of *The Odyssey* as punishment."

Niko looks at me quizzically. I shrug.

"Ummm," I begin, and I turn to Sophia: "I think this is something we can problem-solve."

Niko shines. "Yeah. Problem-solve it, Sophia." (*So he knows her name, but does he know mine? or am I just the one-who-knows-about-baths girl?* And of *course* I want to form a texting alliance with Niko, but I need to tread gently around Sophia and her obsession with having a perfect GPA, even if ~ to do it ~ she has to hang out with all the dumb kids.)

There's more refusal from Sophia, and her glance starts to dip back down to her *kanji*, but I see my shot:

"How about we join a texting alliance, but we don't text about *Wright*. We text about *Dante*. That way, if Wright catches us, he won't go all *Inferno* on our asses ~ "

"What do you mean?" Niko looks quizzical.

I'm being academic enough to pique Sophie's curiosity, and I hear her say "Hey, hey!" and see her mental wheels turning before she offers the hypothesis: "This could work. For reals. Like, we could do a modern-day *Inferno* ~ "

I jump in, "Yes, you know, Tweet-It-Out as if we're actual characters descending through the nine circles and live-streaming Hell."

"It's Purgatory now," Sophia corrects.

"Ok. You're right, but we can't *start* in Purgatory, can we? That makes no sense." I look at her imploringly. "What do you say, Sophia? Yes?"

Sophia looks at me, then at Niko ~ her *kanji* is temporarily ignored ~ and then at me again, and I see some recognition in her eyes. "Yes," she concedes, a little *too* excitedly.

"Then let *The Inferno* Games begin!" I declare. "First we need to choose our characters."

There's a certain blankness in Niko's eyes that makes him ~ temporarily ~ less than luminous, so I clarify, "We're all choosing names of characters from the epic, and we're going to set up accounts in their names as if we *are* that character, and I call Dante."

"I'm Beatrice," Sophia smiles.

"That leaves Virgil for me." There's a little light in Niko's eyes, but I have a feeling he might not understand what he's gotten himself into.

The warning bell is ringing. Sensei doesn't look up from his laptop and calls, "Niko Kaneko, get out of my room."

"Love you, too, Waters Sensei," Niko croons.

Niko walks to the door, and Sensei doesn't look up. But, even from a distance, I can see that he is smiling.

This afternoon, there are no suspicious extra cars parked in Aunt Lainie's driveway. (Ugh. I should have *noticed* yesterday. All today, awful, bare-chested Manny-images have been popping through my mind), so I open the door with a flourish and sing out, "Are you nehkid?"

But nobody is at home. There is a note on the floor:

> *Busy day.*
>
> *Having lunch at the office.*
>
> *Make yourself a home.*
>
> *XXXO Lainie ~*

I assume she means "at home" and not "a home" because the latter would be difficult.

I slop my backpack to the floor and start to rummage through its contents: trash, trash, work, trash, textbook, old gum wrappers ~ it's a fountain of wasted material. Other students' backpacks always seem to stay organized, their lives folded neatly into accordion folders and three-ring binders. But everything about *my* life is messy. I stare into the abyss of a backpack. I *know* I should take out my Japanese workbook and practice some *kanji,* but... light is glancing off the hardwood floors, glinting across the walls and the ceiling.

I look around. This was Mom's childhood home, too, but, for some reason, Lainie got it when Pop-Pop died, but it ended up ok, because Dad inherited his own family home ~ one that he helped build with his own two hands. I picture him, twelve-years-old, up on a roof, nailing shingles and attaching flashing while caulking anything that might move during a gale.

I have twenty-three minutes before Gabby arrives, so I take some time to snoop ~ you know ~ as you do ~ when your backpack is loaded with work custom-made to keep you busy and suck the life from your bones.

The first stop is the kitchen, but the cupboards are only revealing multi-grain crackers and collections of nuts. (Yawn.) The refrigerator is equally unappealing. I know where the best food goes. I eye the trashcan but decide against it.

In the great-room, there are pictures of Lainie with all manners of men: marathoners and CEO's and motorcyclists and musicians, and in every photo Lainie shines with her shimmering blond hair and her heart-shaped face and her skin that glows ~ I think she wears glitter ~ and when you look at her you understand how beauty can hurt ~ how it can fill a viewer with craving and impossible longing and make us all realize how fully and catastrophically our own bodies fall short.

In the bathroom, there are more lotions and bath salts than there are days of the month and twenty-four shades of lipstick, which, from my perspective, could all simply be labelled "Red." But the bathtub. The BATHTUB! It's one of those enormous, cast-iron, lion-clawed wonders ~ one that a basketball player could easily get lost in, and I climb in with my clothes on and sit and imagine how easy it would be to drift, to close my eyes and wash away, to wake up ~ or not ~ in another world entirely.

After a while, a bathtub with no water becomes less than comfortable, so I get up and wander into the bedroom which shines with linens and pillows and even a fountain. In the bookcase, there are three-ring binders filled with REAL-ESTATE LAW (yawn) and the Spartale-family photo album which I've seen once before, but not recently.

I'm wondering what Mom looked like as a baby, but I can only find photos of Lainie's lovely face, Lainie, who, it seems, has always been gorgeous, even as an infant, and then I wonder where Mom's album is and why I've never seen it, and I hear a blast of wind coming from outside, and it brings me to my senses: Gabby's too small to wait in a storm.

I replace the album and rush to the stoop, but the wind seems silent now ~ the treetops are still ~ until I look at the ground, and it is moving, glimmering, shaking with birds.

In all my life, I've never seen so many. I never knew this many could exist in one time and one place. I step out into the yard, and the birds don't notice ~ they keep shimmering, keep rustling, with me in their midst, until I take one step too many and they take off, alighting, flying, the whole world is fluttering about me, there's a rush and a whir and flashes of flame under rustles of wings, and I hear "Ir! Ir!" in the distance, and Gabby is running on his tiny boy-legs, pointing and shouting as if I don't know the birds are here. They're circling and shimmering and impossible around me.

When Gabby reaches the driveway, it's just me, alone; the birds now are whirling in the sky, going to find a new home to settle, a new person to bless.

"Uh ir ah ow uh eh-ehs," and Gabby cues: "The birds have

found the heavens."

I look at him, and he arches his back to face the sky, and the sun lights up his face, and he holds up his arms and reaches wide and grins.

VIVIAN M. JEWELL

Dani Argyle Takes on the Administration
Wednesday, March 5, 2025
9:32 a.m.

Walking down the halls of Stone Mountain High would be enough to give Dante pause.

That man would be fainting all over the place.

He'd pass by one conversation, start swaying, and drop, only to get up, hear more from others, and faint away again.

Most students want more time between classes. I would like less, thank you very much.

On my way to English, I pass some skinny girls. "I keep sending him a break-up text," one intones, "but he just won't respond."

A jock without a neck is complaining about his allowance. "Who can live on $100 a week?" His indignation is total.

A librarian is livid and giving an administrator the what-for: "But the kids are sneaking into the library!" I hear the administrator's tired response: "We can't lock the doors. It's a fire hazard."

The Chorus is up ahead, a circle of girls as thin as winter. As I pass, I hear, "Some people get all the luck. I wish *I* could be a trauma victim. Then everyone would feel sorry for *me*."

"You'd make a very pretty trauma-girl," the Chorus Leader agrees.

The Graeae had it tough because they had to share a single eye. I wonder if anyone in the Chorus cares about sharing a single tongue.

Then I'm approaching a group of guys. They're snorting and bumping shoulders.

As I pass, I hear, "Moooo."

And then someone pinches my ass.

At first, I feel flattened, like I'm garbage and someone's stepped on me.

And then, I run hot.

I twirl and face the cluster and they're all grinning and sniggering, and the next thing I know, I'm not in control of my arm; my *arm* is in control of *me*, and there's one blonde boy grinning wider than the rest, and all my body is swinging and I punch him hard ~ in the gut ~ and I hear all the air leave his body with an "ooof."

And there's no sniggering now. They're staring ~ goggly-eyed ~ and stunned. Until ooof-boy straightens out and says, "What the hell? You bitch!"

"Oh," I reply, "and I'm a bitch because I fight back?" The Chorus is staring and I nod at them. "I guess the other girls you assault don't know how to punch."

I'm too short to get in his face but I take a step closer and I wish he'd step back in reaction, but he doesn't, so I continue, "Why don't I give these pre-syphilitic balls of yours a pinch and a twist and see who's laughing then?" I don't know where I find courage, but I take another step and whisper, "Try that again, and you'll see how much pain a pair of testicles can cause."

I spin around and start walking. I'm trying not to shake. I hear a "I didn't touch you" shouted from behind and then another voice: "Leave her alone. She's just a fat bitch."

I head to the restroom to settle and breathe. When I walk in, there's a gaggle of vapers leaning on the sinks, and I see more steam rising from the stalls.

Really? I just want a place to be. And breathe. And pee, if I need to.

One of the stalls that was being used for just such an occasion vacates, and I duck in and close the door and lock it and close my eyes.

When I catch my breath and feel my pulse start to slow (and pee ~ I can't let a vape-free stall go to waste), I head to Mr. Wright's room. The bell has already rung, and the halls are empty now.

Thank God. Or whatever deity is on my side right now.

These halls are grim, but at least they're quiet. The panels in the ceiling are missing, and wires twist overhead in tangled clumps. I suppose some surly custodians resented always removing ceiling panels to gain access to the tired wiring, and so, in the English and math hallways, the intestines of the school are always sagging and in sight.

As I approach Wright's room, I see Wright and Mr. Glupov are waiting outside the door.

Crap.

I can't catch a break. Not even for a glimmer. Except for vape-free stalls, there is no privacy here. And no time to just *be*. In high school, there is insta-everything. Insta-Information. Insta-Gossip. Insta-Referral.

Mr. Glupov acknowledges me. "Daniella," he begins, "we need to talk. In my office."

He starts walking, and I follow ten steps behind, and he, like some paranoid Orpheus, keeps turning around to make sure I'm still there.

Mr. Glupov is the kind of bald, squat, puffy man who would not get respect elsewhere in the world, so he enters education to lord his towering mediocrity over teenagers. He was a wrestler in high school and now misses the scramble, so he's become an administrator and legitimate a bully-at-large. I imagine, every night, he goes home to his wife to brag about how much cleverer he is than the high-school kids.

He enters his office and motions for me to sit on a chair. "I hear there was a problem in the hall this morning." He slips in his chair behind his desk and waits.

Since he obviously believes he knows more than I do about

what has transpired, I stay silent. I flop into a chair. And glare.

"I hear you punched someone."

More silence. More glaring.

"Is this true?" He gazes back.

"So, you heard that I defended myself against the guy who grabbed my ass." I see him flinch a little.

There's some startled silence, and he says, "The matter is still under investigation."

"I hope so, since it's only been nine minutes since it happened ~ "

"And a lot of students witnessed the event."

"Well, the ass-grab wasn't as apparent as the punch."

"So you admit you punched him." He looks rather pleased with himself.

"I *admit* that I made sure that he would never again treat my body like it is his own personal joke."

"Daniella, you cannot settle conflict with aggression."

"So when *he* sexually assaults me, that's conflict, but when *I* defend myself, that's aggression?"

"What he did ~ if he did it ~ was wrong, but what you did was wrong, too."

"'*If* he did it.' You think my 5'5" frame goes around punching guys for the fun of it?"

"You know the Students' Rights and Responsibilities ~ "

"States that I get to learn in a harassment-free zone ~ states that I don't have to walk the gauntlet of the school like some Godforsaken Tail Hook."

"Daniella, you need to calm down."

"And the *law* states ~ the State Law of Virginia states ~ that I can stand my ground in this mutual-combat state."

He leans back. He looks tired.

There are some dishes on his desk. I think I've interrupted his breakfast.

"Daniella, no one's accusing you ~ "

"It sure feels that way ~ "

"We want to help you."

"Then let me help myself."

"When trouble arises, you need to come to us."

"*When* trouble arises? *WHEN*? It happens every day" (*you frog-faced tool*) "and what are you going to do? Follow me 24/7?"

"There are other ways to help."

"Bullshi-Bull. You don't want to help me. You want to *control* me. You want me to fit sweetly and demurely into this f-mucked-up cluster"

"Language! Language!"

"of a school where I am assaulted every day with sneers and insults ~ "

He seems to be the one who's ooofing now ~

"and you're more concerned about *my language* than *their actions*, and you want me to grin and bear it and come running to you and this helpless, castrated system"

"Daniella ~ "

"because heaven forbid a teenage girl should fight for herself."

There's a pause. "Okay. Okay," he is saying. "Let's take a break. I'm glad you got that off of your chest."

I stand up and go for the door.

"Daniella. Sit down. Do you want a female administrator in here with you?"

I turn around. But I do not sit. "No," I clarify. "I don't need that. Any person with any compassion should be able to deal with this. No matter the gender."

"I can get Ms. Glover in here if you need her."

"You know what I need? Maybe a conversation that went like this. I'll let you into my fantasy world. It's a good place to hide. You open and you say, 'Miss Argyle. How are you? I hear you were assaulted in the hallways of this school, and I want to know that you're ok.'

"And then I'd respond, 'Thank you, Mr. Glupov. I've handled it.'

"And you'd reply, 'Is there anything that I can do to help you more?'

"And I'd say, 'I don't think there's anything you can do to change the nature of adolescent boyhood, but thanks for asking,' and then we'd say our respective goodbyes and I'd go back to class."

Mr. G. takes a long exhale. "I can see we're not making progress today."

"If by progress, you mean that I do not consent to having my ass grabbed, then yes."

"And I want to give you some more time to calm down and reflect. You can meet me for detention after school."

I scowl. "Fine. And if I don't show?"

"Then it's suspension."

"Awesome! I choose that one. Get me the hell out of this place."

"*In school* suspension."

"Which, in your view, is worse than school? Fine. Fine. One prison is as good as another."

I turn around and walk out the door.

I hear his voice calling from behind: "I'll see you in my office at 3:00."

"Yeah. Sure," I call out over my shoulder. "You wait for me. I'll come running."

When I reach Mr. Wright's room, there's a sign on the door that says, "Quiet: Testing in Progress."

Oh. Right. Grammar test today.

Don't even get me *started*.

We need grammar as much as we need to know the organs in our digestive tract. Somehow, our digestive processes work whether we know how or not, and, somehow, we can use language whether or not we can identify a participial phrase.

I take a deep breath. And I enter. There are hills of students slooped at their desks.

Everyone in the class turns and looks at me. It is possible for stares to wound. Today, they feel like an assault.

But there is a major grammar assessment to be assessed, and my classmates' stares are only temporary. Soon, everyone's gaze is on the test again.

I slip into my desk and take out a book.

I think Mr. Wright senses not to mess with me today. He glances at me, but not for long: he is also engrossed in a book.

When the Scantron bubbles have been bubbled, and the tests have been properly aligned into their proper slots on the teacher's desk, Wright takes mercy on the class and allows us to work in groups. Something about identifying imagery and symbolism in Canto XXXIV.

Niko saunters over to Sophia and me. "I'm in your group," he announces. And then he grins, "You guys get 'A's.' Don't you?"

"Not always," I admit.

"*Yes*," Sophia asserts.

And because she's a good person and a dear friend, and because all the whispers in the classroom seem to have my name embedded in them, Sophia asks Mr. Wright if we can work in the hallway.

He acquiesces (*strange*), and we head out.

After we've settled on the floor, Sophia begins: "Ok, Dani, what the hell?"

I sigh. "I'm not sure I want to talk about it."

"Jason Argano is a jerk," Niko consoles. "If you punched him, he deserved it."

Sophia presses on: "I heard you *felled* him. I hear he whimpered on the *floor*."

"The rumors of his assault have been greatly exaggerated," I admit.

Sophia's eyes widen even further. "And what did Mr. G. want? Are you e*xpelled*?"

Dear Sophia. She's as smart as a rocket scientist, but she tends towards melodrama.

"I think I'm suspended." I shrug.

"He's an idiot. Doesn't he know it's March?"

Niko scowls. "What's wrong with March?"

Sophia takes my hand and squeezes it. "Sleepover. Saturday. No saying 'No.' It's fish tacos at the Brown's house."

I smile weakly.

"Hey, Dani." She bends down to look up at me and make eye contact. "Are you going to be ok?"

I nod. "I have to be. What choice do I have?"

And then in a gesture very uncharacteristic of me, I take Mr. Wright's worksheet and hold it up to look at it.

Sophia grabs it from my hand and starts reading aloud: "1. As Dante moves down the flank of Satan, what is the symbolism of his being turned upside down?"

I grab the paper back and start to write: "Life be like that sometimes."

During math class, the words buzz by, and the room sounds as if it's filled with static. My classes always seem like a radio caught between two stations ~ like two different songs interspersed with static are wrestling for my attention ~ but math is *the worst*.

My math teacher is wonderful, however. I love her. I hate *math*, but I love Ms. Satchel.

Hate the sin, but not the sinner.

Ms. Satchel has the patience of Job and the tenacity of Meriwether Lewis. Anyone who tries to teach me quadratic equations would need to have both. Ms. Satchel is not the soft and fuzzy type, but there is a comfort in her candor: she never demeans her students by talking down to them, and when she says something is true, her students believe her. Everything she says is spoken with the same mathematical authority, whether it's $f(x) = ax^2 + bx + c$ or "Dani, you will pass this class."

I'm staring at a worksheet ~ my eyes are blurry and my ears listening to the ambitious scribbles of other students ~ and Ms. Satchel sees that I'm flustered and makes some assumptions ~ which should be unusual for someone with her clinical nature. She leads me into the hall and begins:

"Dani, don't blame yourself. You're not to blame." The words are crisp. "You say you don't understand. I say you don't understand *yet*. This is complicated. This is hard. And if you're not learning right now, then I'm not teaching correctly."

I pause as I consider her words. *Oh. Thank God,* I realize. *She's talking about MATH.*

I never thought those thoughts would wander through my brain.

I reorient my mind and something fumbles from my mouth: "Yeah. I'm sorry. I'm having an off day. But you know, Ms. Satchel, math just doesn't make sense. I don't understand *anything*. I just don't think this way."

She pauses and looks in the classroom. Then she looks at me again. "Math might be a new way of thinking for you, but it just takes time. Slow and steady wins this race. There are no speed records here. Math is a language that anyone can learn."

I exhale. Sharply. "That's what they said about reading maps and telling time on an analog clock."

Ms. Satchel's jaw opens noticeably. And this might be a first: I don't think I've ever seen the woman show surprise.

Then she starts nodding. "There might be more going on here than meets the eye."

I agree. "Isn't there always."

And then I shift my gaze, and Mr. Wright is silent and waiting, as if he's coalesced before us from the very air. I grin as I realize the implications: There's been a sighting of *Mr. Wright*! In the *math* hallway!

He's standing five feet away from us, and we turn to face him. "I don't mean to interrupt," he explains. He sounds so... *conciliatory*. So un*Wright*ish. He looks first at Ms. Satchel and then at me, but he doesn't turn his neck when shifting his gaze: he pivots his entire body.

Ms. Satchel huffs lightly. "It's fine," she explains. "I need to get back to the students." Her words are even and matter-of-fact ~ as if everything she discusses is obvious. Since the world around her is just another manifestation of a mathematical theorem, her tone is as flat as an algebraic equation. She turns and disappears into the classroom without a 'good-bye.'

Mr. Wright stands ~ in a very typical Mr.-Wright-Way ~ with both hands behind his back while tipping upwards on the balls of his feet.

"I've heard Mr. Glupov wants to give you a detention," he begins.

"Yup," I concede.

"It seems to me you don't do detentions."

"Nope," I concur.

A pause. He's nodding gently. Then he purses his lips and asks, "Would you like to come to *my* classroom after school? Some other students are dropping by for help on their essays. I could tell Mr. Glupov that it's a detention, but you could just come, and," he pauses. "*Read.*"

I think for a while. I'm processing Mr. Wright and his un*Wright*smanship.

I'm considering slowly while I gaze at the ground. Then I look him in the eye. "I'll need to text my aunt to see if she can pick up my little brother from the bus stop... but if she can... then..." I shrug. "Yes."

"Good," Mr. Wright confirms. He starts to pivot on one foot but then pivots himself back, facing me again. "I'll email Mr. Glupov and ask if you can serve detention with me."

It's quiet. Typical Wright silence. Of the awkward variety.

"Only you and I need to know," he concludes, "that this isn't detention. It's only reading time."

And then he turns and disappears down the hallway.

In his classroom, Mr. Wright is sitting at his desk, reading a weary copy of *The Catcher in the Rye*.

I pause by the door, but he doesn't say a word or glance in my direction. The room is bare except for a desk with three books: *The Odyssey*, *The Inferno*, and *The Purgatorio*.

I take my seat and gaze at the covers. It can be hard to know where to begin. Telemachus missing his dad? Dante lost in the woods? Virgil and Dante, crawling out of cracks in the earth, emerging from the stench of Hell?

Ok. In for a penny, in for a pound.

I pick up *The Inferno* and begin at the beginning.

Midway in our life's journey, I found myself
In dark woods, the right road lost. To tell
About those woods is hard ~ so tangled and rough

And savage that thinking of it now, I feel
The old fear stirring....

I'm coming to the line about Virgil coalescing and being hoarse after a long silence, when Mr. Wright shifts in his seat.

I look at him. He's so thin and pale. Prematurely gray, with an ageless face that could be thirty or fifty and no one really knows.

He catches me looking at him and puts down his book.

"Dani?" he begins ~

"Yes?"

There's silence and space ~ as there often are when talking to him.

He takes a breath. "I'm sorry about what happened today."

I stare at him, stunned.

And then I start sobbing.

The lump in my gut expands to my throat and it's as if all of my insides want to get out ~ release into the world their emptiness and ache ~ and I slump to my desk and let the sorrows convulse, feel the snot and the tears sting at my skin, watch the world blur and then dim into darkness.

That was all I needed anyone to say.

VIVIAN M. JEWELL

Dani Argyle Takes on Powerlessness
Thursday, March 6, 2025
2:00 a.m.

It's 2:00 a.m. and I can't seem to sleep.

Tonight, I'm *hoping* my dad will arrive.

I'm sitting up, staring at the door, willing him to appear.

And then I hear some motion by my closet.

I twist instinctively, spasmodically, until I realize I look like a crazy person and force myself to close my eyes, to push away the panic. *Crap. Crap. Crap on a map. Don't let him look there.*

I feel like I'm praying, but I don't know to who. *Please. Please, let him sit by me.* And I'm listening for anything, until I realize ~ like an idiot ~ that I'm listening for a *ghost*.

There's silence and waiting, and I can't stand it anymore, so I open my eyes and lean, lightly, to face the possible catastrophe, but Dad doesn't seem anguished, only concerned.

Dad's back is to the closet, and he crosses the room to sit on my bed. He looks at me, and shimmers.

"You've been crying," he says.

I nod. And sigh. *He hasn't seen anything.* My breath steadies into an "I'm sorry." My eyes are too wide, and I wonder if he feels my fear.

Yet Dad's response is gentle, like a whispered hush: "Why are you sorry?"

The relief I once felt starts sagging, and I feel the old fatigue start to rest on my flesh ~ like a gray fog crawling. "I don't know. I don't know. But everything seems so *wrong*. I feel so inept, so powerless." I bend down, as if I'm talking to the bed linen rather than him. "There's nothing in this world that I can control."

When the silence expands, I look up, and a haze of gold flicks across his skin. He smiles. "But I see you, Dani. You're *trying*. That's doing more than most."

I shake my head. "But no matter what I do, things go wrong anyway. How can anyone *stand* it? Life is so awful."

Quiet. Silence. Then a shimmer. And a voice: "That's right. I don't deny it. But it's beautiful, too."

In a blast of realization, I am horrified. I am complaining about life to someone who is dead.

I feel the tears coming.

It seems Dad wants to touch me, but he can't. "That's ok, Dani. Go ahead and cry. But when you're done, you also need to think: what are you going to *do*?"

So I crumble and I cry and let despair make me ugly ~ feel my eyes puff and my skin splotch ~ until I feel blank inside, until the wound feels scabbed over and all the nerves, numb.

Then I wipe my face on my sleeve, look at him, and sigh.

"So?" he asks.

"So?" I respond.

He smiles. "Dani, what are you going to *do*?"

I blink at him. I straighten up, and then I slouch again. "Dad," I explain. "I got nothing."

He smiles. "Nothing yet. You don't have anything *yet*."

Is he's channeling Ms. Satchel?

"Sometimes people," he offers, "make good sounding boards. You're making some friends. Try talking to *them*. Don't fight this life all by yourself. Lean on a person."

I look at him. "Dad," I pause. "You are a person."

He smiles and shines. "Yes," he nods. "And no."

And then he disappears.

Dani Argyle Takes on Her Mother
Thursday, March 6, 2025
1:57 p.m.

I am walking to ASL when I get more messages from Lainie.

LS Hey, Sweet Gherkin... These were under my bed.

Sophia Brown

Mr. Wright *Good formatting A solid summary:*

English 10 *Well-done! A*

14 November, 2024

Odyssey Book Report

The Odyssey is a classic story of the Greek war hero, Odysseus, and his struggles to get home after he leaves the battles of Troy. To get home, Odysseus has to face many obstacles, including gods, monsters, barbarians, women, and his own ego. After ten years of suffering, Odysseus does finally return home only to find that his country has been overrun by men half his age who do not care about goodness or honor but only about partying and relaxing. Odysseus gets rid of these men, restores order to his country, and is reunited with the woman who never gave up on him, his faithful wife, Penelope.

Dani Argyle

Mr. Wright *Engaging, but work on academic voice* B⁻

English 10 *Late* D⁻

December 2

When Gods Attack or

How Much $#%& Can One Man Take?

In case you haven't noticed, the ancient Greeks want you to understand that life is not fair. In ancient Greece, you can be a skillful warrior, a devoted husband, and a stand-up king ~ and then make one tiny mistake (like taunting a giant one-eyed cannibal who just ate six of your crew) ~ and have all holy hell set loose upon you... especially if the one-eyed cannibal has a father named Poseidon. You see, Odysseus is king of Ithaca, and Ithaca is an island, so if you're trying to sail there, probably the only being in the cosmos who you do not want to piss off is Poseidon. So Odysseus is basically tortured for a decade (although one torturous episode does involve being offered immortality by a beautiful goddess), but the torment has the surprising effect of making Odysseus more humble and less of a jerk. (I suppose long stretches of suffering tend to have that effect on people.) The upshot of all of this is that Odysseus becomes a better person and returns home to a wife and son who still love him.

LS Keep?

DA No!

LS Even Sophia's?

DA ESPECIALLY Sophia's

LS Does Sophia know you have her work?

DA I can neither confirm nor deny that allegation

DA

I place my phone in my backpack, sigh, and see Ms. Watson in the distance.

Gabby's former speech therapist! Praise be to whichever deity is guiding me right now! That woman works miracles.

I sprint past a startled ASL teacher, whirl in front of Ms. Watson, and stop.

Ms. Watson had been walking to the main office, but with my body impeding her progress, she slows to a flowy stop. She's never so much dressed as *robed*, swathed in folds of browns and golds so that, even when she stops, she still seems in motion, regal and flowing and streaming like the sea. She has braids and ribbons swirled around her head ~ she's crowned with her own beauty ~ and she stands before me, slim and imperious, as if a goddess from Olympus deigned to descend from on high and step into the world of secondary education.

"Ms. Watson," I gasp. "Please come back to us. Please. Don't leave. Gabby needs you. He does! I know you said he's gone as far as he can go, but he can learn more and he can do better." My lungs feel rushed and gaspy, so I force myself to look calm and breathe.

Ms. Watson looks smooth on the surface but there is a light in her eyes. She inhales a calm breath. "Dani. Hi. How are you?"

"I'm fine. I'm fine. But Gabby needs you." I stare up at her, pleadingly.

"Dani, I agree. That child is eager to please. And absolutely ripe for learning." Her face looks smooth, placid, in part, I believe, because we're agreeing about everything.

Ms. Watson glances toward the main office's door, but I shift my position so she won't get distracted. My voice is imploring: "Then why won't you teach him? Why have you left and never returned?"

"Dani," she's hesitating. "I think there's a misunderstanding. Your *mother* is the one who said Gabby is done with the learning. *She's* the one who stopped the lessons." Although it should be impossible, she seems to lengthen before me, as if my mother's mortal foible has made Ms. Watson magnificent.

I'm stunned but not senseless. "*My mother? Stopped the lessons?* Ms. Watson, please ~ " I realize I'm babbling but I can't stop myself ~ "It *is* a misunderstanding. Please, please don't leave! Come back! You have to!"

She looks at me warmly, and I think I've won my case, but she has one final message: "Dani, I'd love to, but you need to talk to your mother."

The public school's speech therapist has materialized from the main-office door and calls out to Ms. Watson:

"Latasha! The committee is ready to hear from you now."

And my brother's personal angel starts flowing towards the offices. Then she calls out from over her shoulder: "And when you talk to Penny, tell her she owes me for four weeks' lessons."

Today there is a chess tournament at Green Springs Elementary School, so Gabby will be sweetly crushing his peers and wiping their armies from their chessboards into the evening hours.

I'm in the living room, pacing, glancing at a clock ~ even though I can't really read it.

Part of me can't wait for Mom to get home.

And part of me can.

When she walks in, she's small and slumped, as if her bones are sagging in her skin. She's holding a few bags of fabric and a dingy pillowcase, and even this weight just seems too much.

But today I don't care. Today, she is *wrong*.

I stop my pacing, widen my stance into a power pose, face her, and say, "Guess who I saw at school today?"

Mom looks up. "Who?" She pauses. "Was it Niko?"

"Ms. Watson." I stare.

Mom looks like she's been struck in the gut. Air seems to leave her mouth, and her eyes widen with surprise.

I start in: "How dare you, Mom! How dare you! You lied to me. You *lied*. But I don't care about me. You're crushing Gabby."

Mom walks to the couch and starts draping fabric over the back cushions. She looks at *them* rather than *me*. Then the words form: "Now wait a second, Dani. Think about what you're saying. Gabby still gets speech lessons from Miss Eva."

"Miss Eva? Miss Eva? Mom, I have nothing against Eva. She's sweet, and I'm sure she'll be great one day. But, Mom, she is *lost*. She always looks *overwhelmed*."

Mom is looking at the sofa, smoothing the fabric and shaking her head. "Dani, you're exaggerating."

"No, I'm not, I swear. Mom, I've seen her *crying*."

"Dani, life is not as simple as you think." She tugs at the the corner of the pillowcase. "Miss Eva is fine. And public school is free."

I walk to the sofa so she'll have to interact with me rather than the silks. "Is that what this is about? Is this about the *money*?" My indignation is total.

She's looking at me now: "Is money, you think, something to ignore?"

"No, Mom, no, but last I heard, Gabby's settlement left us with money. Enough to pay for college for both of us. And as for me, I won't need that."

Mom looks horrified. "You're not going to college?"

"Mom, this is not about *college*. This is about *Gabby* and what he needs to make his way in this world."

Mom sighs. "Gabby will be fine. Gabby is perfect." She looks out the window as if she'll find him there.

"Yes, Mom, he's perfect." On this we agree. "Gabby is perfect *now*. But how will things be in ten years? In twenty? Will his speech in the future always appear to be cute?"

"Your brother's got a special soul. He's ~ "

I walk in front of the window. "Mom!" I interrupt sharply. "Where's the money? Where *is* it?"

"What do you mean? There's ~ "

"You know what I mean! The money from the hospital?"

"I have it. It's safe."

"Where is it? Let me see it."

"Dani. Behave. You're forgetting yourself."

"No, Mom, I'm not. I'm protecting my brother. You say we have money; I want to see it. Or the paperwork that says where it is."

Mom's face is reddening and her neck is splotching in angry, red patches. She glares at me. "Dani. Settle."

"Don't treat me like a dog." I start walking to the desk in the dining room.

"Dani, what are you doing? Dani, stay here! Dani, that's PRIVATE!" She's calling behind me, but I will not be deterred. I'm opening up drawers and rifling through papers.

Mom hurries her pace and tries to wedge herself between me and the desk. I grab at some papers and have snagged the checkbook. I turn my back to her and flip through the pages.

Amelia Renown $250

Amelia Renown $250

Dominion Energy $94.73

Amelia Renown $250

Amelia Renown $250

Mom's reaching over my shoulder, grabbing at the checkbook, but it's too late. I turn and face her.

"Mom, who the hell is Amelia Renown?"

Mom pauses, and I see her calculating possible responses. "Daniella, I don't have to explain myself to you." She points towards my door. "Go to your room." And then ~ like a volcano that erupts after mild tremors ~ she screams: "GO! TO! YOUR! ROOM!"

I start at her ferocity, but I double down and look her in the eyes. "No, Mom. I'm not ten. I have a right to know."

Her face contorts and darkens ~ and my beautiful mother turns ugly ~ her eyes are bulging and there's spittle on her lips: "Daniella, do not make me repeat myself. I said, 'Go to your room.' *Now*." And when she sees me stand still in spite of the command, she steps towards me and raises her hand.

I feel myself flinch but then straighten and stare her down. "Go ahead, Mom. Go ahead and hit me. While you're abusing one child, you might as well abuse two."

"You have no right," her hand has dropped but so has her voice ~ it's down an octave and she's not yelling now: her voice is coming out like a growl: "You! You! You fat disgrace!"

When those words leave her mouth, she stands still, shocked. And I, too, am stunned into stillness. Inside and out, I feel my body throb.

"Dani," she stammers, "I didn't mean ~ I didn't mean ~ "

"No, Mom. No. That's ok. Now I know how you really feel."

And I turn around and go to my room.

There is a stage of misery so deep, you don't have the strength to rail against the world.

I've been sprawled face-first on my bed, sobbing and despondent. From time to time, I hear Mom's timid knock on my very locked door. I feel her pacing outside, feel the slip and dip of her gravity on the hardwood floor.

And then I hear a click and a pop and the squeak of a door opening.

"Leave me alone." I muffle my words into my pillow.

Mom sits on my bed ~ I feel the mattress sink with her weight ~ and then she strokes my hair.

Her voice is rich ~ but I'm in no mood to be soothed ~ "Dani, my darling. You are right to be upset. I will never forgive myself for what I said today."

I want to say, "You shouldn't," but I don't have the strength.

I hear a sigh and then an intake of breath. "Dani, I'm afraid you're going to be even angrier at me than you are right now, but it's time for you to hear the truth."

She takes a deep breath. There's a pause. A silence. And another deep breath. And then: "I know someone who knows where Dad is."

I turn over and sit up. I am no longer crying.

"Amelia Renown has a gift. She knows things that no human could ever really know." She looks at me and waits.

"Mom, what are you saying? Are you seeing a psychic?"

"Not a psychic. A *SEER*. This woman is a wonder."

"Oh, Mom." I rest my head on my knees and hug my legs.

My mom breathes in a long, extravagant breath:

"Let me tell you a story. There was a time when your father and I ~ we were upside down. He seemed to only care about his job. He seemed more willing to rescue strangers overseas than to talk to his wife and try to help her.

"So I went to Ms. Renown ~ she gives a consult for free ~ to ask if we should have children. I was scared that your father…"

She trails off. I know where that was going.

"and I walked into her parlor, and I asked her point-blank, 'You know what I want, so what should I do?' She looked me straight in the eye and said, 'You're not pregnant, are you?'"

Mom looks at me as if she's still amazed by this woman's powers.

"Dani, I stopped dead in my tracks. I hadn't said *anything* to her about having a baby. She knew it without me saying a word. But I told her I was *not* pregnant ~ I was only wondering if I should try ~ and she told me I needn't try, that your conception was in the stars."

"Mom," I interrupt, "when a woman of a certain age ~ "

"No, Dani, no! This woman told me about *you*! She told me I would give birth to a girl who would be born with the first flourish of the season, and then she told me your name."

I'm surprised. "She named me Daniella?"

"No. Your middle name. She gave you your middle name." She strokes my hair some more.

I lean away. "Oh, Mom, no. That is *not* a name. That is a *curse*."

"You think that now, but one day, you'll understand. One day, you'll find that the Greek heroine suits you." Her eyes are glimmering in the fading light.

"Suit me, it might. If it doesn't kill me first."

"Dani, dear, don't be melodramatic. But don't you see? My dear Dani? This woman has a *gift*. After I saw her sixteen years ago, I went home and took a home-pregnancy test. It came up negative, as I knew it would. But two weeks later, my cycle never began. Or three weeks later. Or four. And then I knew that she was right."

"So you trust this woman because she guessed you were

pregnant? Or about to become pregnant? It's not an impressive guess. You were the right age to ask. You were wearing a wedding ring ~ "

"No, Dani, No." She puts her arms around me and I don't pull away, although I probably should. "Your father and I had been trying for *years*. But then I got spooked and thought we should quit."

I feel my mom's warmth ~ she always smells of earth and honey ~ but then I feel myself stiffen, and I hear my words before I plan to speak them: "But that doesn't explain why she has all of our money."

Mom's arms drop and she sighs. "When Dad's disappearance hit the papers, she came to me and told me things no one could ever know." She's gathering herself and places both hands in her lap.

I'm shocked into silence, but then the reality dawns on me: "Mom? Mom! *She* came to *you?*"

"Yes. With information about Pop-Pop and Daddy and *you*. She's an incredible woman."

I slump in my seat. I worry that Mom is too far gone to be reasoned with. If I'm going to stop Ms. Renown from ravaging our family's grief for her own personal payday, then I'm going to have to confront her and stop her myself.

But for now, I feel like I have some authority. What happened in the dining room is going to give me some temporary control ~ even if it's thin ~ and I need to use it while I can.

"Mom," I venture, "this woman believes that Dad is alive?"

"*Believe*? No, she doesn't *believe*. Dani, she *knows* it."

"And when they discover his body and find that he's been dead for three years, will Ms. Renown give you a refund?"

Mom stiffens. She shakes her head and sighs. "Dani, Ms. Renown is never wrong."

"Then she has a very poor memory. Or she's only confronting the simplest things. Or she's rewriting the past to fit the present. It's the nature of humans to be wrong *sometimes*."

"Humans. Yes. *Humans*." My mother's voice is tinged with triumph. "But there are more things in heaven and earth than are dreamt of in your philosophy, Daniella."

I rise from the bed and stand before her. Sitting on my mattress, she seems so small, so delicate, so *broken*. But if a lie is keeping her small, then the truth might heal her: "That could be the case, Mom. I just don't think the secrets of the universe have been entrusted to a woman who would take so much time to reveal them that she robs a deaf child of his therapy."

My mom is straightening, lengthening before me. "When she finds him, and she will, Dad will come home, and we'll be a family again. Gabby's having his father back is worth the loss of Ms. Watson." She stands up and smiles and strokes my hair.

I can't win. I can't argue against magic and the unfounded optimism of the human heart.

"Mom," I sigh. "I'm tired. I'd like to see if I can sleep at Aunt Lainie's house tonight."

"Sure," Mom soothes. "I'll help you pack a bag."

I glance at the closet. "No worries, Mom. It's already packed."

I ring Lainie's bell and wait on the stoop, demurely, a bag in one hand, Sailor Moon in the other.

Lainie opens the door with a flourish. "Kitten," she says, "Penny called me. She says you two had a fight."

I'm looking at the ground. "You could say that." My bones feel small, like they're sinking inside me.

"Come in, please. Pierre and I are just starting dinner."

I step in to a dining room that is extravagantly set. There are candles and decanters and serving trays with secrets steaming in the air. I wave sheepishly. "Hi, Pierre. Sorry to intrude."

"Don't apologize, Daniella. I love how your aunt loves you." He gets up and pulls out a chair for me.

I sit down and gaze at my lap. "Sorry if I'm not much for conversation." I glance at both of them apologetically. "But the food smells good, and I'd just really like to eat."

It's a lie. I'm *not* hungry. But I really, really, don't want to talk.

Lainie hands me a plate and tells me to help myself. I'm piling food that I'll never eat on a plate I'm going to stare at all night. I glance up and see Lainie grinning her mischievous Lainie-grin. "And I know something else that you will really like." Her eyes flash bright before she glides into the kitchen.

I look at Pierre. He eats of forkful of ravioli and smiles and shrugs.

Lainie comes back with a mug of hot chocolate. Miniature marshmallows are floating on top.

I take the mug from her hands. "Lainie, thank you." I watch the steam whiffing from the top. Before I was ten, there was no problem that couldn't be cured by a warm mug of cocoa. My grief is no longer so thin, but I cup my hands around the mug and feel its warmth. It feels like comfort. I close my eyes and take a sip.

And then I spit its contents back into the mug.

"Lainie, I'm sorry." I look at her with surprised eyes. "But I think your milk is bad."

"No, it's not, Strawberry. I put some vodka in it." Her smile is playful and expansive and perfect.

"Vodka?" I'm stunned.

"Vodka. Sometimes a girl just needs a little drink." I think I hear her giggle.

I put down the mug. "Lainie, thanks. But I don't think that's legal."

She picks up the drink and puts it in my hands. "Legal? No. But it's right anyways. You're my niece, and I need to take care of you."

"With Vod-ka," I say.

"With vodka," she insists.

I look at the mug as if it's daring me to drink it, and I do. I drink. The chocolate is warm and round and the vodka stingy and sharp, and the drink does a thorough job of making me feel toasty as well as a little sloshy and not as angry and edged as I was before.

Somehow, I feel mushy and bold all at once, so I look at Lainie, and then at Pierre, and then at Lainie again. I think my head is bobbing, a little. "Lainie, I'm sorry if this is not a now-conversation, but do you know that my mom has hired a psychic?"

Her lips purse out and then down and she sighs. "I know, Cocoa. We've talked about it before."

"Have you told her that she's crazy?" I'm trying to focus on Lainie, but she's looking a little sloopy.

"We've called each other crazy." She rests her head on her hand and sighs.

"Lainie." It's hard to reach down and bring ugliness this ugly up to the surface, but if I can't say this to Lainie, I can't say it to anyone, so I stare at my napkin and explain: "Mom and I had it out tonight. Really, really bad."

I feel some tears prickling my eyes, so I bring the cocoa to my lips and take a long, warm gulp.

Lainie's voice is soft ~ it tingles the air. "I believe you, Tulip. But you and Penny have had fights before. Big, long shouting matches, if I recall. So don't you think that things will always be the way they are right now. I know you two. You will forgive each other."

"I don't need forgiveness," I clarify. "She does."

"And you will forgive her." But now she's putting on her aunt voice. "Your mother isn't as strong as she used to be, Dani, and

71

to tell you the truth, you can be rather…" she sighs, searching for a word ~ "*blunt*… when you deal with people."

My head startles up. Lainie is smiling. Even Pierre looks engaged, upbeat, enamored. That's what beauty does: everything Lainie says is stunning and gorgeous because Lainie is the one who is saying it.

Lainie blows a whisp of hair out of her face. "You know I love you, Dani-dear, and I wouldn't want you any other way. But you can be a little…" she pauses again ~ "*Prickly*. And your emotions can go off like a bomb."

I'm too tired to disagree. I'm too tired to *think*. And the room doesn't seem as stable as it should be. Even the walls seem wobbly.

"Lainie," I say, "thank you for the food, and a place to stay, but I'm really, really wiped."

"I understand, Dani-doll. You go rest on my bed. Pierre was just leaving, weren't you Pierre?" She looks at him in a way that says, do-this-now-and-I'll-love-you-forever.

Pierre starts to rise. "I know when I'm superfluous. Miss Daniella, farewell. Helena, be well." He kisses her hand and even bows a little. "I will take my leave."

I hear him close the front door, and then I stand and stagger into Lainie's room, and I don't even take off my clothes. I collapse on my back onto the fully made bed and hear some distant dish-clatter. When the noise ends, I feel Lainie crawl onto the bed beside me.

She brushes the hair out of my face and kisses me on the

forehead. "Good night, Dani-dear. Your mother loves you more than you know. And so do I. I don't know what we'd do without you. Relax, and go to sleep."

And I obey. I drift into a large and listless sleep. The sleep of the defeated. The sleep of the dead.

Dani Argyle Takes on the Weekend
Saturday and Sunday, March 8-9, 2025

I'd been wondering whether I should rethink my sleepover with Sophia. Honestly, I feel too upset to have fun, but time spent with her will be a welcome distraction from the disaster that is my life.

So, I'm walking up my friend's driveway and into a palace of a place. My God, my friend is *rich*.

I'm invited into the front foyer ~ which is huge ~ but the place resonates like a drum. Noise is everywhere.

Up until now, I had wanted distraction. Now, I'm getting it in spades.

Sophia's house is full of clatter: full of bickering and bargaining and barking and dogs.

The dogs are omnipresent. There are only three, but there seem to be more. Every time I turn from a dog, I turn to a dog again. Their snouts sniff my feet, my crotch, my hands. There is no part of me here that seems to be clean.

I see why Sophia has never invited me over before now. All

of our sleepovers have been at my house. Mrs. Brown senses my discomfort and puts the dogs out back. Thank heavens! Why anyone would want dogs *inside* their house is beyond me.

The dining room has a table the size of a barn door, and all of the food is laid out like a feast. There's beer-battered fish and tortillas and a golden sauce; shredded cabbage and tomato and red onion for fixings, and cornbread and coleslaw and some bright fruit I've never seen before. There are six of us around the table, but there is room for more. Our plates are full and the food is tremendous.

But no one seems to enjoy it.

Sophia's little sister is complaining about the coleslaw.

"Eat it or don't," Sophia interjects. "You're such a little brat."

"And you're a mean, mean, meanie," the little one retorts.

There's a big brother, and he joins in, obviously enjoying his authority as first-born child: "Shut up. The both of you."

I chew my taco quietly. I had been hoping for humor, not insipid bullying.

The father is spooning heaps of sauce onto his plate. "The sauce isn't as spicy as it usually is."

The mom sighs. "If you want it spicier, you can help in the kitchen."

"No, it's good," the dad clarifies. "It's just a little bland."

Sophia jumps in: "Dad, something can't be both good *and* bland."

I keep my head low and chew some more.

There are more surly words ~ it's dinner and a scrum ~ and then I hear a throat clear and somebody saying my name.

I glance around the table until I find the owner of the voice.

"I hear you and Sophia are in English together," Mr. Brown is saying.

I nod my head. *Brilliant.*

He raises his eyebrows. "So, it's *The Inferno*, huh?"

I nod some more. My conversational skills are fully on display.

"Do you like it?" He seems genuinely curious, the way adults can be when deciding whether or not their children's friends are companions worthy of their offspring.

"I love it."

The edges of the father's eyes stretch into an impressed smile.

"Why?" The mother sounds wounded. "Isn't it dark? All those people getting tortured forever?"

"It's no more dark than real life," I explain. "Dante isn't really writing about Hell, you know. He's writing about what people are doing to themselves when they sin."

"Nuh-uh," the little sister chimes in. "Sophia says it's about Hell."

I smile at my friend. "Dante makes it *seem* that way. But he's just showing on the outside what people do to themselves on the inside. People think that ~ if they do something bad and don't get caught ~ then they've gotten away with something. But Dante is showing how we hurt ourselves when we do evil. And how easy it can be to stop being in control of your actions, and have your actions start being in control of you. Kind of like an addiction."

"I don't get it." The little one is frowning.

"Ok. Imagine this." I'm smiling at her ~ being a teacher is fun. "Say you're having an affair." As soon as the words leave my mouth, I inhale a jag, but no one seems to notice. I collect myself. "And say you're doing something with your body that you know is wrong, but you feel like you can't help it. You feel like your body is calling the shots."

"Like when I take a cookie," the little one offers.

"Like when you take a cookie. In *The Inferno*, Dante puts these people in a gigantic whirlwind so that their bodies are being blown around in a storm. You see? They lost control of their bodies on Earth, so they have no control of them in Hell." I need to change the topic from the adultery angle, so I begin again. "Or imagine you're an angry person ~ a bully ~ and you like beating people up. Dante puts all of these bullies in a small space together, and they keep hitting each other for eternity. See? Whatever environment you created on Earth, that's the environment you get in Hell."

"It still seems pretty harsh," Ms. Brown asserts. "No one deserves to be judged for one tiny mistake."

"Hell is not for tiny mistakes." I feel my authority swelling. "Hell is for people whose sin defines who they are. When do people who sometimes lie become liars? When do people who sometimes gamble become gamblers? Hell is for people who have become attached to their sin. Not only that," and I'm realizing that all eyes are on me ~ even the older brother's, "Hell is for people who *like* themselves exactly the way they are. So they double-down on their bad behavior and don't *want* to change. The easiest way to avoid Hell is to be a work a progress, or at least someone who wants to be a better person."

"Then no one should go to Hell," the sister is deciding, "because everyone wants to be a better person."

Mr. Brown dissents. "You would think that, wouldn't you, Lexie? But I promise, I've worked with a lot of people who are pretty impressed with who they are. Admitting that they're wrong or that they could improve is not something they are willing to do."

"Well, I want to be a good person," Lexie is insisting. "So I won't go to Hell, will I?" She looks around the table, searchingly.

"Never, Sweetie," the mother comforts. And perhaps to stop her daughter from thinking too hard about such problematic issues, she adds, "Who wants dessert?"

When dinner is done, I thank Mrs. Brown for the delicious meal and take dishes to the kitchen and set them in the sink ~ listen to their clatter and the hiss of hot water ~ and Sophia appears by my side, watching. I don't mind washing dishes ~ I find the entire practice relaxing ~ but the Browns have a dishwasher with buttons I've never seen before. I'm leaning over, squinting at them, when Ms. Brown enters and shoos us away ~ something about guests not working in the kitchen ~ and suddenly, I'm exhausted, as if I'm a balloon that's deflated, and I admit to Ms. Brown that I am tired.

And since the house is huge and I could have my own room if I wanted it, Mrs. Brown asks if I do.

"Mom! What the hell?" Sophia's eyes are wide and embarrassed. "It's a *sleepover*. Dani sleeps with *me*." To prove her point, Sophia grabs me by the elbow and pulls me towards her. Then we head upstairs, and Sophia whispers, but loudly, "My mom is such an idiot."

When we reach her room, I plop on the bed, feel the mattress gutter and shake, and Sophia sits and settles next to me. Is this fun-time? Or deep-talk time? I consider telling her about my mother, about Renown, about the ridiculousness that is my life, but how in the world could Sophia understand? The dysfunction of my house is so very different than the disfunction of hers. Hers are tiny conflagrations that are snuffed out as quickly as they catch fire. Mine is a miasma that is smoldering with char, burning secretly under the soil.

I decide it's time for distraction that's fun, so I straighten up, and Sophia and I take out our phones. But still, I observe ~ off-handedly, of course: "Soph, you're kinda tough on your little sister. And your mother."

"They deserve it," Sophia replies. "One is a brat and the other is clueless."

I sigh. There are too many battles, and I need a break.

I try my best to be immersed in my phone.

The memes flash by, and I feel some excitement kindling my skin.

Then I look up and show Sophia my screen. "By the way," I tell her, "the best singer in the world? She isn't a singer."

She squeaks. "You're lying! She's awesome. Hatsune Miku ~ "

"You can call her CV01 ~ "

"She's beautiful and gorgeous and ~ " her fingers are gliding across her screen. "She's gone beyond what mere humans can do."

"She's human in her core," I'm arguing. "Saki Fajita is in there somewhere."

"But Miku has the better hair." She holds out her phone with a picture of the blue tresses that look like the ocean. "This ninja doesn't need a low-taper fade."

"But I know a lot of people who could use one. Kim Jun Un. Elon Musk."

"Joe Biden."

There's no need for words. We laugh and laugh until our stomachs ache.

Then Sophia startles upright and looks at me mischievously.

"What?" I ask. I try to peek at her screen.

"You'll see," she hunches over her phone and grins.

I look at her quizzically. And then Niko texts. Both of us.

NK how r u doing? any pillow fights

SB YES the feathers are flying

NK Dani is this true

I'm staring at my screen, stuck, ogled-eyed.

"Dani," Sophia hisses, "he's flirting with you."

DA not yet...

  but the night is still young

NK I like

   . . .

   . . .

NK what r u 2 doing tomorrow

DA don't know

SB STUDYING

NK boring

SB required

NK Dani, tomorrow u want to hang at the mall

      Sophia is pushing me while trying to grab my phone.

  . . .

DA k

NK cool

Meet me outside of Macys at 4

I'll show you something I know youll like

      Sophia has given up reaching for my phone and is now a blur and a flash of thumbs.

SB good luck with that one Niko. Dani is one of a kind

NK I can tell

SB Good night Niko. Dani and I have some pillow fighting to do

NK give a guy a break

Sophia is shoving me some more, but I'm shaking my head.

"I *knew* it," Sophia is saying. "He *like*s you. The boy has it *bad*."

"Please, Sophia. Please." I'm shaking my head so that my hair seems everywhere. "He can't like me. He can't."

"Why not?"

"You know why." I'm staring at my phone.

"Because you're smart and funny and beautiful ~ "

"Stop!"

"Why?" She seems genuinely clueless. Clueless and baffled and naive.

Will she really make me say it? Say it out loud?

I look at her. "Because I'm fat, Sophia. I'm *fat*. That's why."

"No you're not." A pause. "Ok, Dani. You're *overweight*, but you're beautiful. I'm not overweight, but I'm not pretty."

"Yes you are," I lie.

"No, Dani. I'm not. But you are." Her eyes look sincere.

"Sophia, please. You can't be beautiful and fat at the same time. It's just not possible."

"Niko thinks so." She shows me her phone with the texting chain ~ as if the issue is settled.

"Stop, Sophia. Stop." I cannot get my hopes up. I can't set

my hopes on anyone, but especially not on Niko.

"It's a *date*. You have a *date* with Niko Kaneko." She pushes me, playfully.

"It's not a date. It's not." I scroll through my own texts with Niko. Then I sigh. "By the way," I ask, "what makes something a date?"

Sophia puts on her thinking face. "It's a date," she declares, "if both people *think* it's a date."

"Ok," I hesitate. "Maybe it's half a date."

When we've memed every meme that's worthy of our time, and listened to "Gangnam Style" and danced like crazy ("Op, op-op-op, oppan Gangnam seutail. Eh, sexy lady"), I'm starting to droop.

At the sleepovers in my house, my bed has a trundle. But here, there's just one big double.

The problem is this: I'm an aggressive sleeper. At night, I've been known to wage war with my mattress.

"Sophia," I explain, "I should sleep on the floor. If you try to sleep next to me, things could get ugly."

"Yeah," she begins, "you toss a bit. But I think I can handle it."

"Good luck," I tell her. "You're going to need it."

When I wake up in the morning, it's hard to know whether Sophia is asleep or just really, really still. The room is quiet so that my thoughts are jostling about and begging for attention. I want to meme again, but my phone is out of reach, so I'm stranded here with my memories and the ruins of my life. Perhaps I *should* talk to Sophia. If she can't *understand,* at least she could *sympathize*? I'm tempted to wake her and tell her about Mom, but every time I take a breath, I can hear her rhythmic breathing ~ the tell-tale sign that she is asleep. It's unfair for me to wake her, and by the time she starts stirring, I've lost my resolve.

Sophia yawns and sits up in bed. She scratches her head and blinks dramatically. Then she turns to me and asks how I slept.

"Pretty good," I reply. Relieved at the small talk, I elucidate further: "But all night, I kept bumping into something that was hard."

She rolls her eyes and sighs. "Dani, that was ME."

"Ooops," I apologize.

"Crap. What the hell?" She's looking at some blood on the elbows of her pajamas.

I sit up and inspect the elbows. "I'm a bad sleeper, I'll admit, but I did not do THAT."

"No, I must have scratched off some scabs in my sleep." She rubs at the stains. "And I *love* these pajamas. How the hell will I ever get this out?"

"Wash in cold," I explain. (I've been doing the Argyle laundry since I was twelve.)

"Really? In *cold*?"

"In cold. I promise."

After our fast has been broken (by both food and phones) and we've fixed the sheets that I tried to strangle on Sophia's bed, I text Aunt Lainie and ask for a ride home.

She appears at the door, radiant and giddy.

"Here," she says and holds out the keys to her car.

"What's this?" I ask ~ ridiculously ~ like an idiot.

"You're driving home, my sweetest one." Since I haven't grabbed for the keys, she's placed them in my hand.

I look at them, confused. "Driving? Are you crazy?"

"Why not? You have your permit." She actually appears to be wounded, as if I've returned a gift she gave me for my birthday.

"Lainie, this is ridiculous. I've never driven before. Shouldn't we start small? You know: I'll get in the driver's seat and *sit*?"

"Don't be silly, Dani-doll. You learn to drive by *driving*." She's shining. She starts walking to the car, and, to prove her resolution, she gets in. The *passenger* side.

I open the door and drop into the driver's seat. My feet don't come close to touching the pedals. I feel like a toddler in an adult's chair. I'm squirming (nothing is comfortable when you're extra large) and trying to reach for the pedals that are too far and too much. I look at Lainie and explain to her that she has more faith in me than she ever should.

"Don't worry, Sprinkles." She reaches under my seat and does something magical so I can move myself forward. When I click into place, I hear her say, "I'm right here. You're safe. We'll take things slow."

She gives me the requisite tutorial on turn-signals and mirrors. How have I ridden so many times in a car and not realized which lever is the turn signal and which is the wiper? Everything about the dashboard seems unrecognizable and foreign. At least I know which is the gas and which is the brake.

I turn the engine over and put the car into gear. We bounce down Sophia's driveway (Lainie had taken the time to back the car into it), and I turn, WIDELY onto the street. Thank the heavens no cars are around on a Sunday morning.

We chug down the road, and I feel myself weaving, stupidly, slowly, first hugging the center line and then the shoulder. Who knew this was so hard? Everyone I know drives with such ease.

Somehow, we make it home without driving into a ditch, but I have a feeling that Sophia isn't the only person feeling jolted after spending her morning with me.

"I'm sorry," I say as I pull into the driveway. Even here, I'm braking too hard, and I feel the nose of the car dip and then pop back in place.

"Sorry about what? You were *brilliant*." Lainie beams.

"No," I correct her. "I was awful and stupid and clumsy."

"And you were clumsy, too, when you were learning to walk." She unclicks her seatbelt and it zips back with a snap. "I was there when it happened. You fell down twenty times a minute before you took off on your own. And look at you now! Walking is so easy, you can do it in your sleep. Right?"

"There's a difference between walking and piloting two tons of metal down a street where *other* people are *also* piloting two tons of metal." I unclick my seatbelt, but there's no zipping anywhere; just an awkward belt that's catching on my clothes. "Lainie," I sigh, "this is harder than I thought. I don't think I can do this." I hold the seatbelt away from me so it can retract on its own.

"Are you kidding? You've already done it!" My aunt is exultant. "No mailboxes were mown down during the course of this adventure."

I startle straight and look at her, quizzically.

"Your mother doesn't really talk about me much, does she?" Lainie laughs. "Penny took me driving a month before my sixteenth birthday. She thought it would be cool to teach her little sister how to drive. I plowed through two mailboxes in one day."

"Impressive," I say. It's my turn to smile.

"I was traumatized," she confesses. "And Penny never took me driving again."

I'm waiting for Niko outside of Macy's. Lots of people who are not Niko pass by me and stare. There are a couple of guys who are close to Niko ~ who *could be* Niko from a distance ~ but when they approach, they reveal their true selves, their complete lack of Niko-ness. I'm running through my mind: how many Macy's are there near Leesville? Am I at the wrong one? Leave it up to me to find the perfect guy and then miss our first date due to poor map-reading skills. But when it's four minutes after four o'clock, I have to confront the truth. Of *course* he stood me up.

That's the purpose I serve in life: to be the butt of other people's jokes.

Then I hear a whistle from the building behind me.

The true Niko exits Macy's and stands before me, resplendent in his Niko-ness.

"You made it!" I say, a little too excitedly. "You're here!"

"In the flesh," he grins and even bows a little. "What are your other two wishes?"

He holds the door for me with a flourish ~ and even attempts some French, something like *entray-vue* ~ and I clomp inside. He joins me in the foyer, and I exert some willpower over my tongue. "Where do you want to go first?" I ask. "Spencer's? Hot Topic?"

"Not today," he says; his eyes are glinting. "Today, we see a movie."

"A movie?"

"A movie."

"Which one?"

"Nuh-uh," Niko clicks. "Today is a surprise!" He turns and starts walking.

I jump to catch up. "A surprise? Why?"

If mischief had a face, his name would be Niko. "Because surprises make life fun." His eyes are gleaming.

We turn down a corridor to the theater, but when we're thirty yards away, he asks me to stop and stands behind me. I feel a blindfold slip over my eyes. Then the world blackens, and I hear whooshes pulsing through my ears, and I feel panic setting in. "Niko! Niko! What the ~ "

"Shhh," he assures. His voice is low, conspiratorial. "Trust me. It's going to be amazing."

This cannot end well. I've been the butt of too many school-yard pranks to trust my classmates. In elementary school, I could wear my embarrassment in my own personal solitude, but now that everyone has a cell phone, a moment of shame can be blazed across the interweb. My own personal horror can amuse the masses.

Niko walks behind me to one side and leads me by the shoulder. Then we stop and I've lost track of where in the mall we could be, and something seems to be happening in low, hushed tones. I'm glad the blindfold is covering my cheeks, or he would see them burning.

"We're here!" he cheers. "Follow me." He places my hands on his shoulders and guides me up some stairs and then we're sloping down somewhere and then we enter a narrow space and he tells me to sit. My butt hits something hard before settling into softness.

"Niko," I feel true panic setting in, "can I take off the blindfold?" My voice sounds more imploring than it should: it's strained and 'uncool' by high-school standards.

Through the hushed darkness, I hear his voice, and, even in the dark, it's smiling: "Not yet. No spoilers."

I'm flustered and sweating. To add insult to injury, I'm afraid of the dark. Anything could be going on around me, and I'm vulnerable to it all.

But then I hear some trailers and realize we are, truly, in a theater. He hasn't posed me by the Easter Bunny or next to lingerie models in Victoria's Secret. He hasn't led me to a make-over counter or a tattoo parlor. I feel my pulse start to soothe, and my breathing doesn't seem as jinky as it was before.

When my blood has settled enough that I can hear again, I start listening to the trailers. Sometimes, you can get a sense of the upcoming movie based upon the type of trailers that come first. But today, I'm a blank. Today, I've got nothing.

Silence. Then I sense that the darkness is getting darker.

And then the blindfold comes off.

I look up at a towering Reese Witherspoon who is sitting despondently at a mountain overlook.

She's taking off her boot and chucking it off the mountain.

It takes a while to process this series of events. "Niko!" I finally manage. "It's *Wild*! You've brought me to *Wild*! How is it back in the theaters? How on earth did you know?"

I want to tell him that *Wild* is the best memoir I've ever read, but before I say a word, he's explaining in hushed tones: "It's an anniversary viewing. And I saw you reading it last year. In the library. Before school."

It's dark, thankfully, so he can't see how gobsmacked I am.

"Niko!" I say. "Niko! I love this book."

I settle in. And watch.

I have to admit, the book is brilliant. The movie? Not so much. Unless you've read the book, you have no real idea why Cheryl Strayed is coming undone.

And, oops. There's some sex.

Graphic, in-the-alleyway. Sex.

But we get through the awkwardness, and I don't care that the movie is mediocre: because Niko Kaneko has taken me to see it.

After it's over, Niko leans in. "I know a place," he explains, "in the corner of the mall. The restaurant claims to be Korean, but they have some really good Japanese food."

"My God," I exclaim. "This day is awesome."

We're seated in a discreet corner of the restaurant. Niko is greeting strangers as they pass by our table. I swear, it seems as if Niko knows everyone, even the owner.

I'm stunned and smiling. But when I look at the menu, the reverie starts to fade. There are so many ways this day can turn south.

Because Niko Kaneko is going to watch me eat.

This cannot end well.

When you're overweight, and you eat publicly, everyone will judge you.

Eat a salad, and everyone who watches will think *If she eats like that, why is she so fat?* Order the fried chicken, and they're tsk-

tsking, as if every supposition they've ever had about you has just been affirmed.

But Japanese food will make things easier. Tempura aside, almost everything is healthy.

I order Teriyaki salmon with rice and broccoli.

Niko orders tempura.

Of course.

When the Miso arrives, I decide to go deep. If Niko liked shallow, he'd invite out one of the Chorus girls.

"You're relatively new here," I tell him. "It can be hard on some people to move in the eighth grade."

"Yes," he acknowledges. "Yes, that's true. Things are different here than from my home back home." He looks a little sad. "I moved here from Japan with my mom. She couldn't stand it anymore."

"Your mom!" I'm surprised, "doesn't like *Japan*?"

He picks up his spoon to take a sip of the soup and then pauses and puts it back down again. "Well, it makes sense. She's not Japanese. She's American. She and my dad met in Switzerland, of all places, on a two-week ski trip. Fell head over heels. Had me. Fast." He's grinning again, as if he is co-conspirator in his parents' engagement.

"But they're no longer together?" Now it's my turn to be sad.

"No, they're not together. But they love each other, I know. They really do." He looks like he'll pick up his spoon again but then leaves it be. "But giving up your country for your spouse is a really big ask. And Mom gave up her language, too."

"Your mom doesn't speak Japanese?" This boy's family is a marvel.

"Not well. She speaks at ~ I'd say ~ a third-grade level. And I get the sense that ~ when she lived in Japan ~ she got tired of always sounding stupid. She could never express in Japanese all the thoughts that were in her head."

I feel the umami steaming from the soup. Yesterday's me would be slurping down Miso, but today's me is wrapped in wonder: "Her language didn't improve?"

"A little. Not a lot. She was so embarrassed because she thought she sounded dumb, so she just didn't speak that much. And you don't get better if you don't speak the language." He seems to have forgotten his soup: his Miso is steaming, alone and neglected.

"I'm sorry it didn't work out."

"It's ok. They still love each other. They do. They just love their own countries more." He smiles a weak smile.

"It's understandable. It's still sad." I push my bowl away a bit. "But why did *you* leave Japan? Why didn't you just stay with your dad?"

Niko sighs. He puts his fingertips on the edges of the table ~ as if it's tipsy and needs to be steadied. "I love Japan. I really do. But I spent my trimester breaks over here, in Virginia, with my American cousins. And it's hard to explain, but I'm not sure I connect with *places*. Deep down, I connect with *people*. And I've always been more connected to my mother than my father." He's studying the table, as if there's a roadmap there that he's trying to navigate. "So even when I lived in Japan, I really loved America... I felt connected to this country because I loved my mom."

"So when you travel through life," I offer, "you follow your loves. That's not a bad way to navigate this world." And then I remember Lainie, and I rethink my position, for I've watched love be an impulsive and mercurial guide. "But Niko," I venture, "where do you feel the most... *free*?"

He stills ~ like a statue ~ even his skin seems quiet. "That's a good question." His voice is low, like a hush. He takes a timid breath. "In Japan, I am always *haf-u*." He traces a ハーフ in the air with a finger. "That's not an insult. It's only a fact. So I'm not sure that I always feel *free* in this country, but America is usually where I feel the most.... *Whole*."

I nod.

I understand.

I think.

"But sometimes," I venture, "I sense that that you are lonely."

His eyes flash wide. He seems stunned silent, but then some words venture out: "How in the world could you sense that?"

I nod lightly. "You can feel people's loneliness. When no one else is watching, they look weary, they look heavy, like they're wearing a lead sweater. It's everywhere around us. But the weight that some people carry is heavier than others."

"I don't know what to say." He glances at his soup, but it's lost its steam. The umami is quiet, resting, still.

I look at him and smile, a little show of warmth. "Maybe it's nice not to be lonely anymore."

We catch an Uber and share it together. Niko jokes with the Uber driver ~ he can make anything fun ~ and when the car stops at my house, Niko is all action. "Wait here," Niko tells the driver as he rushes around to open my car door.

My God! I think as he walks me to the door. *He's going to kiss me. Niko Kaneko is going to kiss ME.*

But he doesn't.

I walk up to the stoop, and, when I reach the top and turn around, he's standing below on the bottom step.

"I had a good time," he says and nods.

"Me, too," I agree.

There's silence, and then he tilts his head to the side and adds, "Ok, then. Well, I'll see you at school," and he shrugs.

And then he turns around and walks away.

I watch him walk to the car, open the door, and climb in. The Uber driver must have said something funny ~ probably something about dating fat chicks ~ because Niko throws back his head and laughs. He pats the driver on the shoulder, and the car pulls away.

I open the front door and take the five steps to my room. When I enter, everything is juggery and a tumble inside me.

What the hell happened? Why am I an idiot? How could I be

so stupid and misread so much? And then the reality glowers before me like a storm cloud clogging the sun ~ Niko doesn't like *me*: Niko likes *everyone*. Niko likes *life* and every person in it. He's vibrant and charming and everyone he meets feels special, feels loved, feels *seen*.

I walk to the nightstand and open up a drawer.

Lainie's bottle is in there, waiting.

I know the medicine doesn't work immediately, and I know it's irrational to bulk up on WellProtran or any SSRI, but I need to do something, *anything* right now, anything so I don't have to feel what I'm feeling.

I open the bottle and swallow two pills.

I wait. And I wait. And then wait some more.

Nothing happens. Of course. There is no cure for ugly and fat, so all I've proven is that I'm an idiot, too.

I clomp to my closet and yank open the door.

It releases with a crack.

There, on the top shelf, is a large duffel bag. It's fully packed and ready for action. Puffy and crammed and absolutely overflowing.

It's ready to go in case things get bad.

And waiting underneath is a long, thin knife. It's pointed and sharp. Serrated. Menacing.

It's ready to go in case things get worse.

Today things are bad but not *that* bad. Besides, I could never do that to Mom and Gabby.

Have them find a corpse, that is.

That gift, such as it were, will be reserved for Aunt Lainie and her beautiful bath.

So today, nothing definitive is needed. There are many ways I can show my body how much I hate it and hate everything inside it. There are many ways to numb this pain into submission.

I close the closet door and walk to my dresser, open the underwear drawer, and scrounge to the back. There's a clutter of snacks hidden away.

I choose a bag of chips, a sleeve of cookies, and a box of Teddy Grahams. I'm about to close the drawer when I decide the day has been bad enough to also warrant some Snickers bars.

I lay out the collection on the floor but then realize my feet are sending me to the kitchen.

Dips. Yes. *Dips.* French-onion dip, and buffalo dip, and caramel dip, and some marshmallow fluff. I cradle the containers in my arms and slip back to my room before anyone can see.

My stomach is tight and angry, but I can fill it until it's warm.

I eat a chip. Then a cookie. Then a graham cracker. Then a Snicker.

But all of this food can be more fun. A chip with onion dip. A cookie with marshmallow. Graham crackers with caramel.

Now a chip with onion and buffalo dip. A cookie with caramel and marshmallow fluff. A graham-cracker sandwich with

Snicker-smash.

My mouth feels full and warm and loved.

I feel the food slide down my throat, and my stomach responds with a blossoming sensation. It's weary of neglect. It's eager for attention.

But there comes a time when the fullness doesn't feel so good. It feels ugly and disgusting ~ sloppy and thick. But it felt good a while ago, and I want that feeling again, so I eat more and more until everything inside me is muddled with junk.

I slump among a waste of wrappers, empty boxes, half-eaten jars.

Dear God, I am stupid and I will never, ever learn.

Dear God, I am ugly and I will never be loved.

So I hold my stomach and rock back and forth. Everything is the same. Nothing has changed. I am still fat. I am still ugly. Only now I am fat and ugly and clotted with slop.

I am horrible, and life is horrible, and I will never be happy while I am within it.

I wonder if some people are just too stupid to live.

Dani Argyle Takes on *The Inferno*
Monday, March 11, 2025
9:44 a.m.

By Monday, everything seems normal again.

Renown is still gutting my family for her own personal gain. My clothes are still dumpy. And I am still dumb.

On Monday, no one is talking about me decking Jason Argano. Any whiff of popularity that I might have had ended up being ephemeral and fleeting ~ a thin distraction. Within three days, the Chorus is already squeaking about other people's lives.

In Wright's class, however, there is a promise of fun. Accounts have been created. Sophia, Niko, and I are poised and ready to Tweet.

Tuesday's Niko is the same as Friday's Niko. Charming. Energetic. Glowing. Nothing sad or vulnerable at all.

The class is chattering its pre-class chatter when there's a flash of white in the doorway and Wright sways into the room to find his stage.

The lecture begins.

There's something about the differences between Purgatory and Hell. In Purgatory, there's art, there's nature, there's community, there's some other things too, and some moving and rebuilding and some sun and some time.

I'm struck by the something about time.

"Hell is an eternal present with no hope of a future," Wright is saying. "The gift of being human is the gift of our relationship with time. Humans can imagine a future that is different than the present. That is something that animals cannot do. Neither can the damned."

I nod in agreement. It's perpetual stasis for animals and the damned. And let's not forget about high-school students.

I get a text, not a Tweet, from Niko. He's staring at me. Resplendent.

NK I'm having second thoughts

...

I think I should be Dante.

DA oh HELL no, sweetcakes

I AM DANTE

SB stop texting and start tweeting

@VirgilInThePhilosopher'sZone

Just got asked to tutor Dante on the consequences of sin. So I'm a nanny now? #demoted

@DanteTheInfernoIsLit

Dominos does not deliver. I just wanted a pizza. Why does Hell suck?

Virgil

Did you read the terms and conditions?

Dante

?

Virgil

Does "abandon all hope" ring a bell?

Dante

Someone seriously needs to Febreeze this place, I feel like I'm dying.

Virgil

Updated Resume:

Philosopher

Poet

Mythmaker

Babysitter

Dante

Why is there smooth jazz playing in the vestibule of Hell? Is that screaming in the distance?

Virgil

Dante's fainted and we haven't even gotten to Circle 1 yet. Who can't handle a few wasps and maggots? #designateddriver

Dante

I've got a GF (she just doesn't know it yet)

@BeatriceGirlzGoneToGod

You've got this Virgie, right? I'm done here….

Dante

BUT WE MADE EYE CONTACT

Virgil

Tone it down, poet-boy. The hot girls don't go for us.

Dante

Sign up for dating site:

Long walks on beach.

Reinventing languages that don't have literary aspirations.

Instant match with Beatrice

Beatrice

Uh. No. smh

Dante

The dating site has willed it to be. I don't make the rules.

Beatrice

Make it to heaven first. THEN we'll talk.

Dante

You should be in the eighth circle with the thieves because you

stole my heart.

Beatrice

Heaven help him. Seriously. NOW.

Dante

How many likes to get you to go out with me?

Beatrice

Get a few mil and you'll have my attention.

Beatrice

Briefly.

Virgil

Is there a mute button?

Dante

How to tell if a dead girl is subtly flirting with you

Dante

I know we actually never met and all, but I want to spend the rest of my life with you. Beatrice, will you marry me

Beatrice

BLOCKED

Virgil

C'mon, B. I need some help over here.

Beatrice

UNBLOCKED

Beatrice

Why do you have so many love poems devoted to me? We've never even met.

Dante

I made some stuff up. I invented Italian literature, so I'm allowed to do that.

The Tweets are continuing, but Mr. Wright is gesticulating and some lecture leaks in.

Was there another bath? A discussion of humility being Dante's special weapon? Gilgamesh gets a battle axe. Odysseus gets a bow. Dante gets a long piece of grass.

You can*not* make this stuff up. Mr. Wright should join the Tweet-fest.

Virgil@ThePhilosopher'sZone

It's Circle II and Dante's down for the count. Seriously, bruh. Are you scared of the WIND?

Beatrice

Man-up and wake up. Girls don't go for nerds.

Virgil

Awww. Cerberus. Go fetch some mud. Who's a good puppy?

Wright is saying something about Cato being the guardian of Purgatory and something about how he died ~ not out of cowardice ~ but out of courage.

It's time for me to talk with my voice and not only with my thumbs.

"No, no," I jump in, tucking my phone in the folds of my sweatshirt. "That's not right. That's not logical. Cato is a suicide, so he should be in Hell."

"Why?" Wright asks.

I'm taken aback. Wright doesn't often yield the floor to interlopers.

Still, I stumble on: "Because he had no time to repent. Because Dante's all about growth, and the only real sin is stasis."

"That's true," Wright acknowledges. "The suicides in Hell are defined by their stasis. They are defined by their *absence*. All of their descriptors explain what they are *not*. But Cato died for freedom, so that others wouldn't live under tyranny. His death didn't deplete the world: his death replenished it. His death was an attempt to influence the *future*, not a desire to erase the past."

"But Cato's death was ultimately doomed" (*it's hard to give up an argument easily*) "so his death was ultimately meaningless."

"Which is why he's stuck in Purgatory's base camp," Niko chimes in, "lecturing about law. He seems very grumpy."

If I was stuck in one place forever, I'd be grumpy, too.

Niko's offer to walk me to math should be helpful. After all, his presence gives some measure of protection from Stone Mountain's gauntlet of guys, but now the Chorus girls have noticed that Niko is spending time with *me*, and man, are they *pissed*.

Their whispers hiss by ~ thin, pinched words that are intended to impale ~ "who does she think she…" and "some scout needs a tent…" and "fat" and "fat" and "ugly fat face" ~ whispers that slap and leave me keening, but Niko seems oblivious, and his voice is light and winking. He stops outside Satchel's room, turns to me, and says, "Leave it to you to make Wright's class fun." Then he smiles extravagantly and disappears into the crowd.

I hear a teacher's tongue ticking. I turn and see Ms. Satchel outside her classroom. "Dani," she's greeting me. Not warmly ~ Ms. Satchel is not the type to emote ~ but genuinely: "I have good news. You got a 'B' on your quadratic-equations' quiz."

I smile weakly and shrug.

"I don't understand," she continues. "Why aren't you happy?"

"I understood the math," I explained, "because you had reviewed it right before the quiz. But if you taught me that math and then sent me *home*, everything would have slipped through me like my mind was some silly sieve."

If Ms. Satchel is concerned, she doesn't show it. She keeps her words crisp: "That's just one more clue in solving this puzzle."

I shake my head. Leave it to me. The biggest mark my brain makes on this educational system is that now it's a problem that needs to be solved.

Dani Argyle Takes on the World
Tuesday, March 11, 2025
12:04 a.m.

It's just after midnight, and if Dad comes to my room this morning, he will not find me there.

Because Dani Argyle's got some vandalizing to do.

Yep. That's what Madam Renown has reduced me to: that woman is turning me into a criminal.

Sneaking out of the Argyle house is a breeze: no rooftop escapes are needed for me. Mom is upstairs ~ oblivious to the world ~ and my bedroom is just seven tiptoe steps from the front door.

The Uber drops me off three blocks from Renown's parlor. After all, if you're going to deface private property, you might as well make *some* attempt to cover your tracks.

I chunk out of the Uber, heave my backpack onto my shoulders, hear the rattles of the spray cans clunking about, and survey my surroundings.

This section of Leesville is dingy at best. Dim buildings sag, as if they are sullen and weary with weight, as if the burden of standing is simply too much. Swollen bags of trash cover the curb, timid streetlamps leak tepid light, and dingy critters skulk through the mess, lugging behind them their lumpy shadows.

I start walking towards Renown's ~ briskly ~ this is no location for a leisurely stroll. And darkness is creepy no matter where it is.

I feel ~ and then I hear ~ a car slowing behind me. My heart stirs urgently, and I scoot to the far end of the sidewalk, hasten my pace, and glance over my shoulder.

Following me, slowly, is a cop car. Of course.

Crap. Crap! Shit on a stick!

Of course. Of COURSE Renown works in the sleezy section of Leesville, the only area of town that requires police presence.

This will not end well for me. The Chorus girls can do what they want, and then they bat their extravagant lashes and slip from all consequences.

No one takes pity on the fat girl from the suburbs.

The passenger window rolls down, and a voice emanates from the driver's seat: "Excuse me, Miss. Can we talk for a second?"

I stop and turn slowly. My heart feels squishy: it's stuttering in my chest. Really, I wonder, what am I supposed to do? I *have* to play nice. A girl like me can't *run*.

Then the voice becomes a form: it slides from the patrol car: a long slippery figure wearing a cop's uniform.

The uniform with its voice walks around the car to the

passenger side, but he keeps his distance from me. I step back, instinctively, and then he does, too, and he leans back against the hood of his car.

"I'm Officer Beacham, and this is my area to patrol." The figure's voice is smooth, rounded lightly with a drawl, and it doesn't even have an edge to an edge. Still, I'm in no position to let my guard down, so I'm tense and ready to react. "You're not in any trouble," the voice drawls on, "but I'd like to talk. I'm concerned about you."

He's still leaning against the car ~ it's the opposite of a power pose ~ but my heart is jostling and juggery inside me. He must see me shaking. He must know I'm a teen who is up to no good.

He seems to be waiting for me to speak. Then he adds, "I'm Officer Beacham. But you may call me Grady." He might be smiling, but it's difficult to see in the shadow and murk.

"Hello, Officer," is my brilliant reply.

He nods his head lightly. "Here's the reason I stopped you. It's 12:15 a.m., and this part of town has problems at this time. Hurricane Mack's is a few blocks away." He nods to his left. "They're nearing their closing time, and the drunks will be driving in a hurry to get home." He nods his head to the right. "And this part of town has a homeless population. Some of these people are salt-of-the-earth, but some are addicts and not always..." He pauses. "*Predictable.*" He seems to be focusing intently on me now. "Let me repeat ~ you're not in any trouble, but I have some concerns. Can I ask why you're out at this time of night?"

My mind is rustling, trying to preview all possible responses. Am I sick? Lost? Heading home from a party? "Hurricane Mack's," I hear myself saying. It's the best I can do. "My uncle is there. He doesn't think he can drive his car home, so he sent out a text-blast to see who could help him." I shrug. "I was awake, so I volunteered."

"Here," he says, and he opens the car door. "Let me give you a ride there."

Crap. Damn. CrapDamnCrap. Why couldn't my excuse be better? I'm only seeing now that I need a sick friend.

The pause is long, so he opens the door even wider. "Please, Miss. You'd make me feel a whole lot better if I could give you a lift. Help me earn my paycheck today?" If I could see his eyes, I'm sure they'd be imploring.

I sigh, nod my head, and climb in the car, careful to maneuver my backpack so its contents don't clatter. I can't believe I'm *willingly* climbing into a cop car. I shake my head, but then I comfort myself: I can let Officer Whatever drop me off at the bar, and then I can circle back to Renown's. This vandalism will take longer than I expected, but it will still get done.

The officer gets in his seat, checks all his mirrors, and starts down the road. My stomach starts to clench: it's remembering all the lessons about strangers and cars, about dangers and real monsters who come out at night. I place my hand on the door's handle.

The cop's driving is slow ~ his eyes, vigilant. They dart back and forth, like they're everywhere at once. I don't know whether to be calmed or creeped out. My fingers clench at the handle, but when we get to Mack's, he smoothes the car to a gentle stop.

Then he turns to me. "Thank you, Miss..." He smiles. "Excuse me. I don't know your name."

"Susan," I blurt.

"Thank you, Miss Susan. Here ~ let me give you something." He reaches in a shirt pocket. "This is my card. If you find yourself in these parts again, and need help, you can give me a call."

I take the card and slip it in my bag. "Thank you, Officer." I'm opening the car door and climbing out when I hear a voice from inside the cab: "And tell your uncle he's got one kind niece."

Hurricane Mack's is aptly named. It's loud, wild, and raucous as a storm.

When I enter, men's eyes dart at me ~ full of expectation ~ and then dim away, disappointed.

I wonder how long I should continue this farce. I walk around the bar ~ pretending to look for an inebriated uncle ~ and wait for Officer Beachman to find another citizen to save.

But he's not going anywhere. The light is on in the car's cabin, and he seems to be doing paperwork and periodically glancing at a monitor on his dash.

It's obvious, now, he didn't buy my story. He looks quiet and calm, but he's waiting to pounce.

And here I am: trapped, caged with crazy drunks, blazing my awkwardness for everyone to see.

I walk in stupid circles around the bar until I feel as conspicuous inside this place as I would without. No one goes to a place like Mack's to walk laps around the room.

And I'm realizing, now, the unappetizing truth: if I'm going to give Renown what she deserves, I'm going to have to sneak out the back of the bar and into an alley.

I'd been planning to graffiti Renown's parlor once a week ~ enough to keep her cleaning and away from my mother ~ but all of this is ending up being more work than I had planned.

Apparently, criminal activity is not as easy as I thought.

Leave it to me to even fail at vandalism.

But it's not over 'til it's over ~ as my Uncle Joe says ~ so I make my way to the back of the bar ~ past some very surprised dishwashers ~ and find a door that leads to an alley.

It's rank back here ~ with smells I do not want to think about too hard ~ and I make my way towards the street... more by feel than by sight.

Luckily, the party at Mack's has spilled onto the sidewalk, and it's easy for me to mingle with the group and then disappear, softly, into the distance.

I keep glancing over my shoulder to see if the cop has spotted me, but if he has, he's playing things cool and biding his time.

It's quiet again, and I'm in the weary part of town. But my heart jigs with happiness when I see Renown's parlor.

Her shop is a squat, meek, dumpy thing. Who would think this shamble could wield such power over others?

But now, Ms. Renown, your days are over.

Your truth will be proclaimed across your walls.

I scrounge through my bag and take out the black can. I shake it and feel the insides rattle.

In huge boxy letters ~ that are bold and unambiguous ~ I write

LIAR

And then

THIEF

Then I change out for the red can for the final reveal:

VILLAIN

I step back, admiring my art. It is towering and true.

I place my spray paint in my backpack and shift its weight onto my shoulders. Who will trust Renown now? Who will visit her…with this indictment blazing throughout the district?

I am smiling, giddy, ignited with excitement when I sense something furtive moving behind me.

I spin, and there's a man stumbling towards me ~ maybe twelve yards away. He has long, stringy hair, but the rest is a blur, a shuffle and a blotch blundering in the dark.

He is plodding towards me, undeterred by the words towering before him.

I want to cry out, but the sound is strangled in my throat.

The shadow stumbles slightly and then stutters out: "Hey there, Girlie Girl. Can you help a guy out?" The voice is thick, slurred with spittle, and the hands seem to be working at the pants, moving up and down.

And I am shocked still, stuck in one place ~ everything is

slowing, creeping about me, and the air itself is silent and stuck, refusing to move or enter my lungs.

The next thing I know, I am screaming. Except I'm NOT. I'm not screaming at all. I'm shouting. I'm yelling. I'm *roaring*.

In *Japanese.*

The words squall out of my mouth and clamor about the buildings, resonating, resounding.

Bellowing.

Emono o korosu no wa dougu demo gijutsu demo nai.
Togisumasareta omae jishin no satsui da.
Wir sind die Jaeger! Honoo no you ni atsuku! Onore o our komete!
Subete o tsuranuiteyuke!

The shadow is stunned still. Even his hands are quiet. He's stopped his advance and sways back, teetering, and thin.

And then I turn and barrel away.

I'm hurtling down the sidewalk, blasting past buildings and sagging stacks of trash.

The world is skirring by, and I'm listening, hard, desperate to know if there are footsteps behind me, but all I hear is my own jagged breath and the low, thrumming blur of the wind.

I don't know where he is, but I dare not look. I can't look, I won't look, not even for a glimmer, not until I reach Mack's. Not until I see people.

Or Officer Beacham? I'm remembering the card he gave me,

but I dare not stop to find it ~ but now, each time I see a side street, I stare down to the end, hoping some kind officer will ask me what I'm doing out at this time of night.

There's no sign of police, and I'm cursing my fate, but then I turn a corner and see ~ blooming in the distance ~ light from Mack's bar, and the sound of music and people laughing.

I blare down the sidewalk to the edge of the party, and I burst into the crowd before I start to slow, like a track athlete breaking through the finish line's tape.

Some people stare at me, but most of them don't ~ as if this display of exhibitionism is seen every night.

I turn and look over my shoulder, but no one is there. The street stretches back in a ribbon of night.

"Sweetheart, are you ok?" A woman with copper hair and impossible heels is staring at me, concerned.

I nod my head but can't form a word.

The air is delicious, and I can't seem to get enough of it. I'm bent double, swallowing it down in big, gulping breaths.

A few more ladies are cooing over my entrance. "Is she hurt?" one is asking.

I stand straight and see a man with platform boots and an extraordinary mustache approaching. His eyes are all over me.

"Nuh-uh, Derek," the copper girl is clucking. She puts her arm around me. "This one is with *us*."

And mustache-man turns around and slithers into the bar.

I wake up startled and spurting ~ there seem to be voices around me, and I'm in a strange space. It might be dark, but I know enough to know that this is *not* my room.

And I sense there is a person lying next to me.

I shock upright ~ my heart stiffening and tight ~ and it's true that I'm in a queen bed with someone who is snoring.

Wait.

Wait!

I close my eyes so I won't have to see this situation.

Where-am-I where-am-I where-am-I?

And who the hell is this?

The snoring continues, and I'm scouring my brain, trying to remember what happened last night.

If panic made a sound, I'd be a five-alarm fire, but my panic is quiet, so some of the snoring is making itself heard. It's small, and warm, like a little pug breathing.

My heart starts to soothe, and I shake my head: I know that sound.

So I turn, and I look, and then I see Lainie.

Leave it to my aunt to even *snore* gorgeously.

Events are flitting through my head, dipping through those spaces between sleep and awake, and I'm trying to tame them, isolate them, bring them to the light.

There's a heaviness in my stomach I do not want to

remember.

Did I have a strange dream? Or perhaps, it was a nightmare.

But my mind steadies, and smoothes, and I remember how I got here.

Did some bum-man ask me for help?

And did I respond to his question by running away?

Leave it to Dani Argyle to mess up a chase scene: to make it a situation where I'm being chased and no one is chasing.

I shake my head softly. But why do I feel something dark and scrabbly inside?

I don't like the sensation, so I lie back down and turn and look at Lainie.

She shifts softly, opens her eyes, and beams.

Then her eyes jolt wide. "Dani," she begins, "you promise me you're ok?"

I'm searching through my memories, trying to find an answer. Lainie is Lainie, so she deserves the truth, but she is also an adult ~ who wants to poke into places that should never be poked.

"Lainie," I smile, "I'm fine. Really." I wear my earnest face. "The only thing wounded is my pride." I feel myself blushing. "I'm just really, really embarrassed."

"Well, if you *promise*." She gleams. "Your cover's safe with me."

My cover? What cover? I'm scrabbling to remember. And then I recall an early-morning text to my mother, explaining that I'd had a nightmare and would be sleeping at Lainie's.

I nod. And sigh. "Lainie, thank you."

She smiles, lifts herself from the bed, and disappears to the *en suite.*

I stretch and stand when I realize my phone is buzzing. I plop on the bed.

Niko is texting.

NK U R not in waters sensei's class. Ive checked.

I glance at a clock. It's later than I thought.

DA R U spying on me?

NK just checking on a friend

Friend. Yes. *Friend.*

DA your friend is fine

DA Just a little tired 😴

  ...

NK kk

Maybe this weekend...

we can go on another date

I stare at the phone. It's my turn to ... *Holy crap.* I'm confused.

Date? A friend?

My head starts to throb. But my stomach seems to be floating and flapping about.

DA Fine. I'm game

NK Cool. Talk later

When Lainie emerges, she's sharpened her figure into professional underclothes. And then she slips on a dress that slides over her body like water over flesh.

"Dani, dear ~ " she's holding both hands to one ear, clipping on an earring that dangles with pearls ~ "are you sure you don't want a spa day today?"

I'm shaking my head. I'm grateful, but insistent. "Lainie, thank you, but what I really need is…" I'm scrabbling through my brain, trying to remember the conversation.

"A check?"

"A check." I'm stretching my mind to last night's discussion. Is this wonder of a woman really going to ~

"It's 725?" She eases on the other earring.

I'm stuttering and stupid: "It would be birthday and Christmas and birthday again ~"

"And a spa day," she giggles.

"And a spa day," I agree.

She's finished with the jewelry, and she takes out her purse and a pen and flourishes a check. She hands it to me, gleaming.

I look at it ~ in all of its three-digit glory. "Lainie ~ " I exhale, "How could you ~ why are you ~ you don't even know what I need it *for*."

"If I know you, and I do," she's smiling and resplendent, "what you do with this money is going to be *brilliant*."

And to prove her faith in me, she crooks me in her arm and

kisses my head.

I hug her back. "In this one case," I begin, "I think that you are right."

Lainie's phoned the school to excuse my absence, so when I return home, I'm alone ~ I am ME ~ and this entire place is MINE.

At first, I don't know what to do, so after posting Lainie's check, I'm waiting for it to clear while walking from one end of the living room to the next.

There is so much to think about, and so many feelings I don't want to feel.

But I know a sure-fire cure-all for any emotional turmoil.

Music!

I scroll through my phone ~ find the playlist marked FUN ~ and channel the music through the house speakers.

The music is LOUD, as it can only be when no one else is around, and it goes through me like a wave. I am no longer Dani: I am all bass; I am all drum; I am all attitude; I am all sass.

This is good when difficulties seem insurmountable. I can dip and sip them into oblivion.

Creepy old men who prowl in the dark? *Take it to the left now and dip with it.*

Renown still in business? *Gon' throw down, take a sip*

with it.

I might be big, but I can still... *Lean back, put your hips in it.*

I'm holding my phone (still waiting for Lainie's check to clear), and my dance has brought me to the dining room where ~ This ain't Texas, ain't no hold'em ~ I am in charge here, so everything is sassy!

And then I glance at my phone and there is money in my account. I squeal and tip up on my toes.

Watch out world!

Cause Dani Argyle is taking you on!

I'm setting my sites for more than just Renown. Renown is small time. Renown is old news. Why go to rat-infested hide-outs armed with cans of spray paint? After all, Dad can't be right about *everything*. And when it comes to Mom, he's often been wrong.

Sorry, Dad, but if I'm going to take care of anyone, it's going to be *me*.

This deserves silence: this deserves reverence, so I mute the music and turn to the computer.

Ok. I have to reload the page because it has timed out, but then, my ticket appears.

My one-way ticket-to-the-hell-out-of-this-place:

The Philadelphia Institute of Design and Art
Online Course Leading to Certification:
Event Coordination

I press "Purchase" and I smile. Yes. And yes.

Finally!

Ok. So it's a two-year ticket. The course is thorough and supposed to take two years, but if I play my cards right, I can complete these credits in under ten months.

This will be a ticket in ten-months' time. A ten-month ticket to anyplace but here.

The doorbell is ringing. In the middle of the day?

Some poor salesman must be down on his luck.

I open the door and see a man with a cellphone at the top of the stoop.

Behind him, in the grass, a heavily-bearded photographer is waiting.

My eyes flash back to the "salesman." He's smiling like we're best friends, as if meeting him will be the highpoint of my life.

He reaches out his hand. "Ms. Argyle?"

I don't reach back. "Yes?"

He continues, unflustered. "My name is Philip Silverman, and I'm a reporter from the *Leesville Gazette*. We're doing a retrospective on Operation Tomodachi and the status of the hero

Jean-Peine Argyle."

A leaden sensation is slugging in my gut. In an instant, I'm not dancing Dani. I'm focused and quiet.

And I am *pissed*.

He waits for me to say something or to grunt. When he's met with a quiet stare, he continues, "and I'm wondering if this is a good time to talk."

I don't hesitate: "No." I start to close the door.

He steps forward so that he's almost inside the house.

"Ok. Fine." His elbow is touching the door, so I'd have to dislodge him first in order to close it. "Then what time would be more convenient?"

"Never." I glare.

He's not accustomed to hearing 'no,' it seems to me. He's all charm and finesse, as if we could be best buddies at some point in the future. "But Ms. Argyle," he looks hurt, "we don't want Jean-Piene to be forgotten. He's a hero. Don't you want to tell his story? Don't you want him to be remembered in our community?"

Oh. *He* asked the question. I can give him an answer: "You're not interested in remembrance." My words are spittling little fists. "You're interested in *entertainment*. You're interested in *sales*." I hear him try to interrupt, but I will not be mansplained by some charmer with an ego, so I raise my voice. "You and your colleagues exploit people's grief. Our suffering sells news. You pose our grief and then take your pictures so the worst moment in our lives will never disappear. The death of my father is not a retrospective ~ "

"Your father?" His voice edges through.

"it is a brutal, unrelenting reality."

"Excuse me. Jean-Peine ~ "

"J.P!"

"is your *father*?"

"Yes." I pause for a moment while he processes my age.

"May I speak to your mother?"

I step outside and let the door close behind me. I wish I *could* look people in the eye, but I gather my energy and look up at him. Severely.

"Remind me of your name."

"Philip Silverman." He smiles and starts to extend his hand again.

"Philip Silverman. I'm engraving it in my brain so that I will never forget it and so that I can make one thing abundantly clear. You are going to leave this property and you will never, ever contact my mother. If I *ever* get wind that you have spoken to her, I will chew off your testicles and wear them as earrings. Have I made myself clear?"

I think I might have rendered Mr. Silverman speechless. I see him opening his mouth, but no words are emerging.

"Hey, Dog-Man," I say to the photographer with the over-aggressive beard, "take your friend off my property or you too will come to learn the fury of a pissed-off teenage girl."

They both walk backwards before turning around and

slipping into the car. They do not turn the car around in the nearby cul-de-sac. They put the car in reverse and back out of sight.

Dani Argyle Takes on the Rules of the Game
Tuesday, March 11, 2025
3:12 p.m.

After my meeting with SilverBoy and ScruffyBeard, I text Sophia:

DA Bestie come over after school? HORRIBLE day. Please?

SB Sure! B there by 4. Bring Niko?

DA Shrug

DA

I gather some snacks and bring them to the basement. I also cut up some fruit and bring it down as well. Now Gabby will have something to occupy him, too.

At 4:02, Sophia and Niko appear at the door. I hug Sophia and then feel awkward around Niko.

He leans over and kisses me on the forehead.

Why do I feel like I've been kissed *everywhere*? I'm radiating heat like a torch.

I tell them there's food in the basement, so we head down

there and collapse in the monster-sized bean-bag chairs. Sophia and me in one, and Niko in the other.

Sophia starts: "Ok, Dani, what's the poop? What's going on?"

I can't even touch what's happening with Mom or Renown ~ it's still too raw and stingy to discuss. So I say: "Same March melodrama. But this time, it's reporters and retrospectives."

"What's the big secret about March?" Niko looks concerned.

Sophia is as gentle as she can be. "Niko, remember the earthquake that struck Japan three years ago?"

Niko nods. "The 7.5? Yes. My uncle lost his house."

"Dani had a father."

Niko's eyes flash wide. I feel him gazing at me, but I can't look back.

Sophia continues, "He didn't die during the earthquake. He was part of an urban search-and-rescue team ~ located just east of here, in Fairfax, but they were deployed to Kunimi. But Dani's father never came back."

I can tell by his voice that Niko is struck. "Dani, I didn't know."

I'm still staring at the floor. Maybe that's why the words can form: "It's hard to grieve when they can't find the body. I'm finding a way to mourn, but my mother is not. And if more reporters show up, I don't know what will happen to her."

"Oh, Dani," Sophia sighs. "What are you going to do?"

"Answer every doorbell for the rest of the month."

"And Dani," Niko leans forward, "what can *we* do?"

"Nothing," I explain. "What can be done? The Argyles are stuck in this stupid space ~ not quite hoping, but not grieving either. We just need to know which way to feel, once and for all."

"Dani," Sophia is saying, "you don't believe he's alive?"

"No, Sophia, I don't." I really want to tell them about the early-morning ghost visits, but there's no way I can tell them and still seem sane. So instead, I pivot. "You guys are doing all you can. Just by being here. Sitting with me in this." I lean into my friend.

Sophia wraps her arm around me and squeezes.

"But," I announce, "there's no reason to be sad *and hungry*. I have snacks."

I stand and reveal the display with a flourish: a meticulously draped cloth is covering the banquet, and I grab both edges with both hands and yank up ~ with a SNAP.

Gabby leaves his video game and comes jumping over to join us.

"Is this your little brother?" Niko stands up and gazes down.

I speak and cue so Gabby will understand: "This is my little brother."

Gabby beams and gazes up at Niko. "Oo oo igh areeoh ar?"

"Gabby wants to know if you like MarioKart," I explain.

"Are you kidding?" Niko grins. "Miyamoto is Japanese!"

"I'm not convinced that Niko understands that Gabby can't hear him, but that's ok. I can see that Gabby is smitten. He's grabbing Niko's hand and leading him to the Wii.

Sophia's grinning in wonder. "Awww. They're so *cute* together."

"And kind," I add.

"And kind," she agrees.

Sophia rises and we grab paper plates and pile up some heaps of food ~ no need to impress *her* with miserly eating. We giggle and sit and conspire together to solve the problems of the universe.

Of course, Sophia is here for me, but there is also a map quiz tomorrow, so she's smuggled in the supplies that she needs to study: she's hand-drawn blank maps, filled-in maps, and various-states-of-in-between maps.

"C'mon, Dani," Sophia flourishes the papers. "The boys are playing. Study with me!"

I shake my head. "It won't make a difference."

"Of course it will." She puts a map in my hand.

"No. It won't." I put the map down. "No matter how much I study, I'll get a five out of twenty ~ the same number as random chance."

Sophia once explained to me that she *likes* studying because ~ when she completes a project or even part of a project ~ she feels a rush of adrenaline and a sense of accomplishment. But I never feel that. Whether something is done or undone, I always feel the same.

I'm always just me.

But Sophia insists that we study together, and, right now, studying feels better than moping or crying, so I grab a couple maps and try to stuff some geography in my brain, repeatedly, so it will stick.

Niko glides back and plops in the beanbag after his match in MarioKart. His eyes are wide and impressed. "Hey, the little kid can play. The rascal always slows up before the blue shell drops."

"You can't play him to win," I say, "only to have fun."

"Speaking of winning," Sophia interrupts, "Ms. Russel is giving a map quiz tomorrow, and I'm going to win."

"Win?" Niko asks. "You treat tests like a game?"

"They *are* a game," Sophia insists. "The entire *school* is a game. I'm playing it hard, and I'm in it to win it." Then she drops her voice like she's telling us a secret. "You know the best feeling? When I don't learn anything, and I get an 'A' anyway. That's when I've won. That's when I've *triumphed*." Her eyes are gleaming. "Then I know that I haven't just beaten the *test*. Then I know that I've beaten the *system*." She pops a mini-muffin in her mouth and slurs the rest: "Dani doesn't pway the game ~ not even a wittle."

I look at Niko to explain: "Unlike Sophia, I have nothing against *learning* ~ I just don't like having it micromanaged and micro-assessed. At school, everything we do is constantly scrutinized. No wonder our generation is slowly going crazy. Who can ever live like this?" I glance at my plate, but, now that Niko's here, I'm not going to eat.

"You can stay at school *and* stay sane, Dani," Sophie interjects. "'Man is an animal that can get used to anything.'" She looks at me. "Today, I'm quoting Mr. Wright." She eats another muffin.

I shake my head. "Uh, Sophia, you're quoting Dostoyevsky."

"No, I'm not," Sophia insists. "I heard Wright saying it just the other week."

Niko and I look at each other and smile.

"But actually, Dani," Niko seems serious, "you should learn to play the game. At least a little."

I sit up straight. "What if there's another game?" I ask. Now it's my turn to smile. "One I like better?"

"What do you mean?" Sophia is baffled. I know because she's stopped chewing.

"What if my plan is to leave high school in less than ten months?"

Now they're both staring at me. Like I've grown a third boob. On my face.

"Dani," Sophia starts, "you're not dropping out of high school?"

"You say 'dropping,' I say 'engaging-in-life-in-a-meaningful-way.' Tomato. Tomahto."

"Dani. You're crazy."

"No, Sophia, I'm not. The school has only one game, and I don't like it. So I'm joining another. I'm just finding some different rules to live by."

"What 'different rules?'" Niko frowns. "I don't understand."

"You are looking at someone who has embarked ~ " and even though I'm smushed in a bean bag, I do my best to take a bow

~ "on a different kind of academic journey. I've enrolled in a class through the Philadelphia Institute of Design and Art. In ten months, I will be certified to be an event coordinator."

The two of them are silent. They stare at me, saucer-eyed.

"Aren't you happy for me?" I ask.

"Dani, you'll be sixteen ~ "

"On April 19th." I bow again.

"What kind of person will hire a sixteen-year-old to coordinate an event?" Sophia can be stubborn.

"Ok," I admit. "Maybe I'll begin with children's parties. I've been throwing parties for Gabby for years. Who better than me to throw a party for a child?"

"Dani," Niko answers. "I don't want to talk you out of this. I think you'd be an amazing event coordinator. But you need to be real. People go to college to learn how to run a business. They *learn* before they *do*. You need to study things before you do them."

"Niko," I explain, "to be successful, I don't need to read *books*. I need to read *people*. I want to peek into their minds and make what is in there come alive in the real world. I want to create an environment that celebrates them. I want you to be *you*," I look at Niko, "and you to be *you*," I look at Sophia. "I want you to be the *you-est* you've ever been. And besides," I add, "I don't look sixteen."

"It's true," Sophia agrees. "You should buy beer."

"Just today," I ignore her, "a reporter thought I was my mom." I do not explain that the upside of being overweight (and the only upside, I swear), is that the weight makes your age difficult to guess. "And last year, when I walked into world history on the first day of school, everyone in the class hushed and got quiet…until I walked across the class and sat in a student desk. Then I heard people whispering, 'She's not the teacher,' and chaos erupted again."

"Still, Dani," Sophia is insisting, "I don't see how this can work. You can't own a business until you're eighteen."

"Ok. Ok. I thought you guys would be more excited for me. I can intern until I turn eighteen. Why pay a college thousands of dollars when I can have someone else *pay me* to learn?"

"Dani," Niko says, "arguing against you is a losing battle, so I'm not going to try. Just promise me one thing."

"What's that?"

"Promise you won't drop out of high school until you have a job lined up. Don't burn your bridges until *after* you've crossed them."

"Alright," I smile, "but you'll have to admit: the educational system would make some excellent kindling."

Dani Argyle Takes on High School
Wednesday, March 12, 2025
9:33 a.m.

In English class, I slip into my seat and my phone is buzzing.

For some reason, I am popular now?

Kevin Choi wants to know about the quiz questions in history.

In one way, being dumb has its benefits: people rarely ask me to help them cheat.

Kevin Choi, on the other hand, is the kind of smart student who is in perpetual turmoil ~ like a house on fire. To him, a missed test question is an omen of personal doom: a sign that the cosmos is looking at him personally and she is *pissed*. Kevin is willing to sacrifice anything for a grade: integrity, spontaneity, dignity....

Niko is leaning over me; I can honestly feel his heat. And then I hear, "Why is Kevin texting you?"

I put away my phone. "Kevin is being Kevin. Asking about history."

"But why would he be asking questions of *you*?" Niko

wonders.

Yup. That's me. The only person in the class nobody bothers to cheat from.

The Tweets begin before Wright arrives. Team *Inferno* now has five followers: two teens, a housewife, and an amused Catholic priest.

Dante@theinfernoislit

There's a three-headed dog with snot in his beard.

I came here for a good time and I'm honestly feeling so attacked right now.

Virgil@ThePhilosopher'sZone

The first circle is not so bad. We've got clear rivers, bustling cities, interesting conversations, and not a fainting man-child in sight.

Beatrice@GirlzGoneToGod

Everyone in heaven is watching what's going on in Hell. Bets on Virgil losing his rag and leaving Dante behind.

The bell is ringing, but…

Mr. Wright isn't entering his stage. He's standing in the doorway, stiff like a statue, but his eyes are focused on the hallway.

Then Ms. Kim ~ guidance counselor extraordinaire: that woman could teach an Excel spreadsheet how to stay organized ~

joins him, and Mr. Wright seems sad, but then he smiles and says, "Ok, everyone. Today is Sophomore College Day. Everyone who wants to go to the career center, pack up your things."

And the classroom is a rustle and a rush, backpacks are expanding, ballooning, and then, with a whoosh, I am alone in the classroom.

Alone, that is, with Mr. Wright.

He walks to his desk, sits, and flips open his laptop.

Then he looks at me, quizzically, and frowns.

"Dani," he asks, "aren't you going to College Days?"

I look at him and shrug. "No."

"So you already know where you're going to college?"

I shake my head. "Who says I'm going to college?"

I'm glad Wright is sitting down because he's looking a little wavery.

"Dani, are you speaking in earnest? Or are you teasing?"

"No, Mr. Wright. Why would I do that?"

He folds up his laptop and uses his legs to scoot out his rolling chair from behind his desk. He's still on his stage, but he's sitting down now.

"Let me guess," he begins, "you think College Days are a waste of time, so you will use this period to read."

"Correct."

"But you're still going to college."

"Incorrect."

If he were a boxer in a ring, he'd be going down about now.

But he takes a breath, recovers, and begins: "Ok, Daniella, support your position."

And then Mr. Glupov struts into the room: he always acts like he's proud of himself for simply existing. Like the act of not dying is a reason to crow.

"Andrew!" he barks.

I startle, and he looks at me and winces.

Then he addresses Mr. Wright again. "Andrew, you ought to have this period free. Ms. Conner's sub never showed up, and we need you to cover her classes."

"Sorry, Mr. Glupov," I interject, "but Mr. Wright is helping me today. Big test coming up, and Dante is *hard*."

I look at him, pleadingly, and if the man knew a thing about me, he'd know how thoroughly he's being mocked right now.

But understanding students is not Glupov's gift, and he backtracks, quickly, and mumbles some dross, "Of course, of course. Carry on. Of course."

But before he leaves the room, he looks at Wright and says, "Why you bother trying to teach these kids Dante is beyond me."

When he leaves, I laugh. "Mr. Glupov can be fun."

"And you be careful, Dani Argyle. Some people are petty and not prone to forgive."

"I'll take my chances," I explain, "and actually, in a fistfight, I think I could take him."

"But you're not getting out of this so easily, my young Paduan."

"Yes?" I'm trying to match Wright's serious face.

"You're not going to college. Support your position. Go."

I take a breath, gather my thoughts, and begin the argument as Wright has trained me. "Premise #1: College is not for everyone."

"Agreed," Wright concedes.

"Premise #2: There's more than one way to learn."

"Concur," Wright replies.

"Premise #3: in terms of learning, doing a skill is preferable to reading about how other people do it."

"Agreed, with a caveat, but continue."

"Premise #4: in the educational world, learning and certification have become intimately intertwined, but you can have one without having the other."

"Agree. Whole-heartedly."

"Ergo," I conclude, "Learning is possible without certification, and there is more than one way to prepare for real life. I choose the option where I learn by *doing*."

Wright nods, but then he says, "Alright. My turn."

I lean back and wait.

"In the history of the world, there have been people on this planet who are smarter than you."

I stay silent, but I nod.

"They have written down their wisdom so that you may learn it."

Nod. Begrudgingly.

"When you learn from their wisdom, not only do you expand

your mind and character, other people recognize you as someone they can trust."

Still silence. No nod.

"Ergo: Profound learning occurs in college, and the world understands that college graduates have trusted expertise." He pauses, but then lunges one more time into that breach: "And finally, Dani, aside from money ~ which you will get back in droves if you invest in college ~ what in the world do you have to lose?"

I don't miss a beat. "Four years."

He shakes his head and says, "Dani, don't think of college as four years *lost*. Think of it as four years *gained*: a time to experiment; a time to explore; a time to figure out who you really are."

"There's more than one way to pop that cork."

Then Waters Sensei appears in the doorway, right in the middle of the Wright-Argyle College Smackdown.

"Oh, pardon. Didn't mean to interrupt." He looks at Mr. Wright. "Drew, do you still have that article you were talking about? The one about the tsunami that's been translated by three news outlets?"

"Oh, yes, yes, Nathan. I forgot to send it. Wait one minute, and I'll email it to you."

Wright scoots back to his desk and flips open his laptop. He stares at it, intensely.

Waters Sensei seems to be blushing. "Thanks, Drew. You're a lifesaver." And then he turns to me. "Dani," he begins.

"Yes?"

"We missed you in class yesterday."

The air is heavy. He's probably the one teacher in the building who knows about Operation Tomodachi. He's the one teacher in my life who knows about my dad. Everything about his face is communicating pity and concern. But today, I cannot carry his weight and mine as well. Today, my own concerns are all I can handle.

"I'll make up the work," I lie. "Sophia will be able to catch me up on what I missed."

I can tell he's uncomfortable. Other people's grief can do that to you.

Then Wright's posture straightens. "Found it. Sent it." He closes his laptop. "You should have the article now."

"Thanks, Drew. Lifesaver. Really." And he leaves.

The weight of his pity leaves the room with him. Now, again, I can just be a girl. Not the-girl-with-the-father-who-never-came-home.

Wright scoots back to the center of the room. He tilts his head and looks at me. "Daniella," he begins, "there's something here that you're not telling me."

Crap. I gaze at him. *How can he know?*

He's continuing, "So your real reason for not wanting to go to college is?"

It takes me time to process that he's not talking about grief, about loss, about unravelling.

He's talking, perhaps, about ADHD.

And THAT is something I can talk about:

"Those of us who have ADHD ~ "

I watch the recognition flash in his eyes ~

"have a problem functioning within institutions that were created by people who don't."

Wright looks thoughtful in his serious Wright-way. "Granted," he admits, "certain difficulties can arise, especially when students don't take medication ~ "

"Are you telling me I have to be *drugged* to attend school?"

"No, no, no. Let me rephrase." He sighs. "All learning requires a degree of attention. Learning is not possible without it. The issue with ADHD is that you're paying attention to many things at the same time ~ "

"True. We just learn differently than ~ "

"As if your brain has a leaky filter. That doesn't have to be a shortcoming. People with ADHD can thrive in all sorts of situations: emergency rooms ~ "

"event coordination ~ "

"and as an evolutionary trait, it was probably selected widely before the industrial revolution. But even now, it doesn't have to be a weakness: it can be a strength, and a prerequisite for people who consider themselves creative ~ "

"and creativity is a quality the school system *loves* to embrace" (sarcasm/off).

Wright pauses. He employs rhetorical strategy #3: *Concede and Move On*. He moves on: "Granted: a certain amount of rote learning must take place at the high-school level before the creativity ~ the really *fun* stuff ~ can be focused on in college."

"So what you're telling me is that, if I go to college, I won't sit at a desk and take notes for ninety minutes." I glance around for a stack of notes that someone has taken, but the room is empty. I would like to hold up a stack of notes that I've taken in class, but I make it a habit to never take notes. So I look at Mr. Wright and narrow my eyes.

Now there's just an awful lot of staring going on.

"I simply do not want," Mr. Wright begins again, "to see you cut yourself short. You have ADHD, but you don't have to settle for mediocrity."

I straighten. "It's because I do *not* assent to mediocrity that I think it's important to leave education. I have no doubts that ADHD can lead to greatness. Look at da Vinci, at Twain, at Einstein."

"And you can learn more about them in the educational realm."

"But they themselves were conspicuously absent from it. Many geniuses were undereducated according to the standards of their time."

"Evidence?"

"See the list above. And add Shakespeare, and Darwin, and Bill Gates, and Steve Jobs, and," I smile wickedly, "and *Dante*."

That's what you can learn by studying with Mr. Wright. Dante is the trump card. Add him to any argument, and you automatically *win*.

Wright shakes his head. "I worry about you, Daniella Argyle. You're up high, and you're flying without a net."

"But if you want to be free," I smile and lean back, "then that is the very best way to fly."

For March 11, the weather is pretty nice, and I've snuck out of the building to have lunch on a grassy patch with Sophia and Niko.

The sun is bright and feels glorious on my skin. I'm wearing my darkest sunglasses ~ I buy them by the dozen and keep them everywhere: in cars, in backpacks, on porches ~ but both Niko and Sophia can withstand the light and are immune to the assault of the sun. Nevertheless, I'm leaning back to catch as much of it as possible. On one level, I know that this is a terrible day. The people who died three years ago are still dead today. The families they left behind are still stuck in grief. And yet today, the sun is warm. And today, I have found a little whiff of freedom.

Sophia is eating a sandwich and complaining about the map quiz. "And Ms. Russel ~ the beady-eyed bitch ~ she takes a point off because *she* can't tell the difference between an 'a' and a 'd'."

"I think you'll survive," I'm comforting her. "Your GPA still remains unchallenged."

"No! No! No! It's not fair! It's not right!" She's pinching the poor egg-salad sandwich flat between her indignant fingers. "I deserve that point! I'm not asking her for anything that I don't deserve."

"Speaking of deserving," I'm baldly interrupting, "I know of a woman who is really, really bad."

"How bad is she?" Niko interjects like he's setting up a joke.

"Does she work at this school?" Sophia wonders.

"No. It's not that." This is the first time since the blow-up with Mom that I've felt clear-headed enough to discuss Renown. "There is a woman who is gutting my family. She's torturing my mother and keeping my brother from the speech lessons he needs."

Niko and Sophia are silent. They realize this issue is no laughing matter.

"Dani, that's awful," Sophia puts her sandwich down. "Can you call the cops?"

"Unfortunately, no." I'm struggling to explain. "She's evil, but she's not a lawbreaker. If she wants to exploit people's grief, the government will let her do it."

"Then there's nothing that can be done," Sophia surrenders.

"Unless? Dani is involved?" Niko is questioning.

"I need to stop her without hurting my mom. And I might be coming to you guys for advice."

"I'm always willing to help, Dani," Sophia explains, "as long as it doesn't involve anything illegal."

"I'll do what I can," Niko agrees.

I reach out and squeeze both of their hands. "Thank you," I say. "How would I get through the next seven days without you?"

"You'll never have to find out," Sophia says as she glances at the strangled egg-salad sandwich and opts, instead, for a crunchy snack, "but you'll also have to live with-POTATO-CHIP HAIR!" And she drops and handful of Pringles on the top of my head.

"It's better than POTATO-CHIP BRA!" I retaliate, trying to grab what's left of the snack and drop it down her shirt.

Sophia is pushing me away and squealing, and I'm leaning into her and trying to claim my victory, but Niko has a good view of the building, and he's trying to hush us without being obvious.

I look up to see a woman bearing upon us with an angry-teacher walk. Ms. Worthington is striding toward us, glowering.

"What are you three doing out here!" She snaps each word as if they are flags worthy of saluting. "You *know* you're not supposed to be outside!" She doesn't know me, but she recognizes Sophia. "Sophia Brown, I'm surprised by you! You know I could write you up for leaving the building without permission. What are you thinking?"

"I guess I wasn't, Mrs. Worthington," Sophia submits.

"Now go inside, the three of you, before I call security."

We get up, dust off, and head back to the building.

Nothing is as subversive as three teenagers talking in the sun.

Dani Argyle Takes on a Mountain
Saturday, March 15, 2025
8:55 a.m.

It's T minus 144 hours and counting.

One hundred and forty-four hours until the anniversary of Dad's death.

Tomorrow will be supply day. Tomorrow we'll stock up for when Dad's Fairfax friends come to the house on the 18th and the 19th.

That's the problem when you do not know the exact time of death. You don't know what time to focus your mourning. Then the grief expands ~ takes over neighboring days ~ bullies the entire month into a miasma of misery.

But today is not Sunday. Today is *Saturday*.

Today is a respite from grief and preparation.

Today is a Niko-and-a-surprise day.

The thing about surprises is that they leave you unprepared. I've been told to wear layers of clothes and sturdy shoes. Or boots.

Since my bedroom is on the bottom floor and faces the

street, I'm watching from my window for Niko's arrival. But I can't have him *see me* watching for him, so whenever a car approaches, I duck and listen.

A car goes by ~ which sometimes they do, even on a cul-de-sac ~ and circles back around and heads away. And then I peer over the sill and look down the street.

Finally, a gray SUV is approaching, and I duck down and listen to it settling by the curb. I hold my breath, scoot from under the window, stand up, and wait.

The bell rings. When I open the door, Niko is there, looking trim and athletic and ready for a safari.

I look over my shoulder and call to Mom, "I'm going," and then look at Niko, "to Timbuktu?"

He smiles. "Nah. They were booked for a month. So I found the next-best thing."

We climb into the backseat of a car, and there is a woman in front of the nondescript variety ~ the kind whose identity seems to have been robbed by age ~ she's roundish and beige-ish and pleasantly plump. I am assuming that she is Niko's mother.

"Mom," Niko is saying, "this is Dani Argyle. Dani, this is Mrs. Kaneko."

"Nice to meet you, Dani." Mrs. Kaneko is smiling.

"And you, Mrs. Kaneko," I reply, solicitous.

We're off and heading west on Route 7. The land is full ~ expectant ~ with the hope of spring. It seems like everything is holding its breath.

We seem to be in mountains ~ Virginia has those too ~ ancient, stumpy things: the wizened old uncles of the uppity Himalayas. Virginia's mountains rise up 3,000-4,000 feet. They've been stooped with weather and the relentlessness of time. But they're comfortable and agreeable old geezers. They've given up pretense.

We pull in the drive to Sky Meadows State Park. Mrs. Kaneko comes to a stop, even before she reaches the parking lot. "You kids have fun," she says as we scramble out the back. Niko pops the hatch and grabs a backpack and two poles.

He hands one to me. "Are your shoes comfortable?" he asks.

"The best ones I've got."

"Well, I packed another pair in case those don't work out. I don't want you to have your own boot-throwing, Cheryl-Strayed moments."

He sets off, and I follow.

"This way," he calls back to me, "is the fastest way up the mountain."

Up the mountain? UP THE MOUNTAIN!

The trail is graciously hospitable, and I'm keeping up fine. For a big girl, I have endurance. But I will never be spry.

But then the trail becomes ambitious – steep and unrelenting. The trail is rocky and impossibly long and becomes an endless series of mountain mirages. I'll look up ahead-and see the trail flatten ~ and I'll think, "That's it! We made it to the top!" But then you reach that flat part, and you realize that it's not really flat, and the trail remains continuous and mocking.

I reach a flat part that's not really flat ~ just a tease and a joke.

"Niko," I stop and double over and rest my hands on my knees. "Please. I need a break."

"So do I," he lies and takes off the backpack. He reaches inside it and takes out two strips of yellow foam. He unfolds one ~ like an accordion ~ and gives it to me: "The world is now your chair, m'lady. Choose whichever seat you desire."

I walk over to a fallen tree and sit on it with the cushion. Niko joins me, places the backpack between his feet, then reaches in, and produces water.

"Oh, thank God," I say. I leave manners behind and chug.

Niko gestures to the wilderness. "In two months' time, this will be a different world. The trees will be full with leaves. And the Japanese will call all of this a green bath."

"A green bath?" I'm confused.

"That's their word for hiking. It's not merely walking. It's cleaning your soul. It's taking a green bath."

I nod. I could use any kind of bath right now. Green. Clear. Any color will do.

Niko smiles. "When we get to the top, I have something to show you."

"I bet the view is fantastic," I lie. Views be damned. No panorama is worth this pain.

"Oh, it's better than a view." Niko is cryptic. "And take your time with this break. There is no rush. Once we reach the top, the way down is easy."

If there's an easy way *down,* isn't there an easy way *up*? I'm actually gaining some sympathy for Dante. When he was climbing Purgatory, no wonder he complained.

I hesitate. "How much more until we reach the top?"

"We're close," he assures. "A mile. Maybe more."

Does he know a mountain mile is different than a suburban one?

"Ok. I'm ready," I lie. My legs feel on fire, and not in a good way. But we take off walking, climbing, *enduring* this mountain.

I'm trying to distract myself from exhaustion with attempts at conversation. "Your mother seems nice." Small talk has never been my forte.

"Yes," Niko begins, "and she's ecstatic you're here. She loves this place. She'd live here, if they let her. There are such remarkable birds."

"Birds?" I scan the treetops, but they look bare to me. If birds are here, they're hiding. And quiet.

"Oh, yes. My mother is a birder. She follows them everywhere."

A birder? A *birder*? She used to ski the Alps. I picture her, youthful, racing her future husband, teasing him down to the base of the mountain. And she's traded in Alpine excitement for *binoculars*? What is it about life that makes adults so *timid*?

The mirage continues: it's relentless and cruel. The trail acts like it's flattening, but it's never really flat, and then it shoots up ~ vertically ~ taunting me.

And then there's the pain. The ridiculous, horrific, embarrassing pain. How do I handle this? How do I admit to this beautiful creature that I really, really need to pee?

I stop. "Niko," I sigh. "I need a restroom."

"Yeah, so do I," he's scrounging in his backpack. Then he offers a roll of toilet paper the way Lainie offers keys.

"Niko," I begin ~ my hands are at my side, determinedly *not* reaching for the offering ~ "you're kidding, right?"

His arm remains outreached. "Dani, up here, the world is your toilet. You'll be fine. You go over there" (he gestures north, I think) "and I'll go over here. Meet you back on the trail."

I grab the t.p. Seriously, this *date* could not get any worse. Here is a partial list of gross bodily functions you do NOT want to perform on date #2: slurping, chugging, peeing, sweating… but I'm in pain and wetting myself is not an option.

The embarrassment is total because, when we meet back on the trail, I'm sure Niko's been waiting for at least ten minutes, but we trudge up the mountain some more, and I'm about to admit defeat ~ tell Niko I'm done; I'm spent; I have nothing left; we need to turn around; we need to go *down*…but we take a few more steps up and then I'm on a new trail with a different personality.

I look around. Confused. The trail we had been on struggled *up* the mountain. This trail seems to snuggle the mountain, embracing it at the waist.

Niko stands in front of me. "TA-DA!" he exclaims.

I look around, underwhelmed. This is *it*? There is nothing here that's impressive to see. Not even a view.

Niko shines. "Welcome to the A. T."

I look around, bewildered. I actually spin in a circle, like an idiot. "*This* is the Appalachian Trail?"

"The one and only! Look!" Niko points at a sign that identifies the trail ~ one that notes that Harper's Ferry is 34 miles thataway:

"But, but," I'm processing, "I don't understand. I thought the AT was *huge*."

"Not *huge* as in *wide*, just huge as in *long*, and," he gestures so extravagantly that I think he'll break into jazz hands, "and you, Dani, are standing right on it!"

I'm exhausted, and a little dizzy. If there was a leaf-pile, I'd collapse.

"I could not bring you to the Pacific Crest Trail," Niko is explaining, "but if Cheryl Strayed lived in Virginia, her story would begin *here*."

And now I understand. The wonder comes slowly, like a theater curtain's slow rise. Dates can do more than merely be fun. Dates can be thoughtful, an exploration of another's personality. An expedition to see how two temperaments intersect. I feel baby tears stinging in my eyes.

"Here," Niko gestures, "give me your phone, and I'll take

your picture by the AT sign. I promise, when you return to school, you'll have bragging rights for life."

"Or a week," I clarify. "It is high school."

"Or a week. Good enough."

I give him my phone and walk towards the sign. When I turn around, he's swiping right. "You have so many photos of Gabby," he smiles. "That's sweet." Then he turns the camera to me. "Say, 'Spring!'"

"Spring," I echo.

When we walk again, it doesn't feel like hiking. There is nothing rocky or laborious about it.

This portion of the AT is a wonder. It's soft and welcoming and slopes down quietly like a gentle 'hushhh,' and then becomes grassy and wide, like strolling through a meadow. On the sides of the trail, baby crocuses wink at us with their shy, white eyes. The trail is graceful, modest.

Until it isn't.

Until the land drops away and the sky balloons huge, and I can look out and down and see squared plots of pastureland and look out and across and see and layers of mountains frosting the horizon.

"Welcome to Piedmont Overlook," Niko grins. "Best view in the state. And do I have a seat for you." He gestures to a solitary bench nestled at the side of the trail.

I back up to the bench, so I don't misplace the view, as if ~ if I look away ~ it would disappear forever.

I sit, and Niko drops beside me…with the backpack between

his feet. It's open and he's scrounging and squinting and grabbing.

"Found it," he smiles, and offers me a bottle of Ramune.

How did he find this? Japanese soda! But because the Japanese have a playful, whimsical side, it's both soda *and* a toy.

If you can combine food and play, why ever would you not?

Niko's still searching in the bag. "And Poki. I have Poki. And mochi. And fruit."

Then he looks up at me and smiles, "And I have one more thing just for you."

"What's that?" I try to peek into the backpack, but his hand nestles my chin, and he guides my face towards his lips.

And then he kisses me.

It's not long or lingery. It's thin and quick like a little bird's peck.

But it's enough. It's a *kiss*.

"And Niko?" I venture, "I have something for you."

And I lean in and kiss him with a warm, relaxed kiss.

And I don't stop kissing him for an extravagantly long time.

Dani Argyle Takes on Playgrounds. And Preparation. And Unfortunate Truths
Sunday, March 16, 2025
9:17 a.m.

After being with Niko for one extravagant day, it's hard to make re-entry into the Mom-world and touchdown within a Mom-climate. Any glimpse of joy I had with Niko was ephemeral and fleeting ~ like glimpsing a single star in a world oppressed by fog.

When you walk through the doors of the Argyle house, normalcy awaits.

Unrelenting, tepid, normalcy.

Sunday morning, Mom is at her desk, squinting at the Japanese newspapers on her computer screen, printing hopeful articles, highlighting various words, stuffing data and more data into bulging three-ring binders. Then I hear a strange strangling sound in her throat, and Mom's face flushes to life, reddens at the cheeks, but it is a false fire. Hers always are.

"Dani," she calls as I creep toward the kitchen. "Come here. Look at this word. It's '*Aibou*.' That's like friendship, right? It's a synonym for '*Tomodachi*.'"

I pause and squint at the screen. "Not quite, Mom. '*Aibou*' means 'partner.' It can be a neutral word or a loving one. It depends upon context."

"I'm going to mark it anyway." The printer prints. The orange highlighter highlights. Mom leans back with a look of accomplishment. And then she leans towards the screen and squints some more.

That's my mom: a moment away from madness ~ of the tape and red string variety.

Gabby jumps up to me and pulls on my sleeve. "Aah ee. Ay ow, eeee?"

That's Gabby-speak for, "Dani. Playground, please?" He's clasping both little hands in front of him: the classic sign for begging. No ASL required.

Crap. I still have some meals to prep. If I don't do it now, I'll have to do it tomorrow in order to prepare for the arrival of Dad's mourners, and that means I'll have to miss even more school.

Wait.

"Ok, Gabby." I'm signing now, not cueing. "Playground today." I pretend it's for him, but leaving this house is a respite for me.

He jumps up and down, pealing with laughter. For him, joy can't be expressed with a mere mouth or throat: it requires the whole body and lungfuls of air.

We begin the mile trek to Stone Circle Townhomes, enjoying the walk and the whisper of warmth. Gabby runs ahead of me, then circles back, and runs ahead again. When he gets tired of running, he jumps.

I can't let him run too far ahead. I can never let him out of my sight. The issue with caring for a deaf child is that, for the caregiver, everything is scary. If a hearing child gets lost, he can just find an officer ~ or a mother with kids ~ and ask that person if they can help. But if a deaf child gets lost, who can he turn to? Who will listen? Who will understand?

And some kids from the neighborhood are passing us on their bikes ~ whoopingly, daringly, and startlingly unsupervised. But how could the deaf child hear the car behind him? Or react when someone shouts 'Watch out!'"

So playground time is a big commitment. It's not a let-Gabby-play-while-I-read-a-book day. It's an all-attention-on-Gabby-and-ADHD-be-damned day.

When we get to the play yard, I get down on one knee and look at Gabby.

"Gabby," I sign as I speak, "I'm not feeling well."

His eyes stretch wide and he beams.

"I feel that there's something really strange inside me."

He's tipping up and down, bobbing on his toes.

"I don't think that I'm Dani anymore. I feel like I'm someone else." And then my voice deepens, and my signs get BIG. "Run for your life! It's the TICKLE MONSTER!"

Gabby shrieks and flees. I lumber after him with Frankenstein steps and Frankenstein arms, grrr- grrr-ing in the back of my throat.

Soon, there's shrieking throughout the playground as other children gather around. They cheer and they taunt, "You can't catch ME!" and I growl, "Me, monster. Me TICKLE!" and they dart in different directions, flashing outwards like a firework, and I rumble, "ME TICKLE YOU ALL! MWAAA HAAA HAAA HAAA!"

But of course, that's a lie. If I catch a kid, it will have to be Gabby. Parents don't like it when people play with their children.

But after the children have been chased, and some of the older ones have learned that monsters can be grabbed and brought to their knees, the skies start to lower and grumble with thunder, and rain flashes down in fat, dumpy drops before thinning into threads connecting earth and sky.

The walk home is faster than the walk to the playground. Rain makes everyone undignified and sudden.

We stomp into the house with wet, galoshy stomps and start stripping to our skin because ~ being wet is fine, but I draw the line at being wet and cold.

When I change and walk to the kitchen to fix some fruit, Mom is still fixed at the computer, eyes erect, posture slumped.

"Mom," I say, "it's thundering outside. I think you need to turn off the computer."

"Thunder?" Mom repeats ~ blankly ~ and then reconsiders. "Really? In March?"

"In March," I affirm. "It's not what I ordered. I'll voice my grievance and demand a full refund."

And then I return to the kitchen.

These lasagnas are not going to assemble themselves.

I know it's late, and I should try to get to sleep, but if I start Tweeting now, I might have dreams worth dreaming.

Dante

Nothing's as good as seeing your own personal nemesis stuck in the sludge of Styx. #KnewIWasRight

Dante

Virgil keeps staring at me from a distance. Can someone explain?

Beatrice

You're starting to understand....

Virgil

Been on hold with the Help Desk for over an hour. How long does it take for a technician to open a door?

Dante

When you think you smell BBQ but it's just a bunch of heretics on fire.

Virgil

Weird traveling with a guy who's actually alive. So now I have to watch him trip over himself?

Dante

Google is not being helpful:

Why r all the popes mean to me

How to write love poems to the dead

Best tourist spots in Hell

Help, I'm lost in a dark wood

Virgil

Yup. He's alive alright. Just tackled him to save him from the wrath of Medusa #HeroNow

Dante

My heart is too frail. I can't do this anymore...Wait, I see a bad pope over there.

Dante

So the difference between heresy and blasphemy is...?

Virgil

Smackdown between heretics and blasphemers tonight on DisTV

And then I do fall asleep. Deeply. Dreamlessly.

But at two o'clock, even a shift in the light can startle me awake.

My dad's sitting on my bed. Watching. Glimmering.

I sit up and stretch upwards to refrain from reaching for him.

"Hello, Dani-Boo." He smiles and shines.

"Hello, Dad." I squint and blink.

He's waiting and patient. "How are you doing? And how is your mom?"

I shake my head and grab Sailor Moon for something to hold. "Dad, those questions should not be asked side by side. Choose one or the other, but I can't handle both."

"Ok, Dani. Then how are *you*?"

I feel something hard and crampy inside me. Something small and dark and too ugly to be said. "Dad," I manage. "I'm just so tired. Life is too much."

"It hasn't beaten you yet."

"Not yet. But I'm not sure how much longer I can continue like this. Something's got to give, and I think it's going to be me."

"No, you're not giving in. I know you. You're fighting. I see you. You're swinging your hooks to the left and the right. Others would stay down, but you keep getting up. That's something. That's courage."

"Dad, it doesn't feel like courage." I look instinctively at Sailor Moon. "It feels like fatigue. If I'm still standing, it's only because I'm too tired to *care* anymore."

There's a whuff of silence as he processes my words. "I'm sorry to hear that." A pause. Some disappointment? "The fight that comes from not caring isn't courage, Dani: it's desperation. But courage takes place in many forms. The most courageous thing I've ever done isn't releasing the pressure valve on that school's boiler right before it was going to blow; the most courageous thing was taking those last few steps before knocking on Private Lanka's door and telling Mrs. Lanka that she was now a widow. Dani, courage is never a lack of care. Courage is an over-abundance of it. Courage is just one form of love ~ it's love on steroids ~ a love that stares down discomfort because it cares about something more than itself."

I want this to sink in, but it feels hard and foreign and achingly distant.

"Dad, you expect too much from me. I'm not courageous, and I'm not full of love."

Dad's eyes are gentle and smiling. "Yes, you are, Dani. You love your brother."

"Yes, you're right. I love my Gabby."

"You love me."

"I love you."

"And you love your mother."

Silence.

Awful, gaping, desolate silence.

Some truths are too awful to be told.

Dani Argyle Takes on the Broken Things
Monday, March 17, 2025
7:59 a.m.

Monday is a school day, a see-Niko-before-class day, an envy-Sophia-for-her-sticky-brain day, and an all-things-Japan day.

Japanese 2 with Waters Sensei is about more than vocabulary and grammar. It's about culture and cuisine and a country's character.

Today, the entire class is waiting in the hall outside Sensei's room. The bell is ringing and the door is locked and Sensei is nowhere to be seen.

And then he appears, looking oddly flustered, shoulders his way between the students, unlocks the door and lets us inside.

We're barely in the class when there's a collective gasp.

Every beautiful object in the room has been broken. The objects on our desks are all cracked and collapsing. I stare across the room: whenever I look away from brokenness and ruin, I look toward them again.

Who could do this? Who would break every object a student

had identified as beautiful?

There's a collection of interjections and expletives and questions and ~ I swear ~ somewhere in the room, someone is sobbing.

I've never witnessed such a collective scene of adolescent outrage.

Sensei is shouting ~ a rare Sensei moment ~ "Have a seat! Have a seat! Find the desk with your beautiful object."

Beautiful object? Has he seen this place?

"Let's not blame vandals," Waters Sensei is projecting above the dismay. "Time itself is the ultimate vandal, and the process of existing leaves everything that is pristine vulnerable to its predation. But because an object is broken, that does not mean it is ugly, and by no means does damage render everything useless."

"But my cup!" someone in the back is pleading, "How can this be useful? It's broken in *half*!"

And Waters Sensei takes two hands and holds a plate high over his head. "So was this plate ~ at one point in time." I look at the plate: it's creamy and thin with abrupt strips of gold zagging throughout. And he looks up at the plate and says, "Look closely. There is beauty in brokenness."

Then he puts the plate down and explains himself. "The West is preoccupied with perfection. But beauty cannot be so limited. The art of *kintsukuroi* is the art of golden repair. The artist doesn't hide brokenness: instead, the repair is illuminated. *Wabi sabi* teaches that beauty is more than mere perfection. Beauty has the opportunity to create within us serene melancholy and spiritual longing. When brokenness is illuminated, the broken will become beautiful again. It will be more revered than it previously was."

And then we are given smocks and gloves and glasses and glue ~ is it glue? it's part lacquer, part paste, and it glints with gold ~ and we are told to repair the vessel and let its brokenness shine.

Sophia and I are working side by side. She has a plate; I have a vase.

The vase is thin and practically pointless ~ its purpose is for holding a single bud only. It's been snapped at the neck and a chunk of glaze severed. I study its desolation and plan its renewal.

"You know what would have been really fun?" Sophia is saying. "If we got to smash all this stuff all on our own. Now *that* would have been a class to remember."

I finger the vase and blow off some dust.

Poor Sophia. She doesn't yet know.

No one should seek out to purposefully destroy.

Life, in her carelessness, will do that herself, easily, wantonly, and oblivious to the cries of grief around her.

Dani Argyle Takes on Bigotry. And Depression.
And Nostalgia
Tuesday, March 18, 2025
10:02 a.m.

It's T minus six hours and counting.

Six hours until everyone who feels Dad's loss will converge on our house, filling it full with both pity and laughter.

Gabby will go to school today, and when he gets back, he'll play MarioKart to his heart's content. There is no reason for him to get caught up in this particular maelstrom.

But Mom and I stay. And clean.

And wait.

Mom's dusting the mantle, and I'm Swiffering the floor.

Work can be good when conversation is difficult.

"Niko sounds nice," Mom finally offers.

"Yes, I like him." I smile.

"Tell me more." She's holding a small statue of a faceless family ~ two parents and two children, with arms encircling each other ~ she's holding them with one hand, and she's dusting with the other.

"He's so…" I pause to find the words, "in the moment. You know? Like he's just *him* and doesn't care what other people think."

"I know someone else like that." She returns the statue to the mantle and grabs another figurine ~ a Madonna and child. (This child is sweet: not the pious mini-adult of some saccharine traditions ~ this baby is gazing at his mommy's face and reaching up.)

I shake my head. "But I *do* care what people think, Mom. Just not enough to change for them." I'm Swiffering the floor in huge loopy loops. Just because I'm cleaning doesn't mean I can't have fun. "But Niko doesn't care. He just *is*. He's 100% pure, unadulterated Niko."

Mom turns and looks at me. "I'd like to meet him."

I pause and smile. "I'd like to have him over."

"Once all this is over," she gestures to the house, "you can have him over for dinner."

"Thank you, Mom. And if it's the weekend, he can stay." I Swiffer some more.

I sense Mom is confused. "What's that again?"

I pause. I want to talk slowly, like I'm talking to a child, but I refrain. "Niko. He could stay the night. You know, like a sleepover."

Mom has been shocked still. Not only is she not dusting, she's not breathing. The air seems heavy with unspoken words. Then I hear a 'no,' and Mom is shaking her head lightly, as if she's having an internal disagreement that I am not privy to. "No, Dani.

No."

"Why not?"

Mom still looks struck, positively dumb. She blinks a couple times as if the scene will transform. "Well," she begins, "I could call his mother. He could sleep in Gabby's room."

"Mom," I sigh. "That makes no sense. My bed has a trundle."

Mom seems stuck, like a car in snow. She's trying to gain traction but is not moving forward. "Dani, I said 'no.'"

"Why not? We won't have sex."

Now she's flustered, reddening. "Because, no. Because no. Because we don't entertain boys in the bedroom."

"Sophia stays over." *Must I remind adults of everything?*

"That's different." Her voice is stronger now, as if she's spoken something true and incontrovertible.

"Why?" I wait.

There's silence. Confusion?

Mom seems lost, glancing around the room like she needs a new compass.

"Mom," I continue, "you know I'm pan. I came out to you in the fifth grade for goodness sake, but you never seem to take me seriously."

Now that we're on ground that we've rehearsed before, Mom's words flow easier: "That's not true, Dani. I understand that you might be bi, but," and she takes a deep breath and lowers her head, "you also might not be as bi as you think you are. I don't think these conclusions can be reached in fifth grade."

"Don't patronize me, Mom." I turn to attack the floor with the Swiffer. Why do adults believe it is their right to tell us who we are? "I knew in the fifth grade and I still know now: I am attracted to personalities, not penises."

I sense Mom flinch, but soon she recovers: "Dani, adults are not as obsessed with your sexuality as you think we are. My job isn't to define how bi you are. My first job as a parent is protection. Dani, I need to protect you."

I drop the handle of the ridiculous Swiffer. "Protect me from what? Protect me from *Niko*? I don't need protecting." Why parents can never let their children become adults is beyond me. Isn't the whole point of having children to make sure they become independent? Who has kids to keep them kids forever? "Mom, I can take care of myself. And why would I need protection from one friend, like Niko, and not from another, like Sophia? Why would it make a difference whether Sophia stays over or whether Niko does?"

"Because it does. Because it does. Because, like it or not, girls listen to cues. They take 'no' for an answer. They rarely become sexually aggressive."

I stare her down. I want her to feel the burn of my glare: the staggering weight of her own hypocrisy. She will not denigrate fifty percent of the world's population without feeling uncomfortable about it. My words are tight and biting: "Shame, Mom. *Shame.*"

If Mom at one point had lost her composure, she's regained

it now. She's straightened in her skin. "Say what you want, Dani, but you're not entertaining boys in your bedroom. After Niko comes to dinner, you two can go to the basement or stay in the dining room. But those are your choices." She returns to dusting the mantle. In her opinion, the conversation is over.

"Never mind, Mom." She will not get the last word. I will: "I don't want Niko over."

She shakes her head and squints at me. "So if things aren't 100% your way, you're not willing to compromise?"

"Why bother? These are other people's rules. Not mine. And I will never consent to bigotry and bias." I pick up the neglected Swiffer and start cleaning again. Aggressively.

"That's me, Dani," Mom begins, "the world's most intolerant and bigoted mother."

She said it. I didn't. And those are some last words that I will allow her to have.

The house is pretty full when Joe Chalk arrives: Dad's best friend and a personal repository of all things Dad. But ~ since he's Joe ~ you have to get him drinking in order to get him talking.

I know my Uncle Joe.

We'll be eight people squished around a table meant for six, so there's not much room for extras ~ like water pitchers or centerpieces.

But I did make room for a single bud vase.

"What a funny little holder," Lainie insists as she sits at the table.

"I like it," Joe explains. "It looks like it's been loved."

I look at Joe with grateful eyes. "It has been, Joe. Broken things can be beautiful, too."

When the lasagna has been eaten ~ I'm glad I made two; the second is already half devoured ~ Joe turns to Terrel, and to Chris and Micah.

"Remember that time," (he's had his second beer, so the dad-stories are starting to come) "when we were in Jacksonville excavating that apartment?"

"And the looters beat us there," Terrel offers.

"And we're jacking up the supports to keep the whole damned building from coming down, and this group of teens ~ "

"They were a piece of work ~ "

"they stumble upon us with guns in their waistbands, and *they* tell *us* to leave?"

"And J.P. keeps jacking the beam like he didn't hear a thing ~ "

"And the biggest guy in the group turns to J.P. and shouts, 'Hey. Boomer. I'm talking to you!'"

"And J.P. whispers to me ~ but loud enough for everyone to hear ~ 'Hey, Joe. What's a Boomer?' At first I'm stunned because I don't see his play, but then it just comes to me, and I say ~ "

And all four chime in at once ~

"J.P. You're 40! You really don't know what a Boomer is?"

"And he shrugs, 'Hey, Joe, if you don't know the answer, just say so,' and he keeps on working the jack, and I think the kids all thought we were crazy, because they just turned around and walked away."

"Your father," Terrel is saying to me, "could always pull crap like that."

"Just keep talking." Joe is explaining Dad's philosophy. "And don't give anyone a chance to think. He would never confront people head-on ~ although he could have: the man's muscled like a Mack Truck."

Now it's Chris's turn to jump in. "Remember when we were in Paraguay? And this guy thought that we wouldn't go in the house to rescue his wife unless he gave us money, and he was holding out cash, and J.P. was trying his Spanish, trying to tell the man to step aside and he didn't want the money, and then the man shouted, 'Take it! Take it! And screw you!' and J.P. didn't miss a beat and said, 'That's Mr. Screw-You to you.'"

There's more laughing and joking and then Micah raises his glass: "To J.P. Argyle: no matter what this world threw at you, you handled everything with cleverness and style."

And then the world stops and drops into silence. My eyes widen and I want to say something ~ anything ~ but there's a heaviness stumped in the back of my throat. The silence is expanding, gaping, oppressing.

Everyone glances at Mom. Her eyes are blazing. "Handle, Micah, han-dul." Mom's words seem quiet but they steam. "Do not speak of my husband in the past tense."

The world seems to be holding its breath. At least everyone sitting at this table is. We all stare at Micah. His eyes droop and we hear his voice ~ hushing out the words ~ "Of course, Penny. Of course."

Joe clears his throat and raises his glass. "To J.P. We miss you every day."

That's a sentiment my mother will toast. We all raise glasses and clink. Quietly.

Lainie stands and starts clearing dishes. "Who wants dessert?" she offers.

"It's just chocolate ice cream," I add. "Dad's favorite."

"Two scoops for me!" Terrel calls out. "I'm with your dad on this one. Who needs fancy things when you can have Breyers?"

And the four men start chanting, "Ice cream! Ice cream! Ice cream!"

It's loud enough that even Gabby senses something and emerges from the basement. He signs a big sign: "I hear fun!" And I pick him up and twirl him around.

And so there's joy and life and laughter again.

Joe and Terrel will stay the night; Chris and Micah are driving back to Fairfax ~ so Joe will get my room and Terrel will get Gabby's, and the Argyle family will all sleep in Mom's room.

I'm showing Joe my room. He has no idea what a Herculean

task it was to get my room ready for company. I like to LIVE in my room, thank you very much, but some people feel uncomfortable with clutter. At least I have a big closet. Let's hope no one opens it, or there might be some avalanche issues.

"There's towels over there ~ " I'm pointing to the dresser, "and an extra pillow there ~ " I gesture by the bed.

He sits on the bed and pats the mattress next to him. I sit.

He's looking at his knees, fixated and glum. "Dani," he sighs, "I owe you an apology."

"Uncle Joe ~ "

"No. Hear me out. Your father was my responsibility." He's still looking at the floor.

"He was a grown man. He took care of himself. And he was never one to play by the rules."

"That's true. But they can't create rules for every situation out there. His ability to improvise was exemplary."

I nod. "It was until it wasn't. Joe, he died doing what he loved."

His voice slows and deepens. Trying to say the unsayable can have that effect. "That's no excuse for me to lose track of him."

"Joe ~ *he* left *you*." My words are *not* slow and *not* deep. They are energetic and crisp ~ poised and precise in a way that can only be truth. "*He's* the one who returned to base and then tried to catch up to you again."

"So he should have been somewhere between the base and our expedition. But I didn't even know to look for him."

And then words seem useless ~ how can air comfort? ~ so I circle my arms around his shoulders and hold this man who is heavy with guilt. And he rests his cheek on my head and holds me back, and we sit together in our sadness and ache.

Joe could probably hold me forever: he's always done the night shifts and never seems to sleep until the dawn appears ~ until the sun and stars go to battle for the sky ~ and his most difficult jobs (the death notifications and discipline reviews) always begin at dawn, but I am tired, and there is a point in time when even a hug becomes uncomfortable, so I pat Joe on the back and make leaving noises. He releases his grip, and I stand and stretch. I hear a fluffle around the nightstand, and then I hear, "Dani!"

I turn around. Joe's watch is dangling from his hand, poised over the opened nightstand drawer and ready to drop, but he's staring down.

He reaches in and pulls out a bottle of prescription pills. He turns the label to me and then says, "Explain."

"They help," I offer.

"They're not yours," he asserts.

"True. Lainie gave them to me to see if they would help."

"But Dani, they're *not yours*!" His voice has energy again ~ it's the upside of indignation. "These things are not candy. They need to be taken with oversight. Besides, WellProtran does not cure situational depression."

I sigh. It's hard to argue against someone who is both right and wrong at the same time. "That's true, Uncle Joe, but this medicine helps *me*, so it's helping with whatever depression I have, and when I turn eighteen, I'll get some on my own."

"So Penny won't take you to get you evaluated?"

My eyes widen. "If you haven't noticed, Uncle Joe, she's rather preoccupied. But I do have Aunt Lainie, and sometimes she sees things that I do not."

"So *Lainie's* the one who thought you were depressed?" Joe's voice sharpens. "Not you?"

"It's not that simple, Joe. I was depressed, but I didn't *know* I was depressed." I feel my voice tightening, and all of my muscles clench like a fist. I want to lash out ~ to bend him into the realization that I AM RIGHT, but I force myself to pause and find the right words. I sigh. "Joe, do you know what a difference it makes to just have a name for your condition? Without a name, I felt overwhelmed and helpless. I felt like I was fighting a ghost." I blush at the word "ghost," but I don't think Joe notices. "Without a name, the malaise just becomes so normal that I didn't even know I needed help." I'm staring at the floor and shaking my head. "Joe, I have been broken so long, I couldn't even imagine becoming whole. But now that I can name this thing, I can also fight it."

Joe sighs. He seems to be softening, but he's still holding the bottle, not returning it to the drawer. "I'm glad Lainie cares, Dani, but I care, too. I care enough to be concerned. How long have you been taking these?"

"Not long. About two months."

He looks at the bottle, as if the label itself will tell him what to say. "And they're already working? These things take time."

I rattle-off the prescription information: "SSRI's need two to six weeks to start being effective," and then add with a contented: "But yes, Uncle Joe, they are working."

"How do you know?" Then he looks at me, waiting.

I probably shouldn't mention how, before the medicine, I obsessed about suicide every day, but now I'm considering it more on a monthly basis. Adults never react well to information like that. So I find a truth that *can* be said: "Because I feel like I've emerged from a fog. Because there was a part of me that I always kept hidden ~ hidden from everyone except a few chosen ones ~ and now she's out. Now she's free. Now she's visible to everyone."

Uncle Joe chuckles. "Oh, I've seen that little devil. She ran rampant around the house from age three to ~ " He stops short.

"To twelve." I nod. And then I smile a little. "It's nice to have her back. For a while now, I've been missing her."

When I trudge upstairs to Mom's room and open her door, she's in the middle of the king-sized mattress, lying on her left side, arms outstretched to Dad's side of the bed, and Gabby is snuggled up to her back, a tiny arm around her waist.

I swear, that child is smiling in his sleep.

I look at the bed and wonder how I'll fit. I can't sleep on Dad's side, but if I try to squish myself behind Gabby ~ on the edge of the mattress ~ every time I shift, I will wobble and tip.

So I grab an extra pillow and lie down on the floor at the foot of the bed. I try to make myself small so that any late-night trips to the bathroom will not end in disaster.

My mom starts to whimper and I hear a thrashing and a "No! No! I see you! I'm coming!" and a guttural sound from the back of her throat.

I listen to the sounds of grief, of pain, of nightmare, and I wish they were always limited to our sleeping hours. But nightmares persist, stretch their rotting fingers into all the hours of our lives. Even when we're awake, the monsters snatch from us, consuming and devouring what we love the most.

There are so many ways our mothers disappear.

Dani Argyle Takes on the Bullies
Tuesday, March 25, 2025
7:43 a.m.

Sometimes, it's interesting being invisible.

Before school, I can hang-out in the common area ~ waiting for Sophia and Niko ~ and all kinds of conversations are whirling around. The pretty girls pay no attention to someone like me.

"Did you see Ryan?" a Chorus member is asking.

"He is so messed up," the leader's laugh scrapes the skin. "He's telling people he fell down the stairs."

"You don't want to cross paths with Julian Jones. That guy will mess you up. Why did Ryan let his guard down?"

"Everyone has to pee."

I'm sitting right next to them, texting their conversation to the Loudon County Public Schools' Tip Line, and I'm getting names, dates, times ~ all the information LCPS would need in order to conduct a thorough investigation.

If they ever wanted to bother, that is.

Niko sneaks up behind me. "Who are you texting?" he's asking, taking the phone from my hand and scrolling through my summary of the Chorus girls' discussion. He whistles and drops an arm around my shoulder: "Damn, girl. You are *brave*."

I don't feel brave, but I do feel a little…conspicuous.

Sophia shouts from across the common area: "Dani! Niko!" She titters up to us and gleams.

And the three of us feel so right together ~ like a three-legged stool that will never tip. And, when Sophia's around, Niko's not so… hands on.

We sit on the floor and take out our phones. Tweets will be tweeted.

Virgil@ThePhilosopher'sZone

Just told my first 'You so ugly' joke. Minotaur just got PWND.

Dante@theinfernoislit

Got a glimpse of Alexander the G up to his nips in boiling blood.

The Greeks X

The Romans ✓

Beatrice @GirlzGoneToGod

Dante just slipped down a hill in Circle 7. Please don't make me watch anymore.

Dante

I see a forest up ahead. Where's my GPS?   #walkingincircles

Mr. Glupov is passing with Ms. Spira. "Look at them," he's saying. "These kids. They don't even *talk* to each other. They just sit around and text on their phones."

"And they're sitting right next to each other," Ms. Spira agrees.

Virgil

The souls here lack basic reasoning skills. Nothing to see here. Move along. Move along.

The warning bell is reminding us aggressively that school is not about friendship and creativity but about punctuality and order and very loud reminders, so Niko gives me a long kiss goodbye and Sophia and I head off to class.

Before we duck into Waters Sensei's class, Sophia is gushing, positively gloating, "You and Niko are so perfect together!"

"Really? You think?" I drop to my desk.

"Of *course*! Oh, my God! He's cute and you're brilliant." She slips into her seat. "You're like, the perfect couple."

I laugh inwardly. "Well, Sophia, one of those statements is certainly correct."

She beams. "I know. I know. I'm so happy for you."

After school, I'm in Ms. Satchell's class, trying to shove some math into my brain.

Bless that woman. When it comes to teaching, she's indefatigable. She's tutoring me privately after school and then giving me tests immediately after each lesson.

I might just pass Algebra II. Give that woman a Nobel Prize.

When I finish and walk outside, Lainie is leaning ~ gorgeously ~ on the car. I swear, even the teenage boys are stopping to stare.

She holds out her keys. "Here you go, kiddo. Show me what you've got."

We climb into the car, and, I will admit, my driving is not as chunky as before. It's not smooth, I know, and I think I hug the right side of the lane, but everything feels safer over there ~ and I have yet to drive into a ditch or plow through a mailbox.

I park the car in front of Gabby's school. "Be right back," I tell Lainie. I glance at the clock in the middle of the dashboard, "They should be done with chess and beginning the clean-up."

When I enter the cafeteria, it's vacantly quiet. There's no one around except one devoted chess coach and some open chess boards.

"Miss Argyle!" he calls out. "I sent all the kids out to the playground. The day is nice and the natives were restless."

"Really?" I ask.

"Well, not Gabby, of course. I want you to know that I promoted him to the league for fourth through sixth graders. He'll never get better unless he plays against people more skilled than he is."

"I think one reason he's so good," I offer, "is that he can concentrate longer than other first graders."

"I think," Coach offers, "there is more than that. Gabby remembers every lesson that I teach, and he uses the lessons in innovative ways." He looks at me seriously. "That kid has a gift."

"Agree to agree," I smile. "And Coach Zhang, thank you for taking the time to challenge him." I turn and start to walk to the exit.

"Always a pleasure," he calls out behind me.

I'm walking to the playground, and I hear in the distance, "Make him talk again! He sounds funny!" and another voice, "You think you're so smart, playing with us."

My feet start running before I even really register what those words mean. When I reach the playground, there's a group of big kids encircling Gabby.

Someone pushes him from behind. "Who's the show-off now?"

Gabby's staring, wide-eyed, looking from big kid to big kid, trying to smile at them, trying to get them to adore him, when the biggest in the group pushes him ~ hard ~ and Gabby falls on his butt with a crunch and sits there.

I blaze into the play-yard and scoop up my brother, holding him close and cradling his head. Then I spin around and glare at each child.

"You there, with the face," I spit at the big kid who pushed him the hardest. "Raise your hand if you think it's cool to make fun of deaf kids. Go on! Own it! Do you also like tripping up old people in the dark?"

And I spin when I hear something stir behind me. "You! With the other face! This is what I want you to do every day until the time you die. Look at yourself in the mirror and say, 'This is a person who thinks he's a bad-ass for hitting first graders.'" I step forward and feel ~ scalding inside me ~ a rage so intense, I could disembowel someone and eat intestines for breakfast. I clench my jaw, "You look at that vomitous mass on the end of your neck and remember how disgusting you are inside and out!"

Then I spin at all of them ~ collectively ~ "Run away now, or I will leave behind bloody piles of tiny children parts."

And they back away, slowly at first, and then dash decisively in different directions.

I carry Gabby back to the car and give a stunned Lainie the keys I once loved. Gabby and I slip into the back seat, and no one says a word on the long ride home.

After I give Gabby a bath and wash his sweet face and towel him dry, I ask him which pajamas he wants to wear.

"Mario," he cues.

So I find him his MarioWear and tuck him into bed. I know I should know just what to say, but I don't, so I kiss him on the head and pull the door closed.

In my room, I have some last-minute Tweets:

Dante

Wishing I took up archery. Some people need an arrow up the ass.

There's a scratching sound at the door, and, when I open it up, Gabby is there.

"Can I sleep over in your room tonight?" he signs.

"Of course." I turn on the light because darkness makes him mute, and I pull out the trundle and grab a blanket. Then I sit on my bed and pull up my knees.

He sits on the trundle, but he doesn't lie down. His face is taut and serious with concern.

"I'm not sure I like chess anymore," he explains with his hands.

"Gabby," I cue, "chess is great, and so are you." Then I change to sign so I can be more expressive, "Chess is good, but some of the boys in your school are butts."

He smiles weakly and lies down. I hear him sniff, and he's

upright again. "Dani," he's signing and pointing to his room, "I think that maybe monsters are real."

"Gabby," I reply, "Do you think they're hiding in your closet? I can go and ~ "

"No!" he's waving his hands and interrupting. "They're not in my room." And he pauses. "Just. Places."

I slouch in my bed and try to think.

"Dani," he's signing, "do *you* believe that monsters are real?"

What do I say? I feel blood chilling through my veins, and I see a flash of a man with long hair and a hand jerking up and down. I have no idea what to say. I have nothing to offer but the knots inside me.

But I take a long, deep breath to settle myself. This is not about *me*. This is about *Gabby* and what he needs. If only I knew what that was….

"Gabby," I try, and I stop, and I close my eyes and sigh. "Gabby, yes, I think some monsters are real. But they're not as strong as they think they are. No matter how mean they are, I can be meaner." Then I grin wickedly and lean forward as I sign, "I can make them whimper with a twist of their balls."

Gabby snorts and leans back and grins at the ceiling. Then his sits up straight with a serious face. "Then Dani, does that mean all the monsters are boys?"

Crap. I didn't see that one coming.

I stare at the wall as if the answers are there. Then I nod slowly. "Most of them are. The scary ones, anyway," and I watch some light dimming from his eyes, so I add on, emphatically, "but do you know who else is made up of boys?" I look at him and blaze.

"Who?" he asks.

"ANGELS!" I sign, booming my hands.

He looks up at the ceiling, like they're hovering overhead. "Where are the angels?" he wonders.

"Everywhere," I gesture. "There's Uriel, and Michael, and Gabriel."

He flashes with excitement and raises his hands. "THAT'S ME!" Then he rises to his feet and jumps.

"Yes, my Gabby. Gabriel is you." I reach out and tickle him under his arm.

He spins around and stops and then starts hugging himself. Then he plops on his knees on the trundle and signs, "Dani, I think my eyes are tired."

"I understand. Lie down. Close your eyes. I'm here."

He smushes into the mattress and pulls up the blanket. Then he takes out his hands from under it and explains, "I think it's time for me to wear my full name."

I lie down on my side and brush his face with my hand. "Ok, my dear Gabriel," I cue. "You wear your full name. It fits you beautifully."

And I stretch out and dangle my arm down to him. He pulls it to his chest and cradles it gently and closes his eyes and smiles.

Dani Argyle Takes on Finances. And Renown
Thursday, March 27, 2025
3:59 p.m.

I'm sitting on Lainie's stoop, waiting for Gabby ~ no, *Gabriel* ~ to come jumping up the street.

But when it comes to Tweeting Dante, there is no time like the present:

Virgil

I'm gazing down into a pit of poop. People are scratching it into their skin. You can't make this stuff up.

Dante

Virgil keeps getting tricked by demons. I want a new tour guide.

Beatrice

Go Virgie! Nothing says 'fun' like a game of tag with demons.

Dante

Ha! Virgil keeps experiencing culture shock. "The demons lied to me? They can do that?" 😂

Gabby's running up the sidewalk, arms outstretched. Today, he looks like a plane.

I meet him by the street and hold his left hand. He walks on the edge of the grass while I navigate the road. Our road narrows after Lainie's house, and there's not a sidewalk in sight.

Deaf children should not have to walk in the street.

When we reach our driveway, I pick up the mail and rifle through its contents. Bill. Trash. Ad. Trash. Trash.

And something that feels like a credit card.

Some poor creditor is woefully mistaken. The Argyles are strictly anti-credit.

Dad and his father built this house bit by bit, so they'd never go into debt. They dug out the basement and lived there for two years while saving the money to frame out the main floor. When they got more money, they added more rooms. The house just kept expanding. Like a Lego set.

I look up and see Mom's car. She's home in the middle of the day. I'm tearing up the junk mail ~ I double as a personal shredder ~ and Gabby ~ GABRIEL ~ is signing about Mario when we enter the house. He's off like a sprite to the basement and the Wii.

Mom's in the dining room, sitting at the desk, looking through a binder, hand poised over it with a bright orange highlighter. She looks up. "What are you doing?" she asks, startled.

"Hello, Mom. How was your day? Mine was fine, thank you. Oh yeah. I'm just sorting through the junk mail."

Her arm is reaching toward me. "Dani, that's not yours. Give it to me."

"But I always ~ "

She's up on her feet and snatching the papers from my hand and opening the envelope from the optimistic creditor.

I watch her pull out a credit card and flip it over from front to back.

"Mom," I ask, "what are you doing?"

"Dani, sometimes it's nice just to have a cushion." She sits back down. She's looking around for something, shuffling through papers filled with Japanese *hiragana*.

My heart starts swamping, and it's not until I feel it beating so huge that I realize I'm concerned. "Mom ~ Dad always says that credit makes people lazy ~ less likely to live within their means. For him, it's a point of honor to live debt free."

"Your dad is an idealist, but we need to be practical." She finds a pen, flips the card over, signs the back, and sighs.

I'm trying to catch her gaze: she should be looking at me, not admiring her signature. "But why would we ever need a credit card? The house is paid for. So is the car."

Mom turns in her seat. "Dani, please, you don't need to

know. Enjoy your childhood. Leave the adult world to me."

I want to say that would be nice for once, but my stomach feels twisty and suspicious. There's something I want to say, but my voice is stubborn and suddenly shy. Still, I clear my throat and give voice to my concern: "Mom, are you paying Renown with a credit card now?"

"No," she insists, but she's looking at the floor with some guilty eyes.

I snatch the card from her hands and start bending it and twisting. I watch pale creases zig through the plastic.

"Dani!" she jumps up and reaches for my hands. "Stop that! Give that back!"

"No!" I insist and turn my back to her. "I'm getting a job this summer." Fold. Fold. Twist. "If you need extra money, come and ask me. But do not ask" I glance at the card, "the Bank of America."

"Daniella A. Argyle. Stop it, *now!*" She's reaching over my shoulder. "You will not lecture me on how to spend money. Not when we're so cl ~ "

I turn to face her. "Mom!"

"You give that to me." Her hand is out. "I forbid you to do any more."

I give the card one final crease, throw it on the floor, and look up to face my mother. "Forbid all you want, Mom, but if I have to be the adult in this family, I'm up to the task."

And then I grab my backpack and head out the door.

As I'm walking down the street, I'm texting my friend-group: Sophia and Niko.

DA I'm ubering to Amelia Renowns right now. That bitch is going DOWN.

...

...

SB Dani don't do anything stupid

NK Dani we can meet you there. Sophia, give me a lift?

...

SB Niko I'm coming

Dani ~ be SMART

Sophia, I want to say, reason can only get you so far. The only thing con artists ever respond to is *fear*.

Somehow, Niko and Sophia have beaten me to the parlor ~ even in the light, it's a tired, squat building with a door so small, it seems like you have to hold your breath in order to squeeze through. They're standing underneath a faded sign that reads:

MADAME RENOWN

SEER. PSYCHIC.

IN-HOUSE READINGS

THURSDAY-SATURDAY OR BY APPOINTMENT

OR VISIT US AT THESTARSALIGN.ORG

Sophia runs up and stands in front of me ~ as if her tiny frame could ever slow my stride.

But Niko joins her, and I might not want to take both of them together.

"Dani," Niko is saying, "gather your thoughts. You don't want to go in hot."

"Dani," Sophia adds. "Identify your goal. What is your goal?"

Leave it to Ms. 4.0 to turn my family's dissolution into a lesson on rhetoric.

"You want to know my goal, Sophia? You want to know my damned *goal*? My goal is to *destroy* her. To leave her quivering in a giant glob of goo."

"C'mon, Dani," Niko is insisting, "you need a Plan B."

"Then how about she keeps her hands off my family and leaves us alone. Let. Us. Heal!"

"Better," Niko concedes. "How do you reach that?"

"By crushing her soul and spitting in the vapors," and I'm off ~ through the doors ~ bells jangling behind me.

A strangely serene woman gazes up from a couch ~ she has a round body and dangling jewelry and a pack of cards splayed across a table along with horoscope guides and phrenology charts and college brochures and mints. She looks up at me and smiles.

"Look at you! Daniella Argyle!"

I stop in my stride and stare, stunned. How could she know?

We've never met.

Sophia is waiting by the door, but Niko's by my side, whispering in my ear, "Dani, she's seen your photos in the paper."

So I smile and say, "And oh! Look at you! Amelia the fraud!"

She smiles like I've told a joke. "It's ok, Daniella. The gift of hope has not been given to all."

"If by 'gift' you mean 'curse,' then yes, I agree. And if by 'hope' you mean 'robbing-people-blind,' then yes, I make it a habit not to treat people like purses."

Madame Renown gazes up at the ceiling. "Oh, Daniella, the spirits have told me that you're entering into turmoil."

I'm not looking at the ceiling. There's nothing for me there. I stare straight at her. "Not the brightest bulbs in the spiritual world, those daemons of yours. A deaf preschooler would have said the same thing."

Renown closes her eyes. "They want you to find peace, to find rest."

"Fine. If they want me to calm down, there's one thing that needs to happen. You stop stealing from my family."

Her eyes open slowly, and she's looking at me. "Daniella, I'm not stealing. There are no felons here. Only souls who are growing and seeking the truth." She reaches out as if she's embracing the parlor.

"But not just any truth. Only truths that come with dollar signs."

"Daniella," she sighs and rests her hands in her lap, "I don't want to fight with you."

"The words of someone sorely lacking in logic skills."

"Not all things can be explained by logic. The most important issues in life ~ the issues of love, of hope, of meaning ~" she gestures to the room, "those issues will never be proven with logic."

I take a few steps forward and smile. "So you admit there's no logical proof that my dad is alive."

"There is no proof that *you* would believe." She gestures to the cards.

"But you do."

"Yes."

"So you'll give us all our money back when his body is discovered."

She blinks several times as if she's coming out of a trance.

"What?" I taunt her. "No snappy rejoinder? Put your money where your cards are."

"Daniella, this is not an exact science. I get different visions when the stars change alignments."

"And when your *vision* sees a death certificate ~ which no stars will dispute ~ will you return the money you bilked from a widow and her son?"

She raises her face towards the ceiling and sighs. "The money isn't really mine. It belongs to the cosmos."

I march towards her and regret there's a table in my way:

"You slimy disgusting vulture!"

Niko is trying to place himself between me and the table, saying, "Dani, we need to go."

I crane my neck over his shoulder. "I should apologize. I just insulted vultures. At least they do a service removing rot from this world." My voice is a blaze.

"Dani, it's over," Niko is whispering. "It's time for us to go." He's pushing me back ~ out of the shop ~ but I feel like I'm all muscle and heat and no agility or grace.

Sophia follows us outside, and I'm still facing the shop when Ms. Renown exits. She holds her arms out and says into the air, "Dani, I will ask for the spirits to bring you peace."

And that's when my body becomes only a body and not a mind or a soul or anything else, and it's grabbing rocks and hurling them at the building. I hear thumping, cracking, but my body doesn't stop, it heaves, it launches, anything it can find, and it doesn't want to stop until the shop is a heap.

Ms. Renown crosses her arms across her chest and looks at me and shakes her head.

Sophia is speaking. "Dani, stop! You're making *her* look like the victim now."

So I pick up a rock and aim it at Renown.

Niko practically tackles me. He whispers in my ear, "Dani. Dani. We need to regroup. Nothing good is happening now. We need to go home. We need to plan. This time, plan *first*. Then we bring her down. We bring her down *hard*."

I drop my rock but I don't drop my stare.

And Renown shakes her head and walks into the parlor.

Dani Argyle Takes on the Vermin. And GPAs
Thursday, March 27, 2025
5:34 p.m.

In the Argyle basement, Niko and Sophia have commandeered different bean-bag chairs.

Crap.

On top of everything else, I have to choose between them.

But it's ok, because today, I'm agitated and twitchy, so today seems like a good pacing day.

"We need to brainstorm ways to take Renown down," I'm saying. I grab a broom and use it like a NASCAR flag. "Ready? Go!"

I'm met with silence and some anxious eyes.

"We could picket outside her parlor," I offer. "The three of us could make signs and shout."

More silence. More skeptical eyes.

"That would work, Dani," Sophia begins, "if we had more people... OR if we could sustain it. But realistically, how long do you think we could picket her shop? Two days? Maybe three?"

"Let's think about it another way," Niko is saying. "Your goal is to have her stop swindling your family. How do you accomplish that?"

"Make it more trouble than it's worth," I explain.

"Good. Good," Niko agrees. "And how much is your family worth to her?"

"I don't know," I admit, "but it might be a thousand dollars a month."

Niko's eyes widen, and he exhales so loudly, he whistles. "Dani, I don't know what you can do to get Renown to give up that kind of money."

I turn to pace again, and a scurry of brown flashes by my feet. I glance as it goes, and Sophia jumps up from the beanbag and screams. Eventually, her screech changes form and becomes understandable: "Dani! What the hell! Is that a MOUSE?"

I shrug. "It WAS a mouse, Soph. It's gone now. I promise, it is more afraid of you that you are of it."

Sophia's eyes are wide with fright. "Dani! This is not funny! You are living with vermin!"

I want to tell her that *she* is living with *dogs*… which are much more intrusive if you ask my opinion, but it's obvious that my friend is in no mood to be placated. Even Niko seems quiet with concern. So my words become gentle, soft with reassurance: "No worries, my friends. There was a cold snap last night, and critters come in when the temperatures drop. Wait here. Wait a sec."

I disappear into the furnace room and reemerge with a small

square of peanut butter and a mousetrap: a white and black plastic contraption with a serrated top and a vicious hinge. I take a nubble of peanut butter and place it in the trap's well.

Niko looks concerned. "Dani? What are you doing?"

"Setting a mousetrap." Duh.

He gets up to inspect my work, as if I do not know what I'm doing. "Aren't mouse traps wooden? And don't you bait them with cheese?"

I finish setting the contraption and place it by the cabinet where the mouse had been hiding. "Niko," I begin, "mousetrap technology has improved since the 1950's, and, no, don't bait them with cheese like a *Tom and Jerry* cartoon. Use peanut butter."

"Peanut butter," he repeats, and we're all standing now ~ although Sophia is keeping aloof ~ looking at the mousetrap as if the thing will close on its own.

I turn to face them. "Guys, mice are harmless. They live on scraps and I always get them in the end. But Renown is not harmless. She's eviscerating my family and eating us alive. We need to trap *her*. Think about it. *Think.*"

My friends are looking at me with blank eyes.

"We could write about her online," I offer. "Write horrible reviews. Blackmail? Arson? Come on, guys, brainstorm. There are no bad ideas, so the sky's the limit." I pause and wait. When the silence becomes smothery, I decide on a different approach: "I'm not getting beaten by someone who's never heard of Copernicus."

"Come again?" Sophia looks confused.

"The astrologers," I explain, "still chart the sky as if the Earth is fixed and the stars all revolve around us." I step to a beanbag and sit down, exhausted. My friends sit, too, but they're silent. Confused. I clarify: "They haven't caught up with Copernicus, for God's sake, much less Einstein. C'mon, guys. THINK."

Something is stirring in Niko's eyes. "Then maybe we're going about this all wrong. Don't take down Renown. Take down *astrology*."

I sigh. This boy is beautiful, but he could focus a little more on his logic skills. "Niko," I shake my head, "it's been proven false time and again, but people really *want* their lives connected to the stars. For some reason, it makes them feel safe. I don't understand why enslavement to the stars is preferrable to any other form of enslavement."

"Then change your mom," Sophia is trying. "The problem is over if *she* is convinced."

I deflate like a balloon and plop backwards on the beanbag. I might as well teach a boulder to sing.

And then I hear a shout from the kitchen: "Daniella A. Argyle!"

"Ooooh!" Sophia's taunting, "Your mom just middle-initialed you."

And again from above, "WHAT'S THE MEANING OF THIS?"

I pop upright, and we look at each other with a collective

gasp. *How could Mom have heard about Renown's so soon?*

Mom clomps down the stairs and my stomach is hanging ~ heavily and thickly ~ like I've swallowed something heavy and it's oozing through my core.

Mom stands over me with her smart phone in her hand. "What do you have to say, young lady? Do you call these things *grades*?"

It takes my mind seconds to adjust from bracing for doom to rehashing the old tuffle about school and GPA.

My mom's face is a fire. "Daniella Antigone! You have four 'C's' and a 'D!'"

I stand up. "And two 'A's,'" I remind her. "Credit where credit is due."

Her voice is raw and scrapey. "I don't care about English and ASL. You could get 'A's' in those courses in your sleep. But any course that requires any effort ~ that requires studying and memorization ~ it's just beyond your ability to even *try*!"

"That's not true, Mom. I try. I really do."

"Really? Then how do you get a 'D' in P.E?" She blows some hair from her face and awaits a reply.

"Mom, it's not fair that students have to strip ~ "

"Enough, Dani. Enough. You refuse to interact with the world unless it is exactly the way *you* believe it should be. You do not get to remake the world in your own image. You have to give. A *little*."

"I do, Mom. I try. Just ask Ms. Sa ~ "

"You can fool your teachers with your helplessness crap, but you can't fool me. If you tried ~ really tried ~ you'd do better than this." She waves the phone in front of my face.

And I'm beaten again. There's no evidence that she will accept. *Post hoc ergo propter hoc*: the effect is true, so it must prove the cause. According to my mother and every educational system known to man, failure never comes from a lack of ability, but only from a lack of effort. All failure is proof of laziness, so if learning is hard, you better be ashamed of yourself.

"I don't know how I can ground you anymore," Mom shouts as she marches up the stairs. "You have nothing you love that I can take away."

That's true, Mom. Very true.

Most of that has been done already.

My friends are looking at me with worried eyes. So I put on my brave face and tell them the truth: my mom is a liar.

I sit down to look at them. "There are still things I love that have not been taken away," I explain. "You, and Gabby, and reading, and," I pause and grin victoriously, "and ANIME!" I jump from my seat and find a remote.

The TV flashes on with its fizzing blue light.

I cue through the menu and find *One Punch Man*. Both Sophia and Niko are squirming with excitement until Saitama's bald head shines on the screen. Then we shout out together: "ONE PUNCH!" and cheer until all the air seems alive with light.

On the screen, Carnage Kubuto is ravaging the world, and

he's taunting Saitama with the prophecy that Carnage will remain in rampage mode for a whole week, so he will be deadly and invincible until next Saturday. By then, all the citizens of Earth will be dead.

"Damn it!" our hero is realizing: "I've made a terrible mistake. He said he'll be on a rampage until Saturday. That means *today* is Saturday, too. That means today is bargain day at the supermarket. I've messed up. Because the store closes at 10:00."

So he dispatches Carnage with a single punch. Saitama must hurry because, after all, his coupons aren't going to redeem themselves.

Some people laugh at Saitama because he's a bored superhero. I laugh because it's silly to think enemies can be destroyed with only one punch.

The episode ends, and from the corner of my eye, I see a scuttle of brown. There's a whuff of movement and then a jagged crack.

Sophia startles and looks at me. Her eyes are concerned.

I smile and explain: "Sophie, it's ok. There's a war in this house, and I'm liking the outcome. It's Dani 1; vermin 0."

Dani Argyle Takes on Assumptions
Friday, March 28, 2025
8:47 p.m.

The kick-off to spring break is annually celebrated at the Argyle house. Sophia is here, and there is food to be eaten and sleepovers to be slept.

Traditionally, spring break is my yearly Get-Out-Of-Jail-Free Card, my don't-let-school-get-in-the-way-of-my-education reprieve, my read-and-be-me-and-the-hell-with-hypocrisy holiday.

It is my own personal resurrection from the dead.

This week I will channel *Frozen* and Let. It. Go.

Renown? Gone. Grades? Nope. Students who bully deaf first-graders?

Ok. I'm still a little pissed about that.

But the trundle is out, Sophia is here, and she generously kicks off the festivities by playing Gabriel in chess… while I'm also playing Gabriel in chess.

Two boards. Two games. One spunky six-year-old kid.

He beats Sophia easily, but I manage to trap him into a

stalemate.

I count it as a win.

Gabby bounces back to his room, and I pull closed the curtains to my room. Niko is texting.

NK Wish I was there

SB   me 2 we have muffins

DA   and me 2 mom is an idiot

NK Just don't forget me #moretolifethanbooks

DA I can figure out a way to have you over

...

NK ?

DA Not today. But sometime

NK Awesome #mademyday

Sophia is sitting on my bed, smiling at me. "So you two are serious? Yes? Like 'Dani and Niko sitting in a tree….'"

I shake my head. "Niko is nice."

"Nice? That's all you've got? *Nice*?"

"Sophia, these days, 'nice' is not a given. 'Nice' is rare. How many adolescent boys do you know that you would call 'nice'?"

Sophia is thinking. "It depends upon who they are with. One on one, most of them are nice, but put them together in a group ~ "

"And 'nice' becomes a nightmare."

DA Trust me. Vee have vays of getting you over….

Dani Argyle Takes on Volunteering
Monday, April 7, 2025
9:47 a.m.

We've finished Purgatory but will not enter heaven.

The year is short, and *something* must be cut.

Today is the first day we will study *Othello*.

So farewell, Dante and Beatrice: your love was sweet and ardent and divine, but now there's Othello and Desdemona, and things are about to get *interesting*.

"Awww," Sophia sighs as Wright passes out books. "Last year, we read *Romeo and Juliet*. I liked that play. I want a love like that."

"No you don't," I correct her.

"Yes, I do," Sophia insists. "Their love was perfect. It wasn't their fault they came from crappy families."

Poor Sophia. I think she needs to study some sociology. The percentage of people on this planet who come from perfect families? 0. The percentage who come from crappy ones? Much, much higher.

Since *Othello* is a play, students are volunteering to read various parts during class.

I have this volunteering thing *down*.

The goal in volunteering is to choose a role that doesn't seem dinky but that has no lines after the opening of the play. In terms of volunteering, if you wait too long, you might get roped in to a really big role. And personally, I *hate* reading aloud in front of others. It's like my brain can only do one thing at a time: vocalize the words or understand their meaning. My brain can*not* do both things simultaneously.

So, the trick is to choose a role that is over quickly. Strategy is paramount: if I get stuck with this Iago guy, I will never understand the majority of the play.

I'm raising my hand and waving enthusiastically. "Mr. Wright! Mr. Wright! I can be the Duke!"

When roles have been assigned ~ Sophia is Amelia and Niko is Cassio ~ Kevin Choi starts texting me about history. Again. Niko is leaning over, staring at my phone.

Then Niko straightens and starts texting me, too.

NK Dani ~ ignore kevin that guy is bad news

DA Annoying? absolutely. ridiculous? yes. bad? no

NK Trust me Dani I know this guy

DA I do 2

NK I'm just trying to help you

And then it's my turn to read, because it's

Othello, Act I scene iii

Duke of Venice/Me:

"There can be no compensation in these news

That gives them credit."

Sigh.

Saved by a fortuitously timed Shakespearean line.

By the time the bell rings, I'm liking Othello. He's adventurous, poetic, awe-inspiring, and gentle, and he expects his wife to speak for herself.

Niko's walking me to math, which I still appreciate ~ even if the Chorus girls' eyes stare at me and then thin into slits ~ even if Niko's arm is draped around me, even when he is still strangely fixated on Kevin Choi.

"Dani, please ~ just please ~ just trust me on this one. Kevin Choi really hates me. If he thinks, for a second, he can get to me by going through you, he will not hesitate to do it."

I turn around and face him, tip upwards and kiss.

My goal was to stop his thoughts, but he has stopped mine.

Our kiss is a bright, sparkly, thrumming thing, and my stomach flutters as if it's full of wings. Light expands, skims through my blood and glimmers in my skin.

But then another feeling commandeers my gut, and I feel a weight scrabbing about my stomach.

I pull away and look in Niko's eyes. "Niko, trust *me*. Kevin Choi is harmless. I don't think he has feelings for anyone but Kevin. He's in love with his mirror. If he could figure out a way, that boy wouldn't do anything but hump himself."

And I kiss him once more and walk into math.

Dani Argyle Takes on Doubt
Wednesday, April 9, 2025
6:53 a.m.

I awake from strange dreams and cryptic texts from Niko.

NK meet me before school in the courtyard. Third bench in the amphitheater

This is very specific for pre-dawn texts.

DA kk

And then, to be romantic, I try to sound sweet:

DA Daffodils are in bloom #flowerstalker

NK #youamazeme

I am not sure how to respond to that. The  emoji is the closest to my feelings, but I settle for

DA

When I arrive in the courtyard, Niko is already there. He jumps up when he sees me and seems to crackle and fizz with sudden energy.

He takes both my hands and leads me back to the bench. We

sit, but his legs are jittering and bouncy.

"You have a birthday coming up," he says, as if this is a revelation worthy of blazing.

I nod, confused. "That's true. ish. It's in three weeks."

"But something else will come before that." He grins.

I shake my head. Have I forgotten *his* birthday? I start glancing around the courtyard ~ as if the answer is in the shrubbery.

"Happy anniversary!" He holds out a long thin box that is delicately white.

"We have an anniversary?" I respond. Lamely.

"March 9 was our first date. We saw *Wild* and you blew me away." And he's excited, even his torso seems bouncy now. "Here," he raises the box. "Here. Open it. Open it."

I take the present and look him in the eye. "Niko, I don't know what to say. That day was unforgettable. Except, apparently, I forgot the actual date." I sigh and slouch. "I didn't get you anything."

"Don't worry about it." He's fizzing in his seat. "Open it. Open! It!"

The lid lifts off, and there's a charm bracelet inside ~ glinting, flashing ~ with three perfect charms: a mountain, a book, and a party hat.

"Niko," I say, "it's stunning."

"Here, let me put it on you." He leans over, squints, and clasps it on my wrist.

It's not a wimpy color ~ not like white gold or silver ~ it's deep and bold and burnished like a sunset.

"It's not easy to find jewelry in copper," Niko is admitting. I look at him stunned. He smiles. "Sophia told me that copper's your favorite."

I look at my wrist which glistens like the dawn. I even shake my arm and hear the charms rustle.

This moment should be perfect, except I feel a little tipsy, like the world is off kilter and leaning a little, as if Niko exerts such a gravitational force, I'm rendered a lump that is caught in his orbit.

But the charms glisten more, and I shake them again.

"Niko Kaneko," I look him in the eyes, "I think that I love you."

"Daniella Argyle," he replies with a smile, "I know that I love you."

In history class, Sun Yat-sen is overthrowing an empire, but all I can think about is Niko and the "L" word.

DA Soph ~ u there?

SB Always

DA I have news

SB ???

DA Niko and I said we love each other

SB omg omg omg omg!!! I am so happy for you!

DA but I have a question

SB ?

DA What is love?

SB ur kidding me, right?

DA If ive never been in love before, how do I know if I am now?

SB ...

SB ...

SB Girl, you've got to chill that brain of yours.

DA But...

SB NOW

In Wright's class, it's obvious what love is. It's everywhere and booming ~ it can't be contained.

A storm has almost drowned Othello and wrecked his ship, but he still strides on shore and takes his wife in his arms, saying:

O my soul's joy!
If after every tempest come such calms,
May the winds blow till they have waken'd death!
And let the labouring bark climb hills of seas
Olympus-high and duck again as low
As hell's from heaven! If it were now to die,
'Twere now to be most happy; for, I fear,
My soul hath her content so absolute
That not another comfort like to this
Succeeds in unknown fate.

Yes, Othello. I know what you mean.

Dani Argyle Takes on Awkward Situations
Saturday, April 12
10:34 a.m.

I glance out my bedroom window and see Niko walking up my driveway.

I can be forgetful but not *that* forgetful. We did not have plans for today.

I glance in a mirror and run fingers through my hair. I also shove some old candy wrappers into my sock drawer. *Crap. What is he thinking?*

He knocks at the front door, and I open it, wearing my pleasant face.

He's wearing cargo pants and boots, and I start to feel like we've been here before. But I don't have the energy to climb a mountain today.

"M'lady," he bows slightly. "Your Uber awaits."

"Niko," I ask, "did we have plans?"

"Of course! Remember? Garage Sale at REI."

"Garage Sale?"

"Yes. They have *amazing* deals. And I can get you anything that you want because I am a card-carrying member."

My brain is too scattered to argue. I've already been studying yesterday and today ~ the end of a unit in Event Coordination.

"Oh, Niko," I concede. "Of course I'll go. But I really don't think we talked about this."

"I texted you yesterday. Give me your phone." His arm is outstretched and his hand is beckoning.

I hand over my phone, and he's scrolling through our texts. "Ooops. My bad. I guess I *didn't* say anything. But I promise," he laughs, "I told you in my head."

I call back to my mom and tell her that I'm going to REI. Niko takes my hand and leads me to our Uber.

I'm not into hiking the way that Niko is, so a store like REI can be overwhelming.

There's footwear and bikes and climbing gear; tents and clothing and racks of gadgets. There are socks that are twenty dollars a pair ~ and those are the cheap ones.

I'm trailing behind Niko, who is packing up. He'd need an eighty-liter backpack just to carry the stuff.

I find a pair of socks on the clearance rack. They're made out of Smart Wool (is there a dumb kind?) and are on sale for only ten dollars.

"I'll get these for you," Niko grabs them from my hand. "Socks are important: the most important part of any long hike."

I nod and agree. Who knew?

We're waiting in the check-out line, and my phone is buzzing. I glance at it and see adult concern glimmering on my screen. Uncle Joe!

JC Dani How is Lainie's medication working? Things still alright?

DA 👍 👍 👍 And why r u awake?

JC Don't ask. Bad end to a bad day. That's why I'm checking on you. Making sure you're ok.

Niko is watching my phone. "Who is Joe?" He's concerned. "And why is he texting you?"

I'm squinting at my phone; it's always good to hear from Joe, but now Niko is demanding my attention. I look him in the eyes. "It's my dad's best friend. He's like an uncle to me. He's just checking in with his avuncular concerns." I look at my phone again and consider what to text: Joe seems sad and deserves more than a few thumb's up emojis.

"Well, maybe you should change his contact info from 'Joe Chalk' to 'Uncle Joe.'" He's looking at me and nodding with the certainty of his revelation; then his head tilts slightly. "You don't want people to get the wrong idea."

I'm confused. *Who in the world would get a wrong idea? And why is Niko so obsessed with my phone? And why am I defending a text I received from a man I call my uncle?*

227

I am quiet and inch forward with the check-out line. I send Joe a couple heart emojis and then watch Niko glide up to the register. The final transaction is smooth ~ the cashier is gorgeous and trim and knows Niko by name, and they're bantering back and forth about the merits of steel and aluminum carabiners. The cashier is showing him both types ~ smiling luminously ~ and I realize she has the privilege of a pretty person: no matter what she says, it is interesting and grand. And I still want to text Joe some more ~ tell him my life is now having moments of joy ~ but I stay to the side and smile politely. Then Niko hands me my socks and we head outside.

After we leave, we grab Frappuccinos at a ubiquitous Starbucks. Well, I grab a Frappuccino. Niko gets a Venti-something with double whip, a Double-Smoked Bacon and Cheddar Sandwich, and two glazed donuts.

"I didn't eat breakfast," he explains while he balances a tray, as if boys ever have to excuse their food choices.

"Well, it's lunch time," is my rejoinder, "but you're eating breakfast. There should be a word for that." I smile. "Let's call it 'Blunch.'"

Niko laughs. "Dani, everything you do is fun."

There are two seats available at a small table, and we snag them. Niko's excited and beaming: he doesn't enjoy being still. His torso is upright, but his legs are jumpy. "Ok," he begins. "Where do we go next?"

"Niko," I begin, "you know that I love spending time with

you, but I was not planning on being gone an entire day." I'm stirring my Frappuccino. It's surprisingly artful.

Niko looks surprised. "Really? What is it you were going to do?"

"Actually," I pause, "I was going to study."

Niko laughs. He even snorts softly. "C'mon, Dani. Seriously."

"Niko, I *am* serious. I'm making good progress in my event-coordination course. The course is good and the professor likes me. My goal is to finish the first two units so that I can post my resume online."

"I don't understand." He stops smiling, and his face sags with seriousness. "Are you applying for a job?"

"On April 19th, I turn 16. The government says that I'll be eligible for employment. I have an account on Indeed that is ready to go. On April 18th, I'm staying up until the clock strikes midnight. The second it does, my resume will be loaded, and I'm clicking 'Submit.'" I don't tell him there's a chance I won't be in school on April 21st. Who knows what might happen once my resume gets posted? My days as a high-school student are now officially numbered.

Niko still looks confused. He looks *wounded*. I expect him to argue, but his voice is thin ~ not adversarial: "So that means you can't spend another hour with me?"

I'm stumped. I'm not the type to shrink from a fight, but Niko's not fighting. He's just sitting there, looking helpless. "Niko, not today," I gentle my voice as if he's a child and I'm babysitting: "Next weekend, I promise. By then, the unit will be over, and my resume will be in cyberspace. Besides," I smile mischievously, "*I* will have a surprise for *you* on my birthday."

"Tell me! Tell me! I love surprises!" He's beaming again.

"Well," I take a long sip on my Frappuccino to build suspense, "my Aunt Lainie is leaving for a real-estate conference on Friday. So… her house will be free on the 19th."

"So?" Niko looks confused. He leans towards me. "Am I missing something?"

So!" I begin, "So come over! I'll make you dinner!"

Niko leans back, eyes startled and grinning. "Dani Argyle, you are full of surprises."

"Well, I'm not good at much, but I know how to cook." If I had a mic, I would drop it, but I lean back in my seat and nod with confidence.

He smiles. "I believe you. Happy sixteenth, Dani. I think that this will be a night to remember."

Dani Argyle Takes on Doubt. Again
Monday, April 14, 2025
12:36 p.m.

The sneaky teens are at it again.

We are *outside*. Having lunch in the *sun*.

We're smarter about it this time ~ we found a spot by the track-and-field storage shed, and we're sitting on the far side so no teachers can see.

"I'm looking forward to your birthday." Niko is beaming.

"Me, too! Sixteen! I'll be fully employable!" I raise a bottle of water as if it's champagne.

"Sixteen isn't all it's cracked up to be," Sophia explains with her sixteen years of wisdom. "Can't vote. Can't drink. Can't even book a silly hotel room."

"And you know this how?" I ask her.

She grins and purses her lips. "Wouldn't *you* like to know?"

I'm about to explain that I would, actually, when Niko is talking: "So, Dani, how was your studying?"

Sophia starts laughing. "Dani? Studying? You mean Dani

listening to music and flipping through a book."

I try not to be hurt. I turn to Sophia first, "Soph, I can read books AND listen to music," and then to Niko: "Niko. Thanks for asking. It's going really well. I'm on schedule to finish Unit Two before Saturday.

"So you studied all day?" His eyes are focused.

"All day Saturday and Sunday, too. Some of the lectures are really good when you listen to them double-time." Another lift of the water bottle.

"So you had no time to text me?" He's watching me hard, as if Sophia doesn't exist.

I'm silent and confused. Then I gather some words: "Niko, you know me. I'm easily distracted. When I'm studying, I need to *study*. Not study and text."

"Did you text Sophia?" He nods in her direction.

I look at Sophia. My eyes are wide.

"I asked Dani some questions… about this summer," Sophia admits, "and Dani replied." She looks at me and shrugs.

"But not a lot," I'm explaining. "Not like we, or I, normally do." I look at Sophia and stretch my eyes.

"That's right," Sophia is agreeing. "It's not as much fun without you."

Sophia's giving me a ride after school today. I'm with Ms. Satchel. Again. Passing Algebra II is never guaranteed.

Ms. Satchel has patience of the Herculean variety. The Twelve Labors be damned. Ms. Satchel is teaching me *math*. The math that the government demands that I learn if I'm going to become a productive citizen of this democracy.

Ms. Satchel and I are sitting, studying her textbook, but Sophia has commandeered the back of the classroom. She's spread-out history notes, Japanese assignments, a science text, and *Othello*.

She walks down the row of desks from discipline to discipline. Five minutes on history, then five on Japanese. Then back to history for two minutes, and science for five, and Japanese for two. Then it's flash studying for one minute each.

Ms. Satchel stands up, stretches, announces that she's leaving the room but will be back shortly, and then walks out, so I turn to face Sophia. "Look at you. It's like Henry Ford and the school system got busy and had a baby."

"It's called 'interleaving your studies,'" Sophia explains. "It improves your memory when you jump back and forth between subjects."

"And your copy of *Othello*?" I'm asking. "There's no test in English tomorrow. All we're doing is reading out loud."

"But it's Amelia's big day," Sophia is insisting. "I have to rehearse just a little bit first."

Poor Ms. Satchel is back and re-entering the dumb-zone. "Let's review linear equations," she's announcing in her even, Satchel tone. I have a feeling that ~ whether she's watching fireworks or cleaning the kitchen ~ the quality of her voice is always the same.

I shake my head and gain the courage I need to let her look into my brain. "Ms. Satchel," I begin, "some minds were not made for math. Eventually, you need to give up trying to teach me. You need to have a life, too. Go out. Meet some friends. Have a glass of wine. Some people are just too dumb to learn Algebra II."

There is no pause, and no emotion in her voice. If I'm going to wallow in pity, she will not join me there: "All minds can think mathematically, Dani. Our brains evolved to process math in a way they never evolved to process the written word. So if you are not learning, the only explanation is that I am not teaching you correctly." She makes sure that I am looking in her eyes. "If you do not learn this, then *I* am the failure, not you. And quite frankly," she pokes the desk with her finger for emphasis, "I refuse to be a failure. Now let's review linear equations, and, when you are ready, I will give you a quiz. I have no place I'd rather be than right here."

How sad it is that this wonder of a woman is taking my own stupidity upon her shoulders. From time to time, even Atlas got a respite from the weight of the world.

We're reviewing the same page for the third time when Sophia starts rehearsing her role:

"Pray heaven it be state-matters, as you think,
And no conception nor no jealous toy
Concerning you."

Pause.

"But jealous souls will not be answer'd so;
They are not ever jealous for the cause,
But jealous for they are jealous: 'tis a monster
Begot upon itself, born on itself."

I'm startled from the trance of Algebra II.

"Sophia!" I'm turning. "What is that you're reading?"

Ms. Satchel knows. "That's *Othello*. The tragedy. Jealousy is a green-eyed monster."

And my world is making just a little more sense.

Dani Argyle Takes on Adolescence
Saturday, April 19, 2025
1:47 p.m.

One thing about Mom: she believes in the big birthdays.

No child of hers will enter into a new stage of life and remain uncelebrated.

So after balloons have been ballooned, and streamers, streamed, and gifts have been gifted, the Argyles relax with cake and watch Gabby sing "Happy Birthday" (again) with his hands. Gabriel! My Gabby! When he's done, we applaud him, and I kiss him on the head. He kisses me back, faces the cake, and begins his conquest.

My mom also takes a bite, a delicate taste. "Sixteen is a big one," Mom explains and chews. "Your first step into the world with adults." She squeezes my hand. "So, Miss Mini-Adult, where do you think you'll be this time next year?"

I sigh. It's rather sad. But now is not the time to rail against institutionalized education and explain there will be no difference between my junior year ~ if I have one ~ and my sophomore. And if I tell her I'm making plans to drop out of school and fly from this coop, she might just end up taking it personally.

And she probably should.

"Right now," I begin, "I'm just looking forward to tonight. Sleepovers at Sophia's," I'm lying, "are always fun."

Mom smiles. "You're lucky to have such a good friend."

"Mom," I need to educate my mother about the economics of high school, where each person's value is determined by the size of their friend group: "Every day I'm surrounded by people my age. It's pathetic for me to only have two friends."

"Consider yourself lucky," my mom is explaining. "If you have two friends, you should never complain."

As she starts to clear the table ~ removing everything but cake remnants ~ my world is shifting: I actually feel like I'm in a clock that's rotated, turned, that's set to a different time than it previously was.

I realize that my mom doesn't have two friends.

I remember a time when Mom had friends, and the Argyle house was stretched with visitors. There were parties and cocktails and poker nights and book clubs: our house was the hub that held the neighborhood together.

But the thing about grief is that it embarrasses those who witness the grieving. Neighbors stutter, ashamed, when they see you on the street. Friends who have husbands who are fully alive fade slowly and quietly into guilty silence. When catastrophe first strikes, there's a whoosh of activity, but it's soon replaced with emptiness and ache.

And nobody wants to be too close to that.

So I'm up on my feet ~ "Mom, let me help" ~ and I lean up against her as we drop plates in the trash.

And then she turns and smiles and kisses my head.

Working in Lainie's kitchen is a little like dancing. The space is open, but accessible. Whenever you want something, you just turn and reach.

Eggs in the fridge? Turn and reach. Flour in the pantry? Turn and reach. Spices on the spice rack? Turn and reach.

So the chicken has been dredged, and now, it is baking. The broccoli has been seasoned, so it's ready to grill. And the bread will only need a few minutes to warm.

I'm usually reaching for food, but sometimes, it's for my phone. My resume has been uploaded into cyberspace, and there's a chance that, very soon, my life is going to change.

My phone remains wearily quiet. But then again, it IS the weekend.

There's a knock at the door. Lainie's house is a great room: a kitchen, a dining room, and a living room all rolled into one, with a master bedroom on the main floor. So when I want to answer the door, I can just take a few steps, and then turn and reach.

Niko is standing on the stoop, smiling, with extravagant roses nestled in his arms. I imagine the poor guy couldn't decide which color to choose, so there's three bouquets: red, pink, and white.

"Perfect!" I exclaim. "Lainie has three vases."

I give Niko a kiss hello and lead him to the kitchen where I start trimming rose stems. I'm arranging the roses and realizing I should have made an appetizer. Niko's in the kitchen with nothing to do.

I give him some silverware. "Set the table?" I ask.

He's off, obediently, and I must admit, Niko didn't go out of his way to dress for the occasion. He's wearing a hoodie and a pair of sweatpants.

Meanwhile, I'm cooking while wearing a modest example of a little black dress.

Niko's back in the kitchen, nuzzling me and kissing. He pauses and smiles. "Happy birthday, Dani. Shall me move to the sofa?"

I check the timer on the stove. "Sure," I agree. "Dinner will be ready in twenty-six minutes."

On the sofa, he's kissing me again: my lips, my face, my neck and ~

I lean down and kiss him on the lips again.

And my body feels charged ~ like there's a universe inside me that wants to get out, and I'm lighting, igniting ~ my skin feels like a torch.

And Niko's hand is on my thigh, moving between my legs.

I put his hand back on my hip and hold it there, carefully.

But his body feels warm, needed, and I'm pressing into him.

And then he's moving my hand under his sweats, and I freeze ~ stupidly ~ like some frightened animal, and he wraps my fingers around this hardness which is hot and large and pulsing.

"Niko!" I gasp. "I have to check on the chicken!" And I'm up off the couch.

"Really? Right now?"

"Lainie would not take it lightly if I burned down her house." I turn and walk to the oven.

I've grabbed my phone, and since my back is to Niko, I'm texting Sophia an emergency text:

DA 911 Lainie's house now

...

SB u ok

DA Pls can't talk

SB OMW

And I slip the phone into a drawer, open the oven, and stare into its heat and breathe.

Niko is in the kitchen now, but my head is still in the oven.

"Everything ok?" he's asking, softly.

"Uh huh," I lie. "I just need to baste," I lie some more. "It's a good thing I got here when I did," (go big or go home), "or the entire meal would have been burned to a crisp."

"Well, as long as everything's alright." It should be

impossible, but I can actually feel him standing behind me.

"Oh," I'm remembering (and I still feel like I'm talking to the chicken), "I also have some broccoli to cook. Will you please be a dear and look in the fridge for the butter?" I feel like an idiot ~ talking with my head in the oven ~ a ridiculous parody of an oversized ostrich.

So I give Niko some tasks I could do myself, and then I stand up straight and stretch and hope I can just keep him busy until Sophia gets here ~

"Oh, and I need some ice for drinks," I'm babbling. "Could you grab some ice trays and break out the cubes?" I gesture to the freezer.

"Sure," he says, and I'm dancing in the kitchen again, turning and reaching and chopping and warming, but my dance is frenetic ~ not as languid as before ~ and then I hear ~ thank God ~ a knock on the door.

"Who could that be?" I ask... like an idiot.

And I walk to the front and open the door, and Sophia bubbles in with a "HAPPY BIRTHDAY, DANI-BEAR!" And she hands me a teddy bear as if this has been her plan all-the-day long.

I hear Niko behind me, calling to Sophia from the kitchen: "Hey, Sophia. Dani and I were just having some quiet time together."

"Cool! I'm in!" she shouts with delight. God bless this girl. No one plays clueless as well as she does.

I still hear Niko in the kitchen ~ my back is to him, but I hear ice cracking ~ Sophia is staring at me with extravagant eyes. And I'm staring at her ~ widely, knowingly ~ back.

Then she nods her head, takes my hand, and leads me to the kitchen, saying, "Something sure smells good, and man, am I hungry!"

We're about halfway through the meal, and we're just to the point where things are a little normal again, and we're bantering, bickering, laughing, when Lainie opens the door and enters with a WHEW.

She stares at us for a long second, then drops her suitcase and smiles, laughing, "Hey, Honey. I'm home."

"Lainie!" I jump up and hug her. Then I grab her suitcase and start carrying it to the bedroom. "If you're hungry, I'll make you a plate. I thought you were going to a conference."

"I *was*," I hear her gliding to the kitchen and pouring herself some wine, "but my supervisor got a little handsy, so ~ " I imagine her taking a long sip. "So, oops. Here I am!"

And I hear her moving to the table with Niko and Sophia.

"Lainie," I'm calling from the bedroom, "you remember Sophia, but you've never met Niko."

I know that Lainie is beaming right now. "So you're Niko!" I imagine her reaching out a graceful hand. "I'm so glad to meet you. I think we'll be friends."

"Nice to meet you, Miss… Sparkle?"

"Spar*tale*," I hear her giggling. "I think we'll get along fine. And please, call me Lainie."

When I return to the great room, I can see that Niko is rather stunned by Lainie's beauty. I understand. Seeing her for the first time leaves most people breathless.

I wonder if he's pondering how *I* can be related to *her*.

But after two glasses of wine, the Lainie-stories spill forth.

"The first time I was kidnapped," she's explaining ~ like it's normal ~

"The *first* time! You were *kidnapped*!" Niko's eyes startle wide.

"Oh, it was no big deal." She's waving her hand dismissively. "I was five years old, shopping with my mom, and this old man with Alzheimer's got me confused with his granddaughter."

"*Sure* he did, Lainie." Forgive me for being skeptical.

"And he was leading me out of the store when my mother called security. See?" She looks at us all, individually. "It was no big deal."

"But you said the *first* time." Niko's leaning forward, his food ignored.

"Well, *kidnapping*'s an exaggeration," she smiles guiltily. "I was separating from my husband, and I snuck into our house when I thought he'd be gone ~ I was packing my clothes ~ but my husband *was* home, and he kinda locked me in the basement and wouldn't let me out."

"You know, as you do, when you're a really *good man* and

your wife needs a rest and break from the marriage." It's my turn to be sassy.

"Oh, Dani. Cupcake. We're all good now. All's well that ends well."

I think Lainie needs a primer in story theory. "Lainie, you can only say that at the *end* of the story. It makes no sense at any other point."

"End Othello at Act II," Sophia explains, "and everyone and everything is sunshine and roses."

Sophia offers to drive Niko home, and I offer to help Lainie clean up in the kitchen.

It *is* only fair.

We're washing dishes ~ for reals this time, no paper plates ~ when Lainie starts smiling.

"Niko seems nice."

I smile weakly. I can still feel his hand guiding my hand, and I sigh and feel awkward and shifty and warm.

Lainie stops mid-scrub, and I hear a plate float and settle on the bottom of the sink. "Do you want to have a seat?" She is looking at me with her knowing Lainie-look.

I nod, and we go to the table, and I sit and busy my fingers with picking crumbs off the table and dropping them carefully into a glass.

"Dani, plum, what's going on?" Her eyes narrow with

concern.

"I don't know, Lainie. I just feel off-balance." I don't look at her. I'm still preoccupied with the crumbs. "When it comes to Niko and me, I don't think things are going the way they're supposed to go."

"Well, sweet pea," her words are smiling, "I don't know how things are *supposed* to go. Every relationship is different. But if you're feeling uncomfortable, you need to talk to him."

"No, no, no, no," I stop picking at crumbs and look at her with imploring eyes. "No, Lainie. I can't." I pause and gather a breath. "I think I need to send him a break-up text."

Lainie is shaking her head in a very un-Lainie-like way ~ with urgency and vigor ~ nothing about this is graceful and fluid. "No, Dani, no. Learn from my mistakes. You never solve problems by running away from them. You look that boy in the eyes when you break his heart."

"No, Lainie. I can't." I'm looking at the floor.

"Why not?"

"How could I? He's not a bad person. He's a very good person. I just don't feel ~ " I'm groping, "that we're all that good" ~ still groping ~ "together."

Lainie shifts in her seat. "It can happen, Dani-Boo. I know from experience. Two fantastic people can bring out the worst in each other."

I nod my head and look at her. "There, then. There you have it."

"Not so fast, Missy. My life is not yours. And to tell you the truth," Lainie is pointing her finger at me for emphasis, "you, my dear, have a tendency to jump to conclusions."

"Not this time."

"Sometimes you jump to the conclusion that you're not jumping to conclusions."

I don't know what to say about that.

"Promise me this." Lainie looks serious. "Wait a while. If it's right today, it will be right tomorrow. Let this settle. Whatever happened today ~ "

"It's not just today ~ "

"Whatever's been happening, it should at least be reflected on. And, who knows, maybe you and sparkly-eyes can work this out together." She smiles at me, lavishly, with her full Lainie-glory.

How do I tell her, this isn't about...hands... and it's not about my phone ~ although Niko's obsession with it always leaves me off balance. All of a sudden, all of this just seems too much. This relationship is like a gravity that's pulling me down. Even affection can seem heavy to someone who is trying to be free. It can feel hard to breathe ~ hard to stretch and extend ~ under the weight of an ardent and focused adoration.

And then I hear a knock at the door.

"Speak of the devil." Lainie is facing me.

I open the door, and Niko is there, looking deflated, looking drenched, like he got caught in a downpour but is completely dry.

"I asked Sophia to drop me off back here," he's saying, "and

I've been pacing around outside." He looks at me. "Dani, can we talk?"

This is the very *last* thing I want to do right now. Can't we both go back to our respective homes and start over on a new day? Let ourselves heal? Pretend this evening never happened?

But I'm calling over my shoulder, "Lainie. Niko is here." I pause and then add, "We're going outside to sit on your porch."

We sit on the stoop. It's dark outside, but I can hear the cedar trees hissing in the air, and I feel Niko take my hand. "Dani, you don't seem like yourself today."

"No?"

"No."

I shrug. Why won't he let this go?

"And I want to know." He's struggling, too. "What you wanted ~ what you were expecting ~ what you were hoping when ~ "

"Niko," I jump in, and then everything comes out in a rush of words: "Niko-I-invited-you-over-to-Lainie's-because-I- wanted-to *cook*."

Then there's silence. Awful. Expansive. Gaping. Silence.

He's looking at the ground. "I got a mixed message."

I'm trying to think if I'm the one who mixed it. Am I really so stupid that I offered sex and didn't know? I am grappling with my anxiety, trying to pin it to the mat so it won't squirm and flop about and wrest me of my control, but I feel this chasm breaking, opening, expanding before me, and I feel like ~ if I don't jump ~ it'll be out of reach forever.

"Niko," I'm saying, "I don't feel like this is working."

"I'm sorry," he begins. "I messed up tonight. But we can put this behind us. We're moving on from here."

And the chasm is still expanding. It's seconds until it's unbridgeable. It's growing and stretching and dimming in the distance.

I leap.

"No, Niko, no. You and me, we're not working. I'm sorry, but I think that ~ " and I stand up, and I turn around, and I look him in the eyes, and I edge my voice out. "Goodbye, Niko."

And then I turn around and walk away.

I'm walking home from Lainie's, and my insides are hiccupping. Everything inside me is jagged and black.

It's dark, and I'm trippy, and I'm stumbling along by the side of the street, one foot on the pavement, one foot off, and even the streetlamps are dim ~ dim, distant, and ridiculous ~ or maybe I'm crying, because it's hard to see anything.

I hear a roar from behind and a pick-up blares past me; I feel the wind blast my back and scrunch up my skirt, and the truck is full of guys who are whooping, "YEE HAW MOTHER FUHH ~ " and then a horn bruits through the dark and I stop in the road and think about just how easy it would have been to slip in front of that truck ~ just a little step ~ and then I imagine the relief of my life leaking from me. I could slip into peace. Into silence. Into rest. My highest hope right now is simply to feel *nothing*.

Hello.

My name is Daniella Argyle.

And there is nothing in this world so beautiful and pure that

I, personally, cannot fuck it up.

Part II: Still Life

Dani Argyle Takes on the Job Market. And Plotting
Saturday, October 18, 2025
3:55 p.m.

Being an employee at Little Fish Swim School has its advantages and disadvantages.

I instruct five children in my class, so those are my five advantages. I teach beginner swim, and when I see my students start to love the water ~ keep their face in it without panic or concern ~ I am just as happy as if I accomplished something myself. Then high fives and fist-bumps abound.

But the parents can be a problem. They cannot tolerate seeing their children uncomfortable and want to yank them out of the pool as soon as the kids have gotten in. "I will not let your child drown," I keep insisting, "but I cannot promise there will never be tears."

And the other disadvantage is the lack of breaks. The sessions are fifty-five minutes with five minutes of greetings and transitions. Between school and work, the world is conspiring to infringe upon my right to pee. And then, of course, there is the dressing that is needed for the job: my boss won't let me wear a T-shirt over my swimsuit, so my body feels like it's on display for everyone to see.

But the job pays sixteen an hour. Not what I was hoping for when I blazed my resume to the interweb, but, apparently, event coordinators weren't beating the cyberspace bushes in order to scout for interns, and being board-certified in CPR has certain advantages when it comes to the swim-school industry.

Oh, and siblings swim for free, so Gabriel and I can hang out on the weekends even if, I am sure, he'd rather spend his days playing chess.

Any fascination I once had with the popular kids has been replaced by school, job, and my continuing training to be an event coordinator. Days are full. Even books are a thing of the past.

When the shift is finished at Little Fish, I load Gabriel in the car and drive to the dry cleaners. Someday, maybe, Mom will trust me enough to drive her home, but, these days, when I arrive at her job, she walks to the driver's-side door and says, "Scoot."

So I've scooted and she's driving ~ and I pretend to be offended by this, but I'm really not because the day is beautiful and no one can drive and talk to Gabby at the same time. So I turn and ask Gabby about his lessons ~ he's moved up to intermediate swim ~ and he signs, "I liked class more when there just was a lot of splashing," and I sign, "But now, Gabriel, you get to MOVE," and he signs, "I guess I can move and splash at the same time?"

Mom's phone is ringing, and she's turning right onto Route 7, so she's saying, "Get that, Dani, and tell my boss I'm not behind on my work."

So I answer the phone and hear, "The stars are strong! The best alignment of the year! Come in on Friday and the results will be spectacular!" And I say, "Will do! I will not be left behind!" and hang up the phone and say, "I think Mr. Durant likes you," and Mom grins and says, "He has his moments."

And I feel a fullness inside me ~ a purpose and strength. I no longer have to feel helpless, like my mom is careening out of control. I have a week to plan, and the element of surprise will be startingly on my side. On Friday, Madame Renown will not know what hit her.

It's like a chess game, and I'm playing white against an unsuspecting novice.

There are so many gambits to choose from. I need one that dazzles and leaves opponents dizzy within the opening moves.

I'm thinking Intercontinental Ballistic Missile Gambit.

The black queen goes down in eight moves.

And it's checkmate in ten.

Dani Argyle Takes on Guilt. And Acceptance
Tuesday, October 21, 2025
8:05 a.m.

English 11 with Ms. Abele is whole lotta different than English with Mr. Wright.

Ms. Abele was a theater major in college, so, when she takes the stage, she's putting on a *show*. Her voice resonates ~ it will not be contained by a classroom ~ it echoes down hallways and spills through the school. Her class is not focused on accuracy but upon improvisation and risk-taking, and the person who is always taking the biggest risks is Ms. Abele herself. "You-learn-better-from-your-mistakes-than-you-do-from-your-successes" is Ms. Abele's mantra, and she jokes that, because of this, no one learns better than she does. Nothing amuses her more than her own screw-ups which seem to give her a permanent sense of obvious joy. Her room is not filled with analysis, but with amusement.

And her *laugh*. It's a wonder. Not a timid, apologetic giggle, but a full-bodied BOOM followed by an echo, like a thundery day in the Appalachian Mountains.

This is a space where I almost feel safe. Ms. Abele can almost distract me from others in the classroom. And there's one in particular who has the pierciest eyes, who can sit behind me all through the class and *look*.

I've tried to solve the Niko problem by becoming, in English, a back-row student. Nobody can watch me if I'm in the back row.

But Ms. Abele is a fan of the whole-class change-up. No matter where you begin, you'll end someplace else.

"I'm feeling some different energy today," she's explaining to the class. "Heather and Lucy, come sit up front; Lucas and Parsa, move on back. Niko and Dani ~ why don't you work outside? And Kevin, you may join them."

Today's questions are about guilt and punishment in *The Crucible*: an upbeat little play that focuses on one affair, three land-grabs, and nineteen hangings. I grab my worksheet and slouch into the hallway. Niko follows. Then Kevin.

Kevin doesn't even sit and he's off like a shot. "Hey, Arman," he's shouting at a startled transfer student. "You took the physics test in Stone's class yesterday. What was on it?" And he's dimming in the distance, leaving a trail of panic in his wake.

I sit on the floor and look up at Niko. He sits across from me, looks at me, and slouches. His bones seem to shrink inside within his skin.

"We have a lot of questions to answer," I offer, glancing at my worksheet.

"Yes, we do," he nods.

I squint at the assignment and wonder, "Where do we begin?"

Niko looks at his sheet. "How about number 11, which should read, 'How are you doing?'"

I look at the sheet until I realize he's off-script. I sigh and look at him. "I could say the same of you."

"No fair. I asked first." He smiles a weak smile.

I lean back. I can't tell him it's excruciating sharing a classroom with him ~ as if I always feel watched, hated, judged. I can't tell him my life is just a series of messes, or that he's the most thoughtful boy that I've ever met ~ even if he *is* on the wrong side of clingy. So I settle with something we could both agree on.

"I have a meeting with Renown on Friday."

His eyes startle wide ~ just as I remember ~ and his smile opens and expands, radiates warmth. "Really? Tell me more! You're not going to burn her shop down, are you?"

I chuckle inwardly. "No. 'There are no felons here.'" And then I pull up my legs and hug them and admit, "I don't know my play. Renown thinks I'm Mom."

"Come again?" Niko's eyebrows scrunch with confusion.

"Renown called my mom's phone, but I picked it up. She thought I was Mom and asked me to see her on Friday when 'the stars align.'" I use air-quotes for emphasis.

"You have three days, Dani. Do you need any help?"

This boy never ceases to leave me winded. It's as if his very soul is open and generous. "Thank you, but no. Or, rather, I don't know. I have an idea germinating. I think it might work."

"Well, let me know if you need some support." His smile is so genuine, it makes my bones ache.

I try to smile back. "But Niko, you never answered my question. How are *you*?"

He shakes his head and looks at the floor. "It's torture being near you, Dani."

I'm jarred, disoriented. Since our break-up, he's continued to shine. He sits with the Chorus girls and laughs with them continually. He's never seemed awkward ~ not even for a glimmer. I shake my head and say, "I never could tell."

"There are some parts of myself that I'd rather not see."

We sit in silence, in ache. I rarely let myself settle into such discomfort. If I can kick anxiety's ass, I count it as a win.

"Well, Niko, if it helps," I finally say, "I don't know what you see inside yourself, but when I look at you, I see a person I'm lucky to have known."

"And to know. We still know each other, Dani." He smiles. "We still share a class."

"A class, yes. And we have other things in common."

Dani Argyle Takes on College Days
Thursday, October 23, 2025
7:51 a.m.

I'm startled back to the moment by the school bus stopping, settling. I had been looking through my Japan-Bowl forms ~ the deadline is tomorrow and I've decided to compete this year. My forms are in order, but I don't have time to put them in my backpack before there's a clamor of students cramping through the bus aisle, leaving me stranded in an empty space, alone.

I heave my backpack on my shoulders and step outside.

The day is stunning ~ one of those vibrant clean days you only get in fall. It's barely past dawn, and everything about the day is bright and intense and ~

~ and then I'm wholloped from behind by a backpack and its clumsy owner, and the Japan-Bowl papers go flapping through the air.

Crap. Crap.

Of course.

Of course my day will begin bent over double, chasing

papers in front of my peers who are standing in the bus loop.

I'm tempted to just let them go ~ it's obvious the universe is telling me something: It's the JAPAN BOWL for goodness sake, no dummies allowed ~ but Waters Sensei has been encouraging me to join the team ~ and because we compete as a team so that each person has a different part to play, I can't disappoint a group of my fellow Weaboos.

No more than I already have, that is.

That's the gift Dani Argyle gives to the universe: when people compare themselves to me, I make everyone else look good.

So I go chasing after the scatters ~ like an idiot, of course ~ and I almost have them all except one stubborn sheet that keeps getting summoned by every little breeze, jinking across the field until it finally gets trapped by the wind against the trunk of an ambitious sugar maple.

I grab the paper and straighten myself. Here are three sugar maples ~ granted a pardon by some merciful arborist ~ glinting in a field that is otherwise empty. They blaze orange and red and gold all at once, and the dawn light ignites their leaves until they radiate like flame.

I turn to walk to class, and then a blast of wind gusts straight in my face and I cannot breathe ~ it's as if all of the outside wants to get in ~ and I am still, startled, stupid with air ~ the gust rushes down my throat and I am drowning in air as if my insides do not exist, as if I am not me, but a funnel, and the fullness is choking, so I decide to spin away from the wind, and that's when I see ~

the air is swirling, glistening, filling with color ~ the leaves have broken free from their trees and they are whirling around me so that all of the air is alive with light. I actually reach out my hand and pluck color from the air ~ red and orange and gold gold gold ~ the leaves are alive and whispering against my skin, catching in my hair, glazing me, smoothing me, anointing.

And then the wind sighs and settles and I'm just me again. No longer am I girl ~ lost in golden light. I'm Dani Argyle, and I'm late for class.

I'm struggling towards English, hoping I have all my books, but when I get to the class, it's vacant. There are moguls of backpacks and a surprised Ms. Abele.

She looks up from her desk. "Dani! Hi! It's College Days for the juniors. You can go. And enjoy."

I start to spin, figuring I can slip into the library, but Abele calls out ~ "No can-do, buck-a-roo. The backpacks stay in class."

I'm about to ask why, but it's futile, really, so I sigh, and I smile, and I cram my collected Japan-Bowl papers in the backpack's outer pocket, and I head in the direction of the career center, figuring I can double-back to the library when Abele isn't looking.

I walk a few yards noisily in the direction of the east wing, and then pause, and wait, and wait some more, and then I tiptoe towards the west wing and blur past Abele's class so she'll never recognize who I am.

When I approach the library, I have a plan for infiltration: the library and the computer lab are connected. If a student leaves the lab, then I can slip into that room ~ which is always locked on the outside ~ and then sneak into the library from the lab's back door.

I'm approaching my targeted area when I hear a pleading voice behind me: "Please, please Rochelle, just give me more time! I can't find a replacement in only two weeks."

So I look around, and there's a professional woman ~ tall and poised in stiletto heels with a phone to her ear and a shock of red hair ~ and she has a sticker on her blouse announcing: "Ask me about Gallaudet" and her face is trying to decide whether it should scowl or cry.

She's sounding desperate and sharp: "You know we can't do that! She's leaving, too!" and then I hear: "Do it then! Fine!" and she hangs up her phone, looks at me, and frowns.

"What an interesting piece of technology you have there," I'm trying to lighten the mood. "I've seen those things before, but everyone here uses them with their *thumbs*. You can talk into them, too?"

She looks at me and exhales ~ it's not quite a laugh, but it seems close enough. Then she glances around, as if she doesn't know where she is.

Because, I figure out, she doesn't.

"I'm sorry," she's saying, "but I don't know the new building. When I was last here, it was just three floors of circles around a courtyard, but now they've added these wings ~ "

"Yeah," I interject. "We call them vestibules. They go

nowhere."

"So wherever I turn, I seem to hit a dead-end." She looks winded and blows a whisp of hair out of her face. "Can you please explain to me where the career center is?"

I start pointing and describing, but then I sigh and say, "You know what? I'll just show you the way. Come with me."

I turn and we start off, walking towards the east wing. All of these corridors do look the same, with the same stale posters that are browning at the edges. I'm gullumping in my sneakers, and she's slicing through the air, confident and tall.

The silence is awkward, so I'm brilliant and say, "Gallaudet, huh?"

"Oh, yes. Stone Mountain has a great Deaf and Hard of Hearing Program, so Gallaudet representatives come here to recruit." I hadn't noticed it before, but she *is* wearing hearing aids. They're thin and translucent. She sighs and continues, "But forgive me. I'm not at the top of my game today."

"Yeah. It happens," I reply. "Life could be great... if it weren't for all of these pesky *other* people who get in our way."

She chuckles. And nods. "My project liaison went off and got pregnant ~ without my permission, may I add ~ and now she's informing me of her two weeks' notice ~ the exact same *day* that our intern is leaving."

I stop, shocked still, and turn to face her. "Project liaison? Do you mean event coordinator?"

She stops and nods. "Yes. They're the same thing."

"That's interesting," I volunteer, "because I'm studying to be an event coordinator."

Her eyebrows rise. "Really? Now? You don't enjoy teaching high school?"

And I have to suppress a laugh. "Teach? High school? Let's just say high school and I do not get along."

"Well, normally I'd tell you to interview for the job," she's looking apologetic, "but we only accept candidates who can sign."

"Oh, I sign," I sign, "and I cue," I cue.

Her eyes jump open and then she's scrounging in her purse. "Here is my card," she's saying while she scribbles something on the back. "And this is the number of my assistant. Call her. Today. Let's set up an interview."

I look at her card which announces in crisp script: "Patricia Hardy, Assistant Dean of Students." "Ms. Hardy," I begin.

"Call me Pat."

"Pat," (it's hard to say) "you're an assistant dean of students." I gaze up at her in wonder. "What are *you* doing here at Stone Mountain High? Don't they usually ask *alumni* to work as representatives at College Days?"

She's dismissive of my awe. "Oh. I volunteered to come. I graduated here! It was different back then. You never got lost, but the suburbs are expanding ~ this isn't the country anymore ~ and I guess they needed more room to fit all the students. This place is different, but the same. It's good to come back to the old stomping grounds."

"Ms. Hardy. Pat. It is still true that you're the *Assistant Dean of Students*." Does she not know how impressive she is?

She smiles. "It's not a big deal. Gallaudet hands out titles the way other schools hand out diplomas. But if you want to be impressed, by all means, go ahead. Don't let me stop you."

"Ms. ~ Pat. I'd love to apply, but ~ "

"But why the hell not? You'll love Gallaudet. It's one of a kind."

That is true, I will admit. Let's just hope that Gallaudet thinks that so am I.

Dani Argyle Takes on Scheming
Thursday, October 23, 2025
4:04 p.m.

Gabriel and I are entering the front door, and Mom is home. I walk to the dining room and watch Mom being Mom. She's at her desk, staring at a computer.

Squint. Print. Highlight. Sigh.

Repeat. Repeat. Repeat.

I pull up a chair and sit down next to her. How do I tell her I've duped Gallaudet into giving me an interview? Of course, the liaison position is woefully out-of-reach. But the intern? I sigh.

That's also out of reach.

I'm being naïve and ridiculous and childish.

But Gallaudet is not too far. Maybe Lainie could drive me?

I decide that silence is the best course of action, so I kiss Mom on her head and head to my room.

I have research of my own to complete.

Since I've decided to compete in Japan Bowl this year, I feel like this could be a two-birds-and-one-stone situation. I get to compete in Japan Bowl (which is awesome), but I'm also the team player in charge of researching tsunamis, earthquakes, building codes, zoning policies, gaming centers, and parks. At least some of these items will allow me a glimpse into Mom's obsession.

And it might provide ammunition to take Renown down.

My goal is to dip a toe into the waters of Mom's trauma without allowing this quest to overcome me.

I'm scrolling through articles on parks when my eyes catch the headline:

アパートは公園に成って, まだアパートに成ってしまいました

"Apartment to Park to (with Regret) Apartment Again," and I'm about to click away from the article when I realize my fingers aren't moving. They are stubborn, still, and unmoving.

It's as if my hand is trying to tell me something.

I read the article again. And again. And I realize what my hand is trying to say.

I lean back in my chair, nod, and smile.

To con a con artist, what one needs is information, assurance, and a little sleight of hand.

Dani Argyle Takes on Renown. Anew
Friday, October 24, 2025
4:23 p.m.

I walk into Renown Parlor, and Madame Renown is sitting on the sofa ~ star-charts are splayed before her ~ and she's sitting ~ staring at them ~ and nodding her head. I also glimpse, spread before her, a few of the articles my mom must have printed: words are highlighted in an extravagant orange.

"Penny! You're early!" She smiles and looks up.

And then she startles.

"There's no Penny. Only me." I stroll over and sit down beside her.

"Dani, good to see you." She's doing her best to cover her surprise. On the outside, she seems calm, but I sense agitation inside her as if her skin is holding electricity it can't fully contain. "You seem calmer than you were the last time we met."

I relax into the sofa. "You don't."

"Oh, don't mind me. The stars are very powerful today." She gestures to her charts.

"You can tell by looking at these maps?" I pretend to look and be curious.

"The charts, yes, but the energy is everywhere." She looks up and smiles at the air.

"Well, Ms. Renown... Amelia... I brought some maps of my own to show you," and I splay out aerial photographs and articles on top of her layout. "See?" I'm pointing to a large aerial photograph of Kunimi, Japan, in March of 2022 ~ "This is Kunimi."

"Yes, I know."

"And this is where my dad's base camp was." I circle on the map with an obvious red pen.

"Yes, that's right." She nods in agreement.

"And his expedition left ~ to go to a collapsed building..." I'm drawing a line tracing their movement on the photograph, "but then my dad left the group and doubled back to base camp ~ two of the cadaver dogs were agitated and sick, and so he brought them back ~ "

"Yes, Dani, we know all of this."

"But then he went to catch up with his group, and, on his way, he would have passed this building ~ " and I point to the article that I had printed.

"Here," I hold out my phone. "I put this paragraph into Google Translate ~ see? Here." And I show her the app, "And now I hit 'Translate...'" and a woman's voice drones out:

"The plans to renovate the apartments after the earthquake seemed to be on permanent hold, so the owners turned the area into a park and garden, an area beloved by local residents. But now the new owners are unhappy with stasis and are returning the property to a multi-use building. Excavations in the park begin next week." I turn the phone off.

Silence.

Ms. Renown is waiting. She's too astute to commit to any words now.

"See this building?" I'm pointing again to the aerial photograph. "This was GaijinPot Apartments. Three-hundred yards from Kunimi Base Camp. My dad would have passed it three times that day: going out, coming back, and going out again."

I pause. I look at her. She's staring at the photo, processing.

"But no one was prioritizing this building," I explain. "It was being renovated *before* the earthquake... so no one was living there. But if my dad sensed something ~ and he was expert in that ~ if there *had* been people in that building even though they shouldn't have been, he would have left everything to go assess the situation."

I look at her again. She's still staring at my display.

"And no one bothered completing the renovations," I continue. "People turned it into a park and called it a day."

Ms. Renown's throat is swallowing ~ quietly, slightly, as if there is something inside her that she wants to push down.

"But excavations are beginning next week. And, Mrs. Renown, do you know what they'll find?"

She stares at me ~ widely ~ but her eyes seem empty... until they clear, and she nods, lightly: "That's what the stars have been trying to tell me!"

"What's that, again?" I'm forcing calm, but my stomach is twisting.

"Your father's in the park. That's why he's been so peaceful. So untroubled. Your father loves it there." She's closing her eyes as if she's channeling the cosmos.

"He loves it there?"

She's smiling gently, but then her eyes shock open. "He's about to be discovered! And he's worried about the devastation this will cause your mother."

I feel like all the air has been sucked from the room. I shake my head to reorient myself. "My dad ~ "

Ms. Renown is focused. Sharp. "This is going to destroy her ~ "

(only because you got her hopes up, you fog-headed fraud)

"and there will be no hope left." She slumps in her seat.

I stand up. It feels good to tower over someone for once in my life. "My mom is more resilient than you think, Amelia Renown." I stare down at her. "So ~ " I pause. "Should you tell her, or should I?"

She stares at me, moon eyed, like a frightened animal awakened at night.

I nod. "That's ok, Amelia. I'll be the one to talk to my mom. I love her too much to keep this from her."

And I turn around and walk out the door.

Three blocks away, Niko and Sophia have pulled off to the side of the road, waiting in her car. I climb in the back and feel like I'm shivering, as if all of my insides need to burst out and there's nothing but a veil of skin holding everything in.

"Dani! Dani!" Sophia is saying. "Are you ok? What happened?"

I takes me some time, but I manage to edge out the words, "It's over. I got it. It's all recorded. Every. Single. Word." I pull a second phone from my purse ~ the one Niko had lent me. "Ms. Renown has said her last. She has no scam left."

Sophia squeals and Niko claps his hands ~ once ~ and says, "Yessss!"

There are more words and soft cheering, and then Sophia puts the car in gear and merges onto the street, and then the world starts to smooth and turn into a blur. I think Sophia and Niko are talking in the front seat ~ there is a friendly hum somewhere in the car ~ but none of their words are catching in my brain.

The world blurs some more and then I feel the car turn and ease to a stop. I look up and see my own house in my own yard. I'm sitting still and confused, but Sophia jumps out of the car, so I get out too, and my dearest one ~ my friend and my ally ~ runs to me and hugs me and holds on to me, tight. Then she pulls away and looks into my eyes: "Good luck, Dani. I'm here when you need me."

Niko climbs out of the car and keeps some distance. I saddle up and give him a half-hug ~ side by side ~ and then I pull away and face him. "Thank you, Niko. I couldn't have ~ "

"Dani," he says, "Sophia would have helped."

"No," I insist. "You set the recording app perfectly. It worked like a charm. I'll just need your phone for a little more time." I'm looking at the ground. I know looking in his eyes can be a little bit dangerous.

But his voice feels safe, and his words soothe the air: "It's yours as long as you want. But you know the recording is in the cloud."

I glance at him. "When I talk to my mom, I just need everything to go right. There are so many ways that this could go wrong."

Niko nods, agrees. "Dani," he says, "this will probably go wrong before it goes right. Life has a way of doing that."

I sigh and gaze down. "That would seem to be the case."

And I squeeze his hand and walk to my house.

I've sent Gabriel to the basement ~ a very easy task ~ and I'm in the dining room waiting for Mom to come home. Niko's phone is on the table.

Mom enters the house with an "oof" ~ her arms are spilling with stacks of clothes, and she calls out, "Sewing Day, today," and drops the mound on the back of the sofa.

I hear her re-arranging furniture ~ to make room for machines ~ but I call out from the dining room:

"Mom, can we talk for a second?"

She appears in the doorway. "Is everything alright?" She looks concerned. "Did we do all the paperwork for the Japan Bowl?"

"Mom," I stand up from the dining-room table and pull out a chair. "Mom, please have a seat."

She walks over and sits, but she looks up at me with worried eyes. "Dani. This is weird. What is going on?"

I take my seat at the table. "Mom, I went to go see Ms. Renown today."

She starts. Then she's silent. And then: "Why ever would you ~ "

"And I want you to know I recorded our conversation."

Silence. She says nothing. How could she? She waits.

I lean forward and hold her hand. I'm looking at Niko's phone, but I can't seem to press play. The phone rests on the table, stupid and mute. Every second that it's silent is a second of stillness. A second of stability. A second of contact.

Then I squeeze my mom's hand, and then I let it go. I reach out and press "Play."

The long, arduous, awful conversation plays out again ~ in real time ~ with all the pauses and gaping silences.

I hit stop right after the words, "My mom is more resilient than you think."

They hang there, lingery, obvious in the air.

I brace for tears, for screaming, for hysteria. I have watched the wounded lash out and attack ~ I've watched it too often not to expect it.

And that's why Mom's silence is all the more gutting.

She says nothing. And nothing. And nothing some more.

She rises from the table and turns and walks away. Even her footsteps do not make sound.

She ascends the steps and closes her door.

The only sound from her room is the lock as it's latching.

Dani Argyle Accepts Defeat
Monday, October 27, 2025
8:00 a.m.

I'm leaning against Mom's bedroom door. It's been three days since she entered, and she has yet to leave. The tray I left outside her door is still there, the plate untouched, the food uneaten.

I jaggle the door knob a little. Futilely. Ridiculously.

Guiltily.

"Mom," I'm saying, "just say something to let me know you're alive. Please don't make me break down this door."

I hear something like a moan coming from her bed. But it's not as weak and whimpery as it was yesterday.

It's a moan, to be sure. But at least there is a sense of strength behind it.

"Mom," I'm saying, "I have a job interview tomorrow." I feel stupid talking to a door, leaning my forehead into a mute slab of wood. "I know I won't get it, but it can be useful to gain interviewing experience." I'm trailing off. "You know," I try again,

"You can learn a lot about an industry ~ " I'm shaking my head ~ listening to myself speak is a nightmare, "and Lainie can take me, but we might stay overnight."

I hear rustling, and ugh-ing, and a creaky floor.

There's the sound of footsteps, and then the door opens. My mom is standing there ~ pale and thin ~ she wavers before me ~ as if the act of standing is just too much for her. "Overnight? Where?"

I pause and recalibrate. She's curious about my *interview*? "It's in D.C." I explain. "At Gallaudet University."

She's still thin and wavery. "Gallaudet? Why?"

I wasn't expecting these questions. Will she believe I'm interested in going to college? "They have an internship open for an event coordinator." I pause. "A coordinator who can sign. And cue."

She shakes her head. "And they're interested in you?"

I'm not offended. "No, Mom. They're not interested in me. But they were too polite to rescind the invitation once they found out my age."

"You're only sixteen."

"I know, Mom. I know. But like I said," I sound silly, and I know it, "it's not about the *job*. It's about the *experience*. At this interview I can ask ~ "

"When is it?"

"Tomorrow. Like I said, I can ask *them* questions, like, 'What are you looking for in an event coordinator?' and when they give me their answer, I can use those words in my next interview."

"And Lainie is driving you?"

"Yes. Why?"

She's nodding her head. "Dani, I can drive you."

It's my turn to be silent. Does she understand her offer? "Mom. It's a ninety-minute drive ~ if the traffic is light, so Lainie was thinking we could just stay the night."

"I can take you. We can spend the night. Gabby can join us." She turns around to her room as if there are answers in there. "I've called Mr. Durant. He knows that he won't be seeing me this week."

Then she looks at me. Is she hopeful? What is that look I see in her eyes?

"C'mon, Dani. I'll call Lainie. The Argyles can do this. Let's go get you some experience."

She nods her head, and there is a ghost of a smile tipping at her lips.

Dani Argyle Takes on the Job Interview
Tuesday, October 28, 2025
1:11 p.m.

Gabriel is a rock star at Gallaudet.

You'd think no one had ever seen a child before.

He's running everywhere ~ zagging this way and zigging that ~ talking and grinning and laughing.

We're outside and spinning, whirling as we walk. The campus isn't huge, but it is beautiful in a way that feels expansive and free. Our movement seems less like walking and more like a dance.

Gabriel runs up to two people on a bench who are signing, and he signs, "I like you. I think you're amazing!" And then he zags to two girls walking on the grass, "You're beautiful. You look like the sun!" and then to a lonely boy, reading on a step, "I like your book, and your hair is fun!"

By the time we reach the reception area, we walk to the front desk with an entourage.

Gabby is center stage. He's signing and jumping. All the

college students smile and sign. Their hands are dancing.

I separate myself from the group and introduce myself to the receptionist ~ who is probably not accustomed to such celebration in the waiting room.

"Please have a seat, Ms. Argyle," the receptionist is signing carefully. "Mr. Amico will be with you shortly."

So I sit on a sofa, and Mom sits beside me. She reaches out and squeezes my hand.

There's some movement at a door, and a large bald man in a luminous suit emerges from an office and watches the waiting room while crossing his arms. Then he takes a few steps and signs as he speaks, "Ms. Argyle, I am ready to see you."

I squeeze my mom's hand and walk towards the door.

We enter his office and he gestures to a seat. He settles at his desk. He's massive like a linebacker but moves like a ballerina, and he's wearing a tailored gray suit with an exuberant pink tie. He's vocalizing ~ thinly, flatly ~ and signing at the same time. "So, Ms. Argyle. I hear you're in high school."

"I am. I am. But I'm passionate about this job." I sign as I speak.

"Ok. Tell me more. Why do you want this internship at Gallaudet University?"

"Why wouldn't I?" I ask. "Everything about this job, I love. I want to give a voice to people who do not always feel like they can be heard."

"You have a deaf brother."

"I do. And a more precious spirit never graced this planet."

"I think I glimpsed him in the waiting room. He is very entertaining."

"He's that," I explain, "but he's more, of course. He engages in the world so purely. So directly. There is nothing in him that is touched by guile or malice or a hidden agenda. But not everyone can see this, because they rely too much on their ears."

He's smiling. "I understand. But why do you want to intern for our Project Liaison?"

"Because this is where our humanity shines and becomes resplendent." (I cue resplendent.) "This is where we celebrate you, and me, and everyone. As an event coordinator ~ project liaison ~ I have to listen ~ hard ~ I have to see on the inside what people want on the outside. It is the noblest of challenges: to make concrete the human imagination."

He's staring, stopped, so I feel the need to continue:

"And then, of course, there are the other challenges ~ knowing budgets, knowing deals, figuring out how to provide the best product for the least expense ~ " I feel like this is anticlimactic ~ "because nothing can ruin a day's festivities like going over budget."

I have to stop. I'm signing too wildly. Mr. Amico probably thinks that I'm shouting.

Mr. Amico is nodding slightly. "Ms. Argyle, did you bring your transcript?"

I'm trying not to panic. *Of course* I didn't. I brought no records of my academic life: I want this man to *like* me.

"I apologize. No ~ " but I'm thinking… I have a phone, "but I do have these comments from my professor at PIDA."

On my phone, I bring up my last projects and show Mr. Amico the professor's comments.

"Impressive," he admits. "But a high-school transcript? Can't you access that on your phone?"

Internally, I deflate.

Crap. Of course I can.

I log into my student account ~ and there is my transcript ~ in all of its dazzling mediocrity.

I hand him my phone ~ but he doesn't startle at the grades ~ instead, he's scrolling, and he seems to be counting. "Miss Argyle," he signs, "You have seventeen credits."

I nod. I do. "Yes," I sign.

"To graduate high school, you only need twenty-two."

I stare at him, stunned. "But I'm only a junior ~ "

He interrupts. "You have three credits from middle school ~ two classes of ASL and one class in Algebra I."

I do not flinch at the mention of Algebra I. Oh, the idealism of youth. I sign, "Yes, this is true."

He leans back in his chair, hands clasped at his chest. He's nodding ~ lightly ~ as if he's talking to himself.

He leans forward again, fingers drumming on the desk.

"Miss Argyle. Have you ever heard of dual enrollment?"

"Dual ~ "

"Enrollment. Students can enroll in high school and college at the same time. They take one course, but they get two credits."

"A college credit ~ " I'm confused.

"And a high-school credit."

I hate being slow. My stupidity can shine.

"So it would be possible," Mr. Amico is signing, "for you to transfer to Gallaudet and finish high school here." He pauses. "While you intern."

Really? This can work?

"You only need five classes. Two English, a science, a history, and government. It would be possible for you to take two courses a semester and one over the summer and still intern for our Project Liaison."

"That sounds exciting." I feel myself pleading.

"The decision isn't all mine, you understand, and I have three more applicants to interview today. But if it is possible ~ for you to complete high school while you intern here ~ would you be interested?"

"Interested! Absolutely!" I BOOM my hands.

He nods his head and still seems to be holding an internal dialogue unheard by me.

I'm sitting still and wondering if it's time to thank him and say goodbye when he raps his fingers on the desk and asks me one last question:

"Oh, and Miss Argyle, I almost forgot. Do you have any questions for me?"

My mind flashes hot. Now is *not* the time to mine for the future. Now is the time to focus on *now*.

I feel my hands singing, flashing in the air: "Yes, Mr. Amico. How is my signing?"

I watch as he stills and processes my words.

I continue. "You know, I don't sign as much as the other students here. So I know that, to you, my signs probably seem clumsy. And big. This entire interview, you've probably thought that I've been shouting."

He smiles and relaxes. "Just the opposite, Miss Argyle. Your signs are both contained and quiet."

When I leave the interview, Mom can see I'm burning. I'm ignited, charged, fully alive.

Mom jumps up from her seat and grabs her purse. "You seem happy, Dani. Let's check in at the hotel, and you can tell me all about it."

"Hotel? Mom! Hotel?" How can I tell her that's the *last* thing I need? I need movement. I need motion. Settling in a hotel room is silly and pointless. I grab both her hands. "No, Mom, no! Let's go back home! Let's go! I need to move. I need to go. I can drive if you want."

"But Dani, the hotel is booked. And accommodations like these are never cheap."

I hold up one finger and take out a phone. I dial the number of the Courtyard Marriot. A woman answers. Before the eager receptionist can get through her spiel, I'm saying, with authority, "Manager. Now!"

Another voice is on the phone: "Marcos Marin. How may I help you?"

"Marcos Marin? This is Helena Spartale. I am in your restaurant's restroom, and there's a cockroach as big as an apricot scurrying about in the sink. You will give me a full refund ~ Room 419 ~ and you will do it now, or I'm taking pictures and posting them online."

Ten seconds later I'm hanging up the phone and looking at Mom. "Refund complete. We're going home."

Dani Argyle Watches the Aftershock
Wednesday, October 29, 2025
9:15 a.m.

I know that I should be at school, but I'm jittery and restless ~ like my body has gone crazy on a cellular level ~ and today is just not a learning day.

Today is a jumping and pacing day.

I know Mr. Amico will not call today, and even if he did, the chances of his offering me the job are slim. But a slim chance today is bigger than a zero chance yesterday because slim is bigger than zero by infinity ~ which is exactly how my insides are feeling right now: infinity and infinity and infinity again.

Mom is repairing hems in the living room. I try to sit with her, but I'm jumbled, so I jump up and sit down, and I walk to the windows, and I walk back to the chair, and then I walk to the windows again.

Mom is mending a hem by hand. "Dani? Can you settle?

You're making me nervous."

Oh, Mom. You don't know nervous. Seriously, seriously: you have no clue.

But for Mom's sake, I sit. And jiggle my legs.

My phone buzzes and I jump.

But Mr. Amico would never text. Mr. Amico would call.

SB Dani dear Wheres your paperwork Your packet for Japan Bowl is incomplete

DA What! I handed it all in! Everything! Everything! Everything is signed!

SB Everything except for the actual permission slip. Sorry Dani, but youre disqualified.

And just like that, I'm crashing through a chasm. All my hard work. My months of practice, my audition, my research. All wiped out by a blast of wind.

Crap! Crap! Crap on a map! Why? Why do these things always happen to me?

SB Who needs Japan Bowl Theres always next year

Oh, I hope not.

To hell with this place.

"Dani, dear," my mom is saying, "I'm wondering if you'd like to drive me somewhere today."

I startle back to the room when the word "drive" lingers about. I can screw up my own life cataclysmically ~ that is true ~ but when I drive, I forget about my own life's wreckage. When I drive, my mind is beautifully consumed with motion, with steering, with speed. When I drive, there is a world outside that I can *control*.

"Drive you? Really?" I'm realizing how much I need this.

"Really, Dani. Lainie tells me you've become a good driver. I should have taken you driving more. But ~ "

I nod. "I hear there was an issue teaching Lainie to drive."

Mom laughs. She *laughs*! The hem lands in her lap and she grins at me. "Oh, that girl could not learn. She's never been good at staying between the lines."

I nod. "Yes, Mom, I can drive. I need something to do. Where is it you want to go?"

"To church."

"To *church*?" I shake my head. Crap. "You're kidding me, right?"

Mom's looking wounded. "No, Dani. Why would I do that? On Wednesdays, there are confessions at Holy Trinity."

"No, Mom, no. I'm not driving you to *church*." My feet are tapping at the floor, quickly, jitteringly.

"Why not? Why ever not? You used to love Father Francis."

"And he's dead. So no. And no. I'm not letting you jump from one frying pan into another fire."

Mom is donning her pedantic Mom-voice: stubborn, with a hint of fatigue: "Dani. These are Catholics. They don't demand money."

"But that won't stop them from asking." I jump up and plead. "Please, Mom, no. Just look at Lainie and learn."

"Look at Lainie?"

"Why does nobody remember but me? Manny was awful to her. He treated religion like a weapon to crush her into submission. He brought the entirety of the Catholic Church crashing to her door."

"Dani, you exaggerate."

"He tried to have her *exorcised*!"

"And if you remember, Manny was told 'no.' Manny is very ~ "

"Abusive? Sadistic?"

"*traditional* in his values. But not all Catholics are similar to him."

"And not all Nazis were similar to Hitler."

Mom throws her hands in the air. "Dani! You're not comparing Catholics to Hitler!"

"If the sacramental wine fits ~ "

"Ok, Dani, stop it. You win." She sighs. "Don't worry about

me. I'll drive myself."

I walk to the sofa, drop on it, and slump.

I feel defeated, beaten, which doesn't feel like a victory.

It feels like another way to lose my mother.

Mom's back home with groceries in her hands. She empties bags on the counter: carrots and potatoes and onions and celery and

~

"Mom!" I'm excited. "You're cooking! Beef stew!"

"Beef stew!" Mom beams. She's looking through the cupboards. "The season is here! The weather is chilly and the air is clear."

"It's stew weather," I say and start scrounging through the bags.

She slaps my hand playfully. "No you don't, young lady. My secret ingredient is still a secret. But you can help chop."

And I lean into her while she's arranging the produce.

She leans in too and explains, "Look all you want, Dani-Boo. You won't find it here. It's already hidden."

"Mom! I don't believe you! Who keeps ingredients secret from their own family?"

"Only those people who know family members well." She takes the vegetables to the sink and turns on the faucet. "And oh, by the way, I invited someone to dinner."

Lainie? A boy?

The water is steaming; the carrots are out, and she's starting to scrub. "I invited Father Patrick."

My heart dips; it sags in my chest. So *that* is why my mom is cooking. It's not for me. It for the *church*.

I'm talking to her back. "So," I begin, "if you can't get your daughter to go to church, you'll bring the church to your daughter."

Mom pauses at the sink. "Believe it or not, Dani, this is not about you. I feel like there's something ~ out there ~ you know? That something is possible? I can't put it into words. But I don't want to say 'No.'"

I sigh. Sometimes "No" is the best thing to say.

Father Patrick is not as awful as I thought he would be.

He's old, yes. Or, at least, his skin is. And his hair. But his eyes? His eyes are not old. They are clear and blue. And his voice has an energy that makes him seem young.

Gabriel adores him.

Father Patrick is down on one knee, speaking to Gabriel. He's not cuing, not signing, but Gabriel is watching his lips intensely and seems to understand.

"You're Gabriel! Yes! That's a wondrous name! How do you do? My name is Patrick."

"Patrick," Gabby cues and tries to vocalize. "He ran the

snakes out of Ireland."

Father Patrick smiles. "Maybe. Maybe not. People don't really agree about that. But there is one thing we can all agree on. Patrick was a great man because he was capable of great love, and also he forgave a lot of people."

"Did people hurt him?" Gabby is concerned.

Father seems to understand. "Yes, they did. They sold him into slavery."

"Saint Patrick was a slave?" Gabby's eyes widen with horror.

"He was. For a very long time."

"But he escaped?"

"He did. He escaped." Father pauses. "And then he went back."

"He went back to slavery!"

"He went back to the country that put him into slavery. Patrick wasn't Irish, you know. He was Roman. But the Irish stole him and made him a slave. After he escaped to England and was safe and rich, he gave all that up to go back to Ireland."

"And he chased off the snakes."

Father leans in, like he's telling a secret. "Patrick did something more important than that. Saint Patrick of Ireland ~ he saved the world!"

Gabby's eyes flash wide. "Saint Patrick was a superhero?"

Father laughs. "No. Not like that. At the time, Rome had been bringing peace to the world. But then Rome started to fall apart.

Barbarians were winning. Literacy ~ written language ~ was disappearing. But Saint Patrick made little places where people could read and write. And these people saved the stories and ideas from ancient Rome."

"And is that so important? Did that save the world?" Gabby is incredulous.

"It did, my Gabriel. One day, you'll understand. The ability to tell stories keeps chaos away."

Gabriel nods. Like he does understand.

And, to be honest, I think he does.

Mom is dishing out stew. This stuff is a marvel. You think smell is an abstract thing until you walk into it. Like a *wall*.

We're sitting. Not quite eating. More like bathing in a scent. The food has been blessed, but Father is staring at it ~ like it's manna ~ a miracle from the sky.

He raises a spoon and takes a sip. He shakes his head in disbelief. "Penny Argyle. I've eaten a lot of meals with a lot of families, but this ~ " He pauses. "This is a wonder."

"There's a secret ingredient," I offer. "I'd tell you, but Mom won't let me know."

"It's anchovies," Mom spurts.

Now it's my turn to disbelieve. "Mom, you can't lie now. This man is a *priest*."

"No, it's true. The glutamates in the anchovies make the beef flavor pop." She shrugs. "It's science."

I'm staring at my bowl. "Mom. You put fish in my stew?"

"That's why I never told you, Dani, my dear. Some things sound gross, but they're really ~ delicious."

"Amen to that, Penny." Father laughs heartily. "The miraculous and the mundane cohabit together. Isn't that what the sacraments are all about?" He takes another sip. His eyes close and his face relaxes into contentment.

There's a pause while Mom ruminates. "Speaking of sacraments, Father." Mom has put down her spoon and has her hands in her lap. "You never gave me a penance."

"Penance, my daughter?" Father's eyes are open and a generous blue.

"Penance, Father Patrick. Today, at confession. You prayed for me, but you gave me no penance."

Father Patrick puts his spoon on the table. He leans in, softly, like a lover in love. "Penny, that's because grief is not a sin."

"But I am sinful, Father Patrick."

"But your grief is not." His voice is strong and gentle, like a breeze in the summer. "Penny, grief is just love ~ squaring off against its oldest enemy, death, and telling that sonofabitch that he has not won ~ not this time ~ that love will prevail ~ it will continue and continue and death will not stop it. Penny, understand this, and life will seem clearer. Grief is as much a part of marriage as any other stage. It's as sure as courtship or a honeymoon. When you're bound together with the one who will teach you how to love and be loved ~ eventually one of you will be left alone, on this earth, feeling as if you've been severed in two. But that half of you ~ the one you loved so dearly ~ has not been erased from your life. The way your husband blessed you ~ loved you into being ~ that part of you is still very much alive. You honor him dearly when you feel his loss. But you honor him too when you live into the fullness ~ the fullness that he picked you up and carried you into. And that love ~ that fullness that has grown up inside you ~ that part of you is still very much alive."

I glance at my mom, and she has crumbled, sobbing.

My beautiful mother is shaking apart.

I jump up, and wrap around her, and enfold her, and cry.

And Gabriel squishes between us and holds us both with his tiny hands.

And the world seems to be shivering and crashing into ruins.

That night, we're all in Mom's bed.

That night, we all fit.

Mom's in the middle with an arm around Gabby.

Mom's in the middle with an arm around me.

Gabby shoots two hands up into the air. "Mom, please," he's

signing with a grin. "Tell me about the day I was born."

He's heard this story, but he'll hear it again. Nothing is as fascinating as hearing about a self you cannot remember ~ a self that is you, but not the you that you now know.

Mom arranges herself so that she can sign ~ her words look like wings ~ "Well, my Gabriel, it's only fair that Dani's story comes first. She was born a few years before you."

Gabby yells "Nine!" with his fingers.

Mom's hands take flight. "Your sister has always been stubborn. Even when she was inside me, she refused to come out. I was induced ~ then in labor for seventeen hours ~ and then the doctors came in and pulled her out ~ "

"Kicking and screaming ~ " Gabby remembers the story.

"Kicking and screaming," Mom agrees. "She wailed against the world and the indignity of being born, but when they placed her in my arms, she quieted down. She stared at me ~ with huge blue eyes ~ as if I was the most amazing thing she could ever imagine."

"Me! Me!" Gabby is waving.

"And you, my Gabby, you couldn't wait to come out. You were so accommodating ~ even on your birth day. The doctor and the nurse were standing by me, and the doctor had told me to push for the very first time, so I pushed, and then I heard both her and the nurse shout at the exact same time, 'STOP!' and I figured they had no idea you'd come out so quicky ~ they weren't even ready to catch you yet ~ so then they positioned themselves and told me to push again, and on the third push, you were out ~ "

"AND?" Gabby prods.

"And I thought you were *dead*."

Gabby guffaws.

"You didn't make a sound. So I thought you were stillborn, and I was trying to get up, and I was shouting, 'Is he ok?' and the doctor and the nurse were smiling and laughing, and they were saying, 'He's fine. He's fine. He just looks like he's happy to be here.' And you never made a peep. And when they put you in my arms, you snuggled in tight."

Gabby grins. "I still like to snuggle."

And Mom wraps us both in her arms and says aloud, "Yes, my dear Gabby. And so do I."

Dani Argyle Takes on the Delay
Thursday, October 30

Today is still not a school day. It's a lounge-around-the-house day. It's cocoa and pajamas. It's nap-in-a-sunbeam.

When the phone rings, I'm expecting the Stone-Mountain Attendance Office. The school can still confuse me with my mother.

"Daniella Argyle?" A tinny voice is slicing the air. "This is Philip Amico. Do you have a minute? Have I caught you at a bad time?"

I have no idea how to answer both of those questions, so I reply with a lame "I-have-time-now."

"Miss Argyle, I've spoken to the board, and they've given me permission to offer you the internship."

I want to speak. I do. But my voice is hooked in my throat. Whenever I try to say something, I'm stuck and voiceless.

"Miss Argyle? Are you there? Have we lost our connection?"

"No, no. I'm here. Forgive my surprise."

"I hope your surprise is good," he offers.

"Of course." I can't even tell if I'm lying. "Of course it's a good surprise. This is all I ever wanted ~ "

"So that's a 'yes'?"

"That's a," the word is there but it won't come out. "It's," I'm focusing on my throat but my blood is bullying me to get some attention ~ my blood feels like winter, like my insides have turned into ice and slush.

Finally, I give up. "It will be a 'yes ~ '" somehow, I can say *that*, "but there's one more thing I need to check. Can I give my *final* final answer on Monday? 9:00?"

"That is fine, Miss Argyle. I can wait until then. You are our first choice, but we do have a second."

"You won't need a second," I assure. "But I'm realizing my life is about more than just me."

"Understood. I will hear from you soon." And then he hangs up.

Silence.

My blood still feels all shivery. I rub arms and try to get warm.

J.P. Argyle Explains the Universe
Saturday, November 1.
Early morning. Before dawn.

Dad's on my bed. We've been talking through the night.

Tonight, he's had an awful lot to say.

And so have I.

We've been wresting with the tough issues: the many ways someone (moms included) can get lost, and more lost, and then found again; how schools can squish the intelligence from nonconforming students; how some people (like Joe Chalk) end dangerous nightshifts by purposefully walking into hardships and notifications that other people shun; how one's entire future pivots on whether an answer to a question is a *yes* or a *no*.

"I'm missing Dante," I begin, lightly. I need to shift these topics from the existential experiences I've lived through to the existential experiences of a literary world. "There's no depth that man did not explore." I smile and hug my knees. "Sorry, Dad," I demur. "I know you're more of a *The-Lady,-or-the-Tiger?* type-of-guy."

"Don't go insulting *The Lady, or the Tiger?*" His skin is glowing. "It's a good story."

"Only because you believe that ~ at the end ~ it's the lady who is coming through the door."

"Dani, I've walked with people through the worst catastrophes our planet can give. When chaos strikes, I see the goodness of the human heart."

"I have no doubt about that." I look him in the eyes ~ even if his radiance makes my own eyes water and squint. "But there is real evil, too. That's why I miss Dante. His universe is not all Heaven. And it's not all Hell. But whether he's exploring Heaven or Hell or something in-between, there is always *order*. And that's comforting to me. Like there's a moral gravity that permeates the universe."

"That *is* a consoling thought."

"Everything finds the place that's the perfect moral fit. In the Dantean cosmos, you naturally go to where you most belong."

"But there's also room for mystery. And growth."

"That's true," I'm reflecting.

"Mystery and beauty. Don't forget about them."

"Mystery and beauty. That reminds me of that poem. One of Dante's earlier verses. It predates *The Inferno*."

"Tell me about it." His eyes are smiling.

"Well, Dante is a character in this poem. And he's complaining. He's complaining to the *poem* and apologizing to it, saying he's so sorry. No one ~ he explains ~ will take the time to fully understand the verse. No one will pause to untie all the knots where the meaning of the poem exists."

"And then," my dad explains, "the poem itself gets the last word. The poem replies to Dante and says, 'Peace, Dante, peace. It is enough to know that I am beautiful.'"

I stare, stunned silent. "Dad, you know Dante?"

"I know a lot of things, Dani. I know life is hard. But it is *still life*. And the worst sorrow that life can give is better than the most glorious death."

"You know both."

Dad shimmers and glows.

"And as for you, dear Dani, there is still a lot of life left. And the worst isn't over. But neither is the best."

And then he's gone, in a blaze, like a starburst has blasted across the sky, and I've never seen him leave like that ~ like he's both light and heat ~ both action and flame. The dawn is swelling outside, but there are still stars in the sky, and before me, within reach, there's motion, there's whirling, as if the air is dizzy, the dust motes are shimmering; they're flashing and alive ~ sparking upward, and down, like embers from a fire.

And outside, I sense a whisper of movement. There's breathing, and motion, and the sound of steps, and then a whuff of hesitation and an impression of pause.

And then I hear a knock on the door.

DISCUSSION GUIDE FOR CLASSES, SMALL GROUPS, OR INDIVIDUAL REFLECTION

1. Do you like Dani? Why or why not? Does Dani like Dani? Why or why not? Do you think Dani's issue with self-esteem is unusual among adolescents? What is it about Dani's environment that affects her understanding of herself? Why might Dani's understanding of herself be different than the reader's understanding of her?

2. Discuss Dani and Sophia's differing experiences with school. What are their strengths and weaknesses as students? If you were a teacher, who would you rather teach: Dani or Sophia? Which student do you think is preferred by the educational system? Why?

3. Discuss the conflicts between Penny and Dani. Are any of Penny's accusations against Dani justified? Are any of Dani's accusations against her mother unjustified?

4. Why didn't Dani and Niko's relationship work out? Was Dani correct to end the relationship? Are Lainie's observations of Dani's behavior accurate? How did Dani's understanding of the play *Othello* help her understand the dynamics of her own relationship with Niko?

5. How does Dani change throughout the story? Are these changes significant?

6. Are you sympathetic to Penny? If main characters are judged by the magnitude of their character arc, who changes more: Dani or Penny? How does Penny's change affect Dani?

7. This story explores issues of imprisonment. Penny is trapped by grief and Dani is trapped by institutionalized education. Is Gabby imprisoned by anything? Even with his disability, why might he be freer than other characters?

8. Mr. Glupov is an early antagonist in the story. Why is he so despised by Dani? Do you believe Dani's vitriol is justified? What do you personally think are Glupov's failings? Do you understand his viewpoint in his interaction with Dani? In his interaction with Dani, what is Glupov's goal? Both Mr. Wright and Mr. Glupov have early conflicts with Dani. How do these respective educators handle the conflict? What does their interaction with Dani communicate about them as characters?

9. Bathing imagery is important in the story. Dani takes two partial baths in Part 1. What does the reader learn about Dani from these experiences? Are there any baths in Part 2? How do these images of bathing relate to the meaning of the work?

10. Madam Renown is an antagonist in the novel. What do you think of her? Is it possible that she does not understand herself to be a bad person? Why or why not? What does she believe she is offering to Penny?

11. Discuss the title, *Dani Argyle Takes on the Universe*. Who is Dani fighting? Do her adversaries always know that Dani is fighting against them? Why does Dani feel like she is in conflict with virtually everyone around her? The words "Still. Life." And "Still Life" function as section titles in this novel,

and stillness and stasis serve as a central theme. How is stasis understood in this novel? How does Penny suffer from stasis? Why does Dani, as a student, feel mired in it? How are the words "still life" reimagined by J.P. at the end of the novel?

12. Discuss Gabby. How is he a foil for Dani? What aspect of Dani's personality does Gabi bring to the surface that other characters do not? Are there other characters in the novel who serve as foils for each other?

13. Discuss the role of the ghost in the story. What effect does the ghost have on Dani? on the plot? Why does the story begin and end with the ghost? Is the ghost real or a figment of Dani's imagination? How important is this issue?

14. Throughout the novel, Dani's persistent and primary goal is to leave high school. When Mr. Amico offers her this opportunity, she postpones the decision. Why does Dani find it difficult to accept Amico's offer?

15. Throughout the course of this novel, two characters move away from depression. What effect did their depressive episodes have on them? What is the catalyst for change?

16. Dani hates school but loves her teachers. Why does Dani hate school? Is her vitriol justified? Discuss Mr. Wright, Mr. Waters, Ms. Satchel, and Ms. Abele. What are their strengths as educators? Who would you most like to have as a teacher? What would Dani's ideal school be like? What would Dani's ideal teacher be like? How are issues about learning explored in the novel? Are there other aspects of the novel that do not take place in school but that focus on learning? How might these other scenes relate to the meaning of the work?

17. The chapters in this novel are not only given titles but are also given dates. What is Dani's relationship with time? Why does she seem, on some occasions, to be hyper-aware of the passage of time and, on others, to have time slip by unawares? Time often goes unnoticed by readers: *Othello* might take place over two months or two days, *Hamlet* might take place over three months or thirteen years, and both *Romeo and Juliet* and Episode IV of *Star Wars* take place within five days but feel ~ to the reader or viewer ~ more expansive than that. Why do readers so often lose track of the passage of time within the world of a story? Even with all of the dates and time stamps, did you lose track of time?

18. What does Dani learn about life from her study of Japanese culture? How does her love of the Japanese culture help her?

19. In the last scene which focuses on the Argyle family being together, Penny recalls the stories of her children's births. What can we learn about the characters from these stories? What is the effect of concluding this family's arc with the recollection of these birth days?

20. How does Dani's ADHD color her personality, her perception of the world, and the style of the prose? At one point, Dani explains how many things have to go right in order for her to hand in a homework assignment. What was your reaction to Dani's thought process? Dani also has an undiagnosed learning disability: how does this neurodiversity affect Dani's educational experience? Aside from these issues, why does Dani's school seem to have difficulty dealing with her as a student?

21. Together, writers and readers engage in a social contract: the story that a writer tells in Act III should not be different than the story that began in Act I. A novel, for example, should not open as romance and end as slasher fiction. What was your experience as a reader of this novel? Were there expectations that you had that were not fulfilled? Were there certain tropes that were undermined? If so, was it engaging or disappointing to have these expectations unmet? How might this relate to the meaning of the work? Also, skillfully told stories should leave a trail of hints so that readers can reach conclusions on their own without being directly told by the author. As a reader, did you have any "aha" moments regarding the plot or characters?

22. Dani promised to give Philip Amico her final answer to his offer on Monday at 9:00. What will her decision be? Why do you believe this?

23. At the end of the novel, who is at the door? How did the last sentence of the novel affect you as a reader?

24. R.S. Bishop explained, "Books are mirrors when readers see their own lives reflected in the pages. Books are windows when they allow readers a view of lives and stories that are different from their own. Books become sliding glass doors when readers feel transported into the world of the story and when they feel empathy for the characters." For you, was this novel a mirror, a window, or a sliding door?

Stories Talking to Stories

1. Dani's name is similar to Danea (princess of the Argives) and Dante. How is Dani similar to and different from these two figures? Do you think Dani's middle name (Antigone) is as appropriate to her personality as her mother believes it is? Why or why not?

2. How is Dani's mother similar to and different from Penelope of Ithaca? How is Lainie similar to and different from Helen of Troy? How is Jean-Peine similar to and different from Odysseus? Are there other connections between characters in the story and literary characters?

3. How does Dante's journey through Hell and Purgatory parallel Dani's journey through school and life? How do the trio's Tweets about the *Inferno* (Tweets focusing on incontinence, heresy, violence, and fraud) parallel the action of the text?

4. Section markers consist of birds in Part 1 of the novel and maple leaves in Part 2. How do these section markers relate to mythological symbols? At three points in Part 1 (in Chapters 8, 16, and 23), the birds are facing left rather than facing right. What is the possible significance of this? The novel has thirty-three chapters: is the number thirty three a significant allusion?

5. Dani has various "Virgils" (mentors) in this novel. Who are they? How do these different Virgils protect Dani intellectually, physically, and spiritually?

6. At the end of the novel, Dani and her father are discussing a short poem written by Dante. How does this poem relate to the novel? The novel has various references to *The Inferno*: Philip Silverman, for example, is an allusion to the character Filippo D'Argenti (Dante's real-life nemesis and a character in Circle V), and the photographer is an allusion to Medusa; these are the two characters Dante interacts with before he descends into lower hell. Does a reader need to understand all of these literary allusions to appreciate the novel? Why or why not?

7. When teaching her own students, Vivian Jewell often discusses the "magnanimity of literature": the idea that great literature meets us where we are and generously offers us the fullness of experience that we are capable of receiving at that time. (A nine-year-old, for example, might read *The Odyssey* as a rollicking good adventure story while a ninety-year-old might see it as the story of a life ~ told through three generations of men from the same family ~ all moving from isolation to community and from purposelessness to purpose.) Does *Dani Argyle Takes on the Universe* offer this magnanimity, offering different experiences to different readers?

8. Dani's understanding of *The Odyssey* helps her process her grief. Her understanding of *The Inferno* helps her recognize the types of evil that exist around her. Her understanding of *Othello* helps her perceive jealousy in her boyfriend. And her understanding of *Wild* inspires her to endure when her mother seems lost. Which books have deepened your understanding of the world?

9. Father Patrick comforts the Argyle family with wisdom from C.S. Lewis' *A Grief Observed,* Thomas Cahill's *How the Irish Saved Civilization,* and Kate Braestrup's "Into the House of Mourning." In your life, which stories have comforted you?

10. When Tweeting their witty and irreverent understanding of *The Inferno*, Dani Argyle and her friends acquire a little following. Which individuals or groups in social media have helped you build community? (Note: The brilliant adolescent sass of many of this novel's Tweets originated with E.J, E.C, and B.S.)

ABOUT THE AUTHOR

For decades within Fairfax County Public Schools, **Vivian Jewell** has posed as a teacher, but she has ended up learning more from her students' candor, insight, and wit than they have learned from her.

Vivian Jewell studied English Literature at The University of Virginia where she graduated with high distinction and studied Medieval and Renaissance Studies at Oxford. Her poetry has appeared in *The Virginia Literary Review*, *The Kindred Spirit*, and *The English Journal*. This is her first novel.

Vivian originally went into teaching believing that the career would give her the opportunity to write but quickly discovered that she adored her students too much to short-change their writing lessons by working on her own craft. Vivian devoted herself obsessively to teaching until a pandemic shut-down schools and Vivian decided to amuse herself by writing some stories. No one was more surprised than she when one of those stories got a mind of its own and decided to grow up and become a novel. Vivian has been equally overjoyed and startled by Dani's willingness to commandeer her own story.

Vivian would love to discuss with readers the issues that are brought up by this novel. You may contact her through her publisher's website (ShelteringTreeMedia.com) or her author website https://www.vivianjewell.com/ or her Facebook page.

VIVIAN M. JEWELL

For Further Study

Alighieri, Dante. *The Inferno of Dante: A New Verse Translation*. Translated by Robert Pinsky. New York: Farrar, Straus and Giroux, 1994.

Braestrup, Kate. "The House of Mourning." May 30, 2015. In *Facing the Dark*. Podcast, video, 13:51. Accessed February 24, 2025. https://docs.google.com/forms/d/e/1FAIpQLSc08R3ZMSY mvTPxD66yS7QV4FtyznZUQ6OCMGTdpsUCGo5iLg/vi ewform.

Cahill, Thomas. *How the Irish Saved Civilization: The Untold Story of Ireland's Heroic Role from the Fall of Rome to the Rise of Medieval Europe*. New York: Double Day, 1995.

Hamilton, Edith. *Mythology: Timeless Tales of Gods and Heroes*. New York: Black Dog & Leventhal Publishers, 2017.

Homer. *The Odyssey*. Translated by Robert Fagles. New York: Penguin Classics, 1999.

Lewis, C. S. *A Grief Observed*. New York: Harper Collins, 2015.

Shakespeare, William. *The Tragedy of Othello, The Moor of Venice*. Edited by Barbara A. Mowat and Paul Werstine. New York: Washington Square Press, 1993.

Sophocles. *Antigone*. Translated by George Theodoridis. Accessed February 24, 2025. https://bacchicstage.wordpress.com/sophocles/antigone/.

Strayed, Cheryl. *Wild: From Lost to Found on the Pacific Crest Trail*. New York: Alfred A. Knopf, 2012.

SHELTERING TREE

EARTH PUBLISHING

ShelteringTreeMedia.com